Abandoning Memory
Book Three of Tales of Tasimu
by
Celu Amberstone

I0527539

ABANDONING MEMORY

First edition. July 19, 2024.

ISBN: 978-1990581212

Written by Celu Amberstone.

Dedication

This book is dedicated to all the refugees and displaced indigenous peoples around the world. It is also dedicated to my children and grandchildren. Not being a woman of material wealth, my writing is my legacy to both them, and all the children who are our cherished future. Also in dedication, I offer my eternal gratitude for the traditional teachings of my grandparents, aunties, and the other Elders I've met over the years who have taken the time to teach me. The wisdom and strength of my Elders has always been, and will continue to be, an inspiration in my life.

Acknowledgements

I would like to thank for their support, my four sons, my daughter, and those of my friends who were there when I needed them. Paula, Lila, your friendship and help with proof reading, book covers, and other important book related things, was greatly appreciated.

I would also like to thank the folks at Kegedonce Press for their dedication, hard work, their vision, and their fearless determination to encourage Aboriginal writers of all types.

Note to the Reader:

Abandoning Memory is a work of fiction. I hope you'll read and enjoy it as such. Though I've drawn material in the abstract from places I've lived and from my own mixed race background, any resemblance to people, places, languages and cultures, Indigenous or other, in our world is purely coincidental.

A Brief Summary of the Earlier Books

IN BOOK ONE, *Taste of Memory*, Tasimu, a youth with special gifts he has inherited from his mysterious father, dwelling at the bottom of Big Ice Lake, is forced with his family to move away from their ancestral home when the invaders discover gold in their northern mountains. Tribal members who converted to the invaders' religion signed a treaty in which all the northern peoples were forced to relocate to a newly created Tribal Preserve in a southern desert, a wasteland their conquerors didn't want.

During their traumatic journey to this new Tribal Preserve, Tasimu finds a man who knows of his unique heritage, and can teach him how to use his magical gifts, if he will agree to help him with his own quest for revenge against the converts whom he blames for giving away tribal lands.

Fearing that he also has unwittingly been the cause of his baby cousin's illness and death, Tasimu agrees to end his studies with a man of questionable ethics. Book one ends with Tasimu morning the loss of family members and fearing what will await them in this new southern land.

In Book Two, *When Memory Dies*, Tasimu and his people finally arrive on the barren, water-starved land they have been allotted only to discover that they have been lied to by the invaders who took their northern homeland. The treaty goods they were promised are slow to arrive or never show up at all. They will face continuous starvation, illness and despair in their new home. Caught in the middle between two warring factions, Tasimu endures beatings and scorn by both sides, but he also is defended by a girl cousin who chafes at the confines allotted to women in the new order.

Spending a great deal of his time hunting in the desert to avoid trouble in the convert settlement, Tasimu is able to connect with the spirit guardians of his new home, so when he is contacted by the outlaws who need a person with magical power to help them with their raids on ranches for food and horses, he agrees, and so Tasimu and his unhappy cousin run away to join the outlaws.

Tasimu agrees to use his Gift and help one of the desert tribe's war leaders on a daring raid into the enemy's territory to bring back food beasts for their starving peoples. The raid is successful, but while returning to the Preserve with their plunder Tasimu is contacted by one of his spirit helpers, warning of a danger to his mother and grandfather.

The desert war leader, who is starting to see Tasimu like a son, agrees to help Tasimu and his uncle rescue the pair who are being held for trial at the agency; but during the attempt the war leader is badly wounded and he and Tasimu barely escape with their lives.

Tasimu's story continues in Book 3, *Abandoning Memory*.

A Tribal History of Long Ago, Rushton Archives: third interview with Indigenous Zacatik subject 297

NO MATTER HOW MUCH hardship my people and I endured during that time, or what we continue to suffer, I am still Qwani'Ya Tsa'adi. Whether they are living or dead my kindred surround me with their love and wisdom. I never walk alone. My daughter's mentor says he wants to understand our past and help us. I wonder if he has the courage needed to set aside the lies he's been taught and fearlessly embrace the truth.

We shall see.

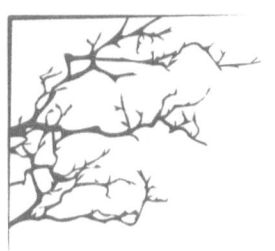

Part One
Chapter One

ON THE MORNING OF THE fourth day after our escape from the soldiers at the Willow Creek agency Utsiyonti was able to contact me mind to mind. <<How is the war leader doing?>>

I had just relieved Uncle on sentry duty and was perched on a high outcrop where I could see the rocky passage to the hidden canyon and the open land and brush covered slopes beyond our refuge. Using Hawk's eyes I saw the warriors as they passed from one juniper thicket to another on a nearby slope. Soaring higher I saw no soldiers or other enemies on their back trail.

<<The war leader is grumpy, but healing. That looks like a big war party for an escort, trying to hide itself among those junipers. You aren't being followed, so come in, but disguise your tracks just in case,>> I said.

He was still too far away for me to see his expression with my human eyes, but I sensed his surprise. <<Look up.>> he did and I sensed the amusement in the mental voice as he took note of the hawk floating nearly above them.

<<These men haven't come as an escort. Most of them are heading east to raid the Chamuqwani for meat and other supplies—as am I. Two among us are the Prophet's initiates, who will go into the Preserve to speak to others about his teachings. Tuumaz, a healer, her apprentice, and two warriors will escort you, the wounded Nachoga and the others of your family back west.>>

<<I will tell them you are coming.>>

<<Good.>>

Thanking hawk for his aid I left him to hunt and returned to my human body. Still perched in my hiding place I told Nachoga of our visitors then watched as they crept closer. As Sun climbed toward the midpoint of his journey, seven people approached the narrow passage and slipped into our hidden sanctuary. The rest of the warriors hobbled their horses and made camp within the junipers on a nearby slope. Getting permission to leave my post I jumped down to help care for the horses.

Arriving back at camp I received some surprises that I wasn't counting on. The first came when I joined the people caring for the horses. I had expected Tuumaz but not Thonna. Dressed in a long tunic and leggings with her hair held off her face with a cloth headband, I thought she was another Kukiya youth till she spoke.

Suddenly rooted to the spot I stared with my mouth dropping open until the spotted horse I was leading nudged me hard in the shoulder, impatient to get to the water. Remembering my task I hastily lead him to the pond, then hobbled him and released him to graze on the long grass and rabbit brush nearby.

Catching up to my friends, I blurted, "Thonna, it's good to see you, but what are you doing here?"

Thonna turned and smiled, then seeing my expression, she put her hands on her hips and scowled. "What does it look like, stupid boy? I'm here to help the warriors when they hunt the Chamuqwani's cai."

"But-but you can't!"

Her scowl deepened and she took a step closer to me. "Why not?"

"B-because you might get hurt—or die!" I stammered, feeling foolish.

By that time our conversation had attracted the attention of a grinning Samiqwas and Tuumaz. "She gonna hit Puhani, if talk more he. Me got pretty green stone me bet."

Samiqwas chuckled. "No bet. Tas isn't smart enough to know when to keep his mouth shut. She's gonna hit'em."

Focusing her glare on them she growled "And you two are next if I start hitting. I have every right to be here. Aunty Ashiqwa gave her permission and my new uncle Talulsit is with the warband out there, so just shut up—all of you."

Pretending to be frightened the others hurried away still grinning. Thonna swore a Chamuqwani soldier's oath and returned her attention to me.

"Thonna I'm sorry; I met no offense—I just..." I let my voice trail off unsure how I wanted to continue.

She glared at me for a moment longer then her expression softened. "My name isn't Thonna, Tas. I left that accursed Chamuqwani name behind when I left my father's home. My relatives among the rebels have gifted me with my true name. I am called Xyilaha now."

Xyilaha, the name didn't sound like a name in our language, so maybe she had received it from the Kukiya family her aunt had married into. "Xyilaha, I will try to remember, but if I forget can I still call you, stupid girl instead? Ow!" she hit me then we both smiled as we walked back to the fire together.

As I took my place in the outer ring around the council fire with the younger people and reached for the hot tea Samiqwas was handing me, I said under my breath, "Good thing you didn't bet him. She did hit me."

The corners of his mouth twisted as if he wanted to grin, but thought better of it when he saw Uncle Tli scowl at us.

Looking around the council fire I saw Uncle, Utsiyonti, Nachoga, Mother and Grandfather, as I'd expected, but then I got another surprise. The woman with gray streaks in her long black hair who had seen the images I could make with my string, named Betsiya, sat next to a scar-faced veteran and another seasoned warrior. Thonna, or should I say, Xyilaha, went and sat behind Betsiya.

I hadn't paid much attention to Betsiya back at the outlaws' stronghold. I had too much to learn in too short of time, but I had heard that, like Grandfather her Gift was healing. Betsiya smiled at me then returned her attention to what Grandfather was saying.

"I have no wish to return west with your people, war leader. I have done all I can for you. But my people need to hear the Prophet's message and learn the prayer songs I can teach them. If you have a horse you could lend me I would be grateful so I can continue my journey."

"Appi, no!" Mother said from her place beside Nachoga. "You are still too weak. When you are rested and have regained your strength then think about continuing your work—" Turning moist, pleading eyes on Nachoga, she begged him to agree with her.

"No, Daughter. I am rested enough it's time I go on my way. On horseback it would be easier for me, but I will walk otherwise."

"We have extra horses, Elder, that won't be a problem, and the one called Sheikai is with us. I believe his mission is the same as yours," one of the newcomers said.

Grandfather smiled. "Yes, I know him. He is another of Iyantsha's emissaries, as am I. it will be good to travel with him for a time."

Nachoga leaned forward to better see him as he focused his cougar eyes upon Grandfather. "It will not be as easy for you to slip among the enemy's camps as before. When you let yourself be ensnared in the trap set by the Evil Ones, you became an outlaw like the rest of us, and the soldiers and the agent's men will be looking for you. They will hang you as they promised if they catch you. Do you understand that, Elder?"

"Yes, I am sure that is so. Still I must go and trust that the Unseen Ones who have sent me, will also protect me."

When Mother opened her mouth to argue, Nachoga shook his head and put his uninjured hand on her arm and squeezed gently. After another moment she closed her mouth and dropped her eyes.

"Ahho, I pray that it is so," Nachoga said, and dropped the matter.

For the rest of the afternoon the men sat around the fire talking war and safe routes through the dry lands to and from the west. Eqwohi, the tattooed veteran warrior who was leading the raid among the Chamuqwani asked many questions about the valley where we had stolen the cai, and the other Chamuqwani held lands Nachoga had seen while away from the Preserve.

Then after a meal of deer meat and coussa root and berries I got my last surprise of the day. When the warriors rose to gather their horses Uncle Tli rose with them. Seeing me stare after my retreating uncle, Tuumaz said so only I could hear, "Nobody make him go war now, but Golannah mad him. Better when uncle come back with meat and gifts for People. Then Golannah be happy again."

Well he had a point. I loved Uncle Tli but I was still mad at him, too. And I wouldn't be sorry to see him gone for a time, either. The only problem was that now we would be left with only three youths, three women, and a wounded warrior if we ran into trouble on our own journey west.

As it turned out, however, only one woman was returning west with us. Betsiya and her apprentice Xyilaha were going with the warband after all.

When Nachoga asked her where she was going Betsiya put her hands on her hips and said, "I'm going with my husband, of course. He will want me to warm his blankets, help with butchering the cai they take, and healing stupid men who get injured. He will need me more than you will, Kukiya brother."

"But, sister, what about my shoulder? Didn't you come to take care of me?"

"I did, but you don't need me now." Betsiya pointed with her lips to Mother standing at his elbow. "Just listen to that one—and do what she tells you. She can care for you as well as I can. And you, I think, will like it better if she does." Betsiya gave Mother a knowing look and the two women shared a secretive smile.

Unable to hide his own grin Nachoga looked into Mother's eyes, then said, "Maybe I will. Go on then."

Eqwohi chuckled and through an arm around Betsiya and walked her to her horse. Over his shoulder he called, "I will send Dotsuwa and Jenaitsi back to see you get to your brother safely."

Nachoga snorted a laugh. Dotsuwa isn't going to be happy with you."

"No, but he will be happy later, because you are going to give him two new horses when you next go raiding. And as for his son, he is in love and afraid the woman will find another interest while he is gone—so he won't mind when you give him a horse, too."

Nachoga laughed. "You have thought of everything. Maybe you don't need me anymore. Maybe I just stay with the prophet's people, eh?"

Instantly throwing all teasing aside, Eqwohi said, "Rest and heal Nachoga, Pride of the Kukiya People. We will always need your wisdom and protection."

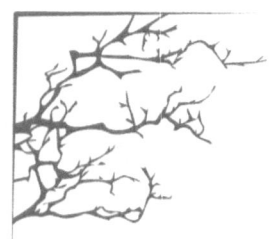

Chapter Two

Our escort showed up at our fire not long after the others left us. I didn't like the muddy colors I could see in their Spirit Fires, and feared we were going to have trouble with them from the beginning. Dotsuwa, the father was a square-built man with streaks of gray in his wispy long hair. He had hard eyes and a haughty expression curling his thin mouth.

A couple years or so older than Samiqwas, his son Jenaitsi was a younger version of his father in looks, but was maybe a little afraid of him. When his father was near he rarely lifted his eyes from the ground and jumped to do his bidding, but at other times Samiqwas and I found that Jenaitsi tried to get out of his share of camp chores whenever he thought he could get away with it.

Thinking that as a Kukiya he was superior to a Qwani'Ya person, he looked down his nose at Samiqwas and me, and told us just exactly what he thought of such inferior people from the north at every opportunity.

I'd had lots of practice while living at the convert settlement, enduring Charlic and his pack of scavengers, so I just ignored him. But the wolf in Samiqwas bristled at every cutting jibe and I feared there might be trouble as our journey west continued.

Catching Samiqwas alone as we came back from caring for the horses one break time, I said, "Don't bother with the puffed up little grouse. It isn't worth the trouble you will make for the war leader if you give the dog turd the beating we both know he deserves. We only have to put up with him and his father for a few days, so let it go."

"Like a lake seal shedding water off its oily fur, eh?"

"Exactly."

Samiqwas smiled, then becoming thoughtful, he muttered, "His father Dotsuwa, I wish we didn't need him to travel with us for our protection, because he is a dust eating dog turd, too."

I agreed with him, but couldn't help wondering if Eqwohi had taken the opportunity to rid himself of such a disagreeable man at the first chance that presented itself—much to our misfortune.

The trouble began that first evening when we were caring for the horses. Dotsuwa wanted Samiqwas to carry his bag and blanket roll back to our fire. Samiqwas was busy and said he would do it when he finished, but that wasn't good enough for the man. Aiming a blow at Samiqwas's head when he finally bent to pick up the man's bag and blankets, he growled, "Lazy, rotten, fish eater, I tell you take my blankets and make me a bed under the trees by fire—now not in morning."

Samiqwas hopped back before the blow connected, said a bad Chamuqwani word then stalked to our camp without looking back, leaving a cursing Kukiya warrior, and his bags behind.

Finished with my mare I came over and picked up the blankets and bag still lying at the fuming man's feet. "We have been taught to respect our Elders, Kukiya warrior," I said as I lifted them to my shoulder. "He would have carried them, if you had asked him instead of yelling and trying to hit him. It isn't our Qwani'Ya way to beat a person to get them to do what we want, nor did I think it was a Kukiya way either. Only Chamuqwani do that."

I would have carried his things, but before I could take more than a few steps Tuumaz came over and took them from me. Tossing the bags at Dotsuwa's feet he said something to him in their language that soured the man's mood even more. Motioning for me to follow him we headed back to our fire together. Looking back I saw Dotsuwa angrily gesture to his son to pick up the disputed things and follow us.

At the fire the rich smells of roasting meat and coussa flat cakes baking on a large flat stone made my mouth water. Mother and Nachoga were there already Samiqwas just sitting down to join them.

"The food smells wonderful, Amima," I said as I sat down beside Samiqwas, Tuumaz sitting on my other side.

Mother smiled at me then pointed with her lips to a grass mat where she had laid out a steaming pile of flat cakes and roasted deer meat. Reaching for the can to pour Nachoga some tea, she said, "You boys help yourselves. Everything is ready."

We needed no further urging.

After they had made their beds and unpacked Dotsuwa and his son finally joined us. Like the rest of us Jenaitsi came over and helped himself to cakes and meat, but Dotsuwa remained where he was—glaring at everyone.

I noticed that Mother had cut up Nachoga's meat to make it easier for a one handed man to eat. Smiling and joking with him she hovered near him, making sure he had everything he needed. Watching them seemed to sour Dotsuwa's mood even further.

When the war leader had finished she handed him another cup of tea then rose and announced, "That tea contains some herbs father left to help you sleep and aid the healing. I will change the wrappings on your shoulder now before you get too sleepy."

As she passed him, Dotsuwa looked to see if Nachoga was watching, then reached out a hand and grabbed her arm. "He can wait for that. Bring me food first, Woman, and be quick about it."

Startled, Mother stared mouth dropping open. Then her mouth shut and she jerked her arm out of his grasp. In a level voice, she said, "As I said, Kukiya Man, the food is ready help yourself. I am neither your wife nor your slave."

Dotsuwa curled his lip. "So you want to be only his slave?"

Mother stepped back in case he tried to grab her again. "I am no one's slave."

As she went to get the clean wrappings Nachoga chuckled and fixed him with his piercing cougar stare. "See that you remember that, warrior. The woman and the other Qwani'Ya peoples here around this fire are honored allies of the People. They are well-loved by me and my brother, so have a care and treat them with respect."

Dotsuwa snorted. "Some say, that unlike a true son of the People your brother has become too friendly with certain Chamuqwani and other outsiders. They say you and he have brought bad Puwa among the People and maybe brought these pale-skinned invaders to our land."

Even in the ruddy firelight I could see Nachoga's face turn red, but he took a deep breath before answering. In a hard voice he said, "Those who have nothing better to do with their time say lots of stupid things. My brother and I have strong Puwa that we use for the good of all. When those who chatter like noisy jays have fed the people and accomplished great deeds in war, then they will have the right to comment about what we do, and who we claim as allies."

We had planned to leave early the next morning, but during the night it rained and our leaving was delayed until the rain slowed next day. We spent a miserable night with only smoky fires for heat, tucked in hastily made branch-covered lean-tos among the pines. When we finally got started it was midmorning. Once outside the hidden canyon we found thick mud in the ravines and gusting winds on the higher slopes which slowed our progress further.

Utsiyonti and the warriors had left with us extra blankets and supplies, which was good, but still Dotsuwa complained about the weather, the slowness of our pace and anything else he could think of, whenever he returned from a scout to report.

Over the following days as we traveled ever westward Sun's heat became fierce, to our northern way of thinking, but the Kukiya seemed not to notice. The land dried, creeks shrinking to only muddy puddles when we could find them at all in the deep ravines. Sagebrush, scrub pine and juniper gave way to bunchgrass and long stretches of red sand on the slopes below twisted rock formations. Traveling in such open country was a challenge for people who wished to go in secret, so often we journeyed at night, or in the gray time before Sun awoke.

In spite of his injury Nachoga kept us going at a grueling pace. Still a newcomer to horseback riding Mother usually rode just behind or next to Nachoga so he could keep an eye on her. When his attention was elsewhere I would catch Mother giving him anxious looks, worried no doubt that he might sicken before we could reach the Prophet's healers if he overexerted himself.

When I could persuade a friendly bird to lend me their eyes I did as much scouting as possible, Samiqwas leading my mare and me tied to her back.

I saw no soldiers, but on my last pass over the trail ahead that day I did notice two Chamuqwani with a pack mule over the next ridge, heading west down the same trail we were traveling.

As I released Hawk and settled once more into my own flesh, I heard Jenaitsi say to Samiqwas, "What matter that lazy boy? Him sick or just want nap?"

Jenaitsi repeated his taunt several times, before he got an answer. Through gritted teeth Samiqwas snarled, "He's scouting."

Jenaitsi snorted. "Look like him sleep to me. My father scout, Tuumaz scout, they good Kukiya men. No need stupid, lazy dog-fucking boy, scout."

At that point I opened my eyes and before Samiqwas could do or say anything, I said, "There are two Chamuqwani with a pack mule over the next ridge in front of us. I need to tell the war leader."

Leaving the dog turd with his mouth hanging open Samiqwas clucked to his horse and we moved to catch up to Nachoga and Mother.

They were walking their horses side-by-side and talking softly and looking into each other's eyes. At our approach they broke apart Mother dropping back at the next wide point in the trail so we could approach.

"What is it, Young Puhani?"

Wounded shoulder and arm in a sling and a blanket thrown around his back and pinned in place across his chest with a stick, he looked tired, but still had the Qwakaiva to look at me with his green cougar eyes as he had always done. "There are Chamuqwani ahead," I said.

His eyes flicked from side to side, evaluating the land for concealment or a place that could be defensible in a fight. There was nothing near to hand but a small thicket of nut pines. Moving off the trail he motioned for us to head for the thicket. "Soldiers? How many Chamuqwani?"

"No soldiers. Only two Chamuqwani, wearing clothes like—like yours when you go spy on rancha men. They have a pack mule with them."

He snorted in disgust. "Probably miners then. In spite of treaty, and this Preserve land, they come." He broke off as he saw Dotsuwa coming down the trail to report.

By this time Jenaitsi, too had joined us, and once again his mouth dropped open when he heard his father's report echo what I had just said.

"What you want do, war leader? I take Tuumaz and my son and we go kill them, eh? You can stay here with woman and children."

Outwardly Nachoga's expression never changed, but I could see the red spikes of anger at the man's implied insult, and frustration at his own weakness. "Or we could just stay out of sight until we see if they are going to cause us a problem," he countered.

Dotsuwa spat in disgust, then he snarled, "What! You think they are your lost relatives, maybe? They are invaders—enemy. Whether they make trouble for us or no, they need to die this is Kukiya land!"

Nachoga's expression remained blank, but he couldn't control the red flush that colored his paler Chamuqwani skin. His hand coming to rest on the butt of the small thunder weapon he still carried at his hip, he fixed the two warriors with his green cougar stare. In his Spirit Fire the big cat snarled. "If you are so unhappy to stay with us in spite of the horses you were promised, then maybe you go back to Eqwohi, eh? We will manage without you.

"True, those men shouldn't be on our land—Kukiya land, but right now there are also many soldiers on our land. If men are killed and soldiers hear the boom of Chamuqwani weapons and find out we kill Chamuqwani miners, then more trouble for the People. I say leave them for now." I could feel his Qwakaiva gathering as he stared down the pair. "So, you and your son go watch the Chamuqwani—or go back to Eqwohi and forget about my horses."

Muttering a curse Dotsuwa wheeled his horse about and with Jenaitsi following they headed up the trail to check on the miners.

I stared after them for a time then broke the silence by asking, "What would you like me to do, war leader?"

He studied me critically with his Spirit Sight for a long moment, then said, "Nothing for now, Puhani. Tuumaz and your cousin can scout our back trail for a time. I may need your Qwakaiva strong later. Don't tire yourself doing tasks others can do now."

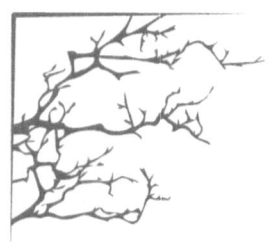

Chapter Three

Two more days passed with no further sightings of an enemy. Moving ever westward into a broken land of rocky ledges and canyons we kept an eye on the minors, but they seemed oblivious of our presence. They acted like they knew where they were going, however, and that aroused our curiosity.

Instead of going around them Nachoga, Tuumaz and Dotsuwa took council and decided to move at their slower pace to try and discover what mischief they were up to. And so Samiqwas and the warriors took turns spying on them.

As we were about to stop for the mid-day rest Dotsuwa and his son rode back to us, both men carrying new thunder weapons on their saddles and Jenaitsi dragging the minor's mule behind him on a lead rope.

Anger darkening his features Nachoga rose to meet them. When they stopped in front of him, he said. "I thought we agreed to leave the minors alone until we discovered what they were up to on our land. What happened?"

Dotsuwa smirked. "They saw us, so we had to kill them. And we know what they are doing on our land anyway."

"Oh? What?"

For answer Dotsuwa removed a small pouch from his shirt, opened its string top and displayed a palm full of yellow rocks and sand for Nachoga's inspection. "Digging for this is what the dog humpers were up to."

Mother gasped. We all knew what it meant. These Chamuqwani had discovered the golden rocks they so highly prised. The golden rocks that had caused so much heart-ache and death for both our peoples—and now, here on Kukiya land, the nightmare was beginning again.

Nachoga's expression hardened. "I was afraid of this. These men must have discovered the golden rock then went to a Chamuqwani village to buy supplies so they could return to our land and dig more rocks."

"Yes, war leader, you speak true and that why we kill them," Dotsuwa said.

Nachoga grunted his agreement, thoughtfully stroking his chin where a golden stubble of hair was starting to grow.

"We can use the extra supplies but we should find their camp and send people back to destroy all evidence of them being here," Tuumaz added.

"It may be too late for that," Nachoga said pointing with his lips to the dusty mule. "They have already been to a Chamuqwani place. They probably didn't tell the people there where they found the yellow rocks, but the gold they had to sell would have made other Chamuqwani interested in finding more. And looking on our land will be one of the first places they come. Did you find their camp before you killed them, or do we need to waste time looking for it?"

Dotsuwa nodded. "We find it." Looking grim he pointed with his lips towards a tawny lump visible through the heat haze on the western horizon. "It is near the base of Red Rock Bute up the slope from Sandy Creek. They make a pit house, but not good, too close to Creek. It would have filled with water when floods come."

"I want to see it," Nachoga said. "Maybe they will have more yellow rocks there for others to find, if we don't take them away first."

"Pit house is not far; we can stay there tonight it have water and grasses for horses nearby. Then we look around more in the morning."

When we arrived at the spot in late afternoon we saw how the miners had abused the Earth with their greedy search. Where grasses and shrubs once covered the lower slope of the butte, now the hillside was pockmarked with several bare patches where the rock had been exposed to the miners' picks and shovels.

Even to my poorly trained eye, the pit house seemed made by an inexperienced hand and ready to cave in at any moment. Garbage was everywhere, rusted cans, empty waskyja bottles, scraps of bone and other awful thrown together in untidy mounds or just left near the house to rot.

Adding to the bad smells and mess, the Kukiya hadn't bothered to drag away evidence of their slaughter. The minors sprawled in a mangled heap just outside their house. A pool of drying blood darkened the sand near the entrance already attracting a cloud of insects. Overhead a few vultures circled waiting for us to leave.

I saw the ghosts of the men watching us with mournful dead eyes, and I shivered as they called out to me, begging me to help them. Thinking of my own dead, I hardened my heart against them. <<No, I won't help you. Look where your greed and theft of Kukiya land has got you, stupid Chamuqwani?>>

They were confused and angry, but also so alien. Much to my regret later, at that time in my life I didn't know how to help them—nor did I want to.

Samiqwas grabbed Mother's horse as it shied at the blood sent. She must have felt the horses' unease as well because she said to Nachoga, "This is a bad place. Do we have to stay here tonight?"

"No, we will camp up the creek. Tomorrow my warriors and I will come back and take away what we can use. Then we will go on our way to the Prophet's encampment"

Mother seemed relieved at that, but when she studied Nachoga her expression was still troubled. When the Kukiya and Samiqwas had wandered away to explore the area, she moved her horse closer and spoke to him softly, "I know you don't want to, but you need to take the opportunity to rest tomorrow. There is still blood seeping through the wrappings at night when I change them. You aren't strong enough to do everything you want to do—or think you should do—and if you catch a fever..."

Nachoga grunted and moved his horse away, calling for Tuumaz to scout up the creek for a good camping spot. Dismounting outside the pit house he bent and stepped inside.

Mother sighed and urged her horse to follow Tuumaz up the creek. To get away from the yammering ghosts I followed her.

Noticing the vultures still circling overhead I decided to do a little scouting and I wanted a protected place away from the disharmony where I could leave my body and search. With the warriors busy with other tasks I called to Samiqwas and Jenaitsi, who were just dragging away one of the bodies into the brush. I pointed to a grassy rock shelf down the creek on our back trail. "I'm going to scout. Tell the war leader."

I retraced my steps, then dismounted and hobbled my mare to graze on the tempting green shoots. Walking to a shady spot I dug out a hollow in the sand and lay down. I was surprised when Rattlesnake slithered out from among the nearby rocks and joined me. She tucked herself next to my side, and said, <<I will keep watch for you.>>

<<Thank you, Honored One.>> Relieved and grateful, I let my Spirit fly up to greet Vulture's kin soaring above.

<<Since you are just waiting around for my relatives to finish,>> I called to them, << how about one of you flying with me and lending me your keen sight for a while? I promise you won't miss the feast they are preparing for you.>>

With Vulture lending me his eyes we flew Creek's ravine in both directions. We saw no enemies, or other relatives. Not wanting to go back so soon, I stayed with Vulture and watched my mother and Tuumaz pick a nice sheltered spot up Creek's sandy bed that had a deep pool of clear green water among a stand of cottonwoods and willows. Circling back I saw Samiqwas bringing our horses to drink at the creek downstream from the cottonwoods.

Up the slope from the miners' house Dotsuwa and Jenaitsi hacked up the now naked bodies and scattered the remains on a nearby slope to make it easier for the deserts predators to carry away all evidence of what had happened to the minors. Nachoga, I assumed, was still inside the miner's dwelling sorting through their things. I could see a growing mound of usable gear piling up outside the entrance.

A while later Vulture and I were circling back from another pass down our back trail when Rattlesnake's angry whir sounded a warning in my mind. Leaving Vulture to his own interests I sprang quickly back into my vulnerable flesh.

What I saw when I returned was Jenaitsi standing over me with a big rock in his hand. An angry snake had risen from my side with head raised and fangs dripping, ready to strike. Remaining still so as not to frighten her further, I said, "If you try to smash my head with that rock she will get you even if you hit me. Toss the rock behind you and walk backwards slowly."

Eyes wide he did as I suggested. "I-I wasn't trying to hit you," he muttered. "The war leader sent me to get you and I saw the snake..."

He broke off as I sat up letting Rattlesnake shift her position to wrap around my chest as I stood. "Mm. Well, you have delivered your message. Best you go now."

He needed no further urging. Smelly fish guts, I wasn't sure I believed him, but now that he knew I was protected by powerful allies, it might give him pause in future if he sought another opportunity to harm me. Thanking Rattlesnake for the timely warning I released her in the brush and went to get my mare.

The campsite Tuumaz and Mother found was restful, the ancient tree and the cool green water a true blessing in the heat and dryness of its desert surroundings. When I commented about it to Nachoga that night as we ate, he nodded and explained, "Sandy Creek is born from a spring deep under the mountain there." He pointed with his chin to a rocky butte glowing red in Sun's dying fire.

Another amazing thing I remember about that night was the sweet golden fruit packed inside one of the miner's big cans that Mother opened. Nachoga said the fruit was called peaches in the Chamuqwani language. They were amazing! Mother made the war leader a tea with herbs and some of the golden liquid that was also in the jar, and the rest she added to a tasty porridge the next morning.

There were more cans that we could have opened, but Mother took charge of them and later when Nachoga and Tuumaz were elsewhere trouble started when she refused to give Dotsuwa and his son some when they demanded them.

Samiqwas and I were just coming back from setting our nightly snares when we heard Dotsuwa's angry voice by the fire shouting at my mother. I would have rushed in blindly to defend her, when Samiqwas put a hand on my shoulder and pulled me back into the shadows.

"I want to see what this is all about before we rush in to help her," he murmured next to my ear. "Besides, Aunty is getting good at taking care of herself, these days."

"...We were the ones that killed those enemies all the plunder is ours by right," Jenaitsi snarled.

"And is it also a Kukiya custom to be selfish and not share?" Mother said as she stood boldly in front of her cash and put her hands on her hips. "When we go to ask for a healing for the war leader we will need gifts, both for the Prophet and the Unseen Ones who guide and aid him. I want to save them to offer for Nachoga's healing—and you want your war leader to be healed, right?"

Dotsuwa spat on the ground. "Maybe, maybe not. Why you always sit by and care for that one? Are you just another cloocha who wants to be a Chamuqwani's whore? He is no real man of the people, only a pretend Kukiya, a ghost. Better you find another man, a real Kukiya warrior. Maybe I kill him and take you be my cloocha-whore? Maybe you like that better, eh?"

When he reached for her Mother dodged, and then snatched up the digging stick Tuumaz had made for her that was resting against the cottonwood. "Don't touch me, you smelly piece of weasel vomit. You are no real man to talk to me like that."

When he would have lunged for her again Samiqwas said, "If you say bad things about my aunty again or try to harm her, I will kill you."

Turning Dotsuwa saw that Samiqwas had drawn his bow and was aiming an arrow at his chest. As fierce as the Wolf who claimed his Spirit, Samiqwas stared unblinking into the man's eyes, his hand and arm steady and unflinching.

Oblivious to the subtle game of power going on between the two Jenaitsi scoffed. Looking for his father's approval, he joked, "Want me to take care of this sassy dog-fucking baby for you, Father?"

"I wouldn't try that if I were you Kukiya," I said and stepped out of the shadows to stand beside my cousin. "If either of you harm my mother or any of my kin, you will die—and most terribly—I promise you that."

Jenaitsi skin turned ashen, visible even in the dim light. He must have told his father about his earlier encounter with my protector, because neither man chose to continue the confrontation. Muttering curses under his breath and calling me a malicer Dotsuwa stalked off, followed quickly by his son.

When they were gone I rushed over to Mother who was trembling violently. Hugging her tight, I said, "Amima, are you all right? Did he hurt you?"

Mother took a deep breath as she tried to relax and control her trembling. "No, no, I'm all right; he didn't touch me—this time. I'm glad you two were here, but I thought you were hunting."

This time?

"We were. Tas and I were just coming back from setting our snares when we heard them talking to you," Samiqwas said and lowered his bow.

"Oh, I'm sorry you had to witness that unpleasantness. How much did you hear?"

"Enough," Samiqwas said, the still snarling Wolf inside him lending his voice a harder and more mature quality than usual. "And that makes me wonder if this is the first time that dog turd has been bothering you."

"You said, 'this time.' I'd been wondering why you were always asking one of us to accompany you while doing simple chores. And why you ride or sit near the war leader as much as possible," I said. "Has he or his son been bothering you? Are you afraid of him, Amima?"

"No. I just don't want to give anyone an opportunity to make more trouble for the war leader," she said. Then needing an outlet for her pent up agitation she began picking up and packing away things people had left scattered by the fire.

"We need to tell Nachoga about his Kukiya warriors' disrespectful behavior," Samiqwas began, "He is their leader and—"

Mother whirled around clutching the can of peaches she was holding like a weapon, ready to hurl it at Samiqwas and me if we wouldn't listen. "No! You will not tell him I forbid you to say anything about this to Nachoga or Tuumaz!"

"But he is their war leader," I protested. "He needs—"

"He needs to heal," she countered, her expression stern. "That is the most important thing right now, insults made by a stupid, ignorant man who his mother is probably ashamed she bore, don't matter."

Her glare was fierce as any mother bear when she next spoke. "Not a word—I mean it. If Nachoga were to find out, then he would have to do something about it. His warrior's pride and honor would demand it. He would be no match for father and son if it came down to a physical fight—and it probably would.

"He told me Dotsuwa has carried a grudge against him for many years so this goes far beyond the insults and petty annoyances of being sent back to Golannah as our escort. I won't add another stick to that fire if I can help it. Right now Nachoga is pushing himself, but he really isn't well, and I don't want to be the cause of..."

Her breath catching on a sob she broke off, took a deep breath and said firmly, I will deal with Dotsuwa, in my own way—if I have to."

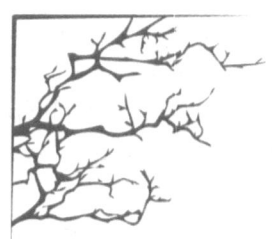

Chapter Four

It was decided to tear down the miner's pit house next day and partially fill the hole with rocks and dirt so it would appear as if it had been abandoned years ago. All the men's unsalvageable clothes and other items they agreed should be taken away and dumped. Tuumaz suggested that the things be tossed in a cave about a half days ride south. "I can do that for you, war leader, if you want," he said.

"Hmm, perhaps we should give that honor to the ones who killed them," Nachoga said and stared grimly at father and son.

Dotsuwa gave him a stiff nod. "I will go, but not that far. There are deep clefts on the butte that will do just as well. No one will find them where I put them. My son can stay and help with destroying the pit house. Then we can leave this place sooner."

"All right, do what you think best. As long as they won't lead the soldiers or other miners to the diggings of the dead ones, it's good with me."

Turning to Tuumaz he next asked, "Do you know where my brother is right now? We need to find him as soon as possible to warn him about the new threat these miners bring to our lands."

"They will most likely be at Saluuli Lake by now," Tuumaz said. "Golannah told Utsiyonti that was where the Prophet and his followers would be camping so they can harvest cattails and other roots that are ready to eat this time of year."

"Good that's only a two or three days ride west of here," Nachoga said.

Next morning the men finished their meal and had started back to the miners' camp, when Mother stopped them and announced to Nachoga that she didn't want to go with them to that evil place again.

Nachoga frowned; I could see that he wasn't happy with her decision not to come with us, but all he said was, "What do you plan to do all day, then?"

Mother gave him a smile, her eyes playful. "Oh, I plan to do lots of things. Cook, mend yours and the boys' clothes—rest, and even sleep, maybe," her smile widened, "you could join me, you know."

He chuckled deep in his throat, his eyes saying he would like nothing better. "Oh I could, could I? That is a very tempting offer." He touched her arm then his mood soured when he saw Dotsuwa and Tuumaz frowning at them. "But not today. You will have to rest alone—today."

Glancing at the others waiting for him her smile disappeared as well. "I don't really plan to lie about, but you should come back and rest at some point, so you won't tire yourself over much. And I do mean rest—because I won't be here to distract you. I actually want to wash clothes and your bandages up the creek, as well as gather willow bark and whatever foods I can find for us to eat while we journey tomorrow."

He thought about it then grunted his agreement with her plan. "I will have one of the young warriors check on you from time to time to see if you need help."

As I started to follow them, Mother held me back with a touch on my arm. "Stubborn man! Try to keep him from overdoing himself if you can, my son. Sometimes he gets so frustrated with his weakness and does too much, and then the injury breaks open and bleeds again."

Annoyed, I grumped, "I'm not sure how you expect me, a mere child, to stop a grown man and my war leader, when you couldn't, Amima?" But then I heard the real worry and concern behind her words, and stopped my complaining. I shared them.

When she opened her mouth to get angry or maybe argue with me, I patted her arm and changed the subject. "I think you really like him, don't you, Amima? Is he the one you will choose to be my new father?"

Startled, Mother closed her mouth and stared at me as if I had grown moose horns on my head. She was silent for a long moment, then when I thought she wouldn't answer, she said, "Marry him? I don't know—hadn't really thought about him that way... Would that displease you, my little Rock Squirrel, my son?"

Would it displease me? I hadn't thought of their growing interest in each other in quite that way, before I opened my big mouth, either. I thought about it for a moment longer, then shook my head and said, "No. it wouldn't displease me at all, Amima. If you want him you have my permission. I would be proud to call him my new father."

She chuckled and gave me a big hug. "Not that I need your permission, as a mere child, of course, but thank you."

When I caught up to the warriors Nachoga, too, put a hand on my shoulder to hold me back. "What did your mother want?"

Grinning I said, "She wants me to keep you from being stupid and breaking open your shoulder again."

"Mm, and how does she expect you to do that?"

I shrugged. "She didn't say."

He walked on for a while, then asked, "She kept you with her a long time. What else did you two talk about?"

Smiling and wanting to joke with him, I said, "I asked her if she liked you, and if you were going to be my new father. I told her that if so, she had my permission if she wanted to marry you."

Nachoga stopped abruptly on the path and whirled to fix me with green cougar eyes. Startled I shrank back. He was shielding his thoughts from me so I couldn't tell if my joking had made him angry, but his intense stare made me nervous. At last he released me and continued walking. Without looking at me he chuckled to himself and then finally said, "What did she say when you asked her those questions?"

"I'm sorry, war leader. I-I was teasing with her when I told her she had my permission to marry you—I meant no disrespect to you or Amima. I would be honored to call you father," I stammered. "And-and she did say she liked you—very much."

He snorted a laugh and caught up to Tuumaz who had paused to wait for us.

Keeping mother's instructions in mind, I stayed close to him throughout the morning, helping the warriors and Samiqwas dig and hall rocks and debris to fill up the hole made by the collapsed pit house. Between Tuumaz and I we convinced Nachoga to leave the stone lifting to us and take charge of leading the mule back and forth while we piled rocks into carry baskets and the little cart we'd found by one of the digging sites.

Samiqwas and I checked on Mother a few times that morning, but she didn't need our help for anything. During the midday heat we all cooled off in the creek and rested in the shade of the willows. At one point I was sure I'd seen the war leader fall asleep—which would please Mother when I told her.

Our work was nearing completion in late afternoon when Nachoga walked over to where I was gathering my last load of stones and said to me in a low voice, "Have your Spirit Helpers given you a warning sign that something is wrong?"

Startled I hastily dropped the stone I'd been lifting into the basket and looked around. Seeing nothing amiss, I shook my head. "No, but maybe I wasn't paying enough attention. Have you had a sending?"

Nachoga stroked his chin, considering my question. "Not a sending exactly, but—something. Dotsuwa should have come back by now. Before you tire yourself too much, with the rocks, can you scout for enemies and see if you can find him?"

A prickle of fear sliding down my spine I nodded. "I will search."

Moving quickly away from that disturbed place I searched, with my own eyes, the cliffs for either a sight of Dotsuwa, or a friendly bird to help me. Vulture and his relatives were busy, but to my surprise a board young eagle clung to a high outcrop, and he was willing to help.

Taking flight we floated on Wind's currents high above the canyon and the surrounding cliffs. There were no soldiers or other enemies sneaking up on us, but also no Dotsuwa on his way back to camp.

I told Eagle to fly a bit lower and do another pass...

There were Samiqwas and Jenaitsi bringing the horses to the creek for their last drink, before hobbling them near the cottonwood for the night...

At the miner's campsite, Tuumaz was holding up a burning clump of sage and circling the disturbed ground. As cleansing blue smoke formed patterns in the cooling air his chanting prayer echoed off the surrounding hills. Nachoga stood by the unharnessed mule, thunder weapon in hand, joining the prayer song, and scanning the hillsides for signs of trouble.

Seeing nothing amiss, I urged my friend to continue up the creek towards our camp. When we flew over I was surprised that the evening cook fire hadn't been rekindled. Lighting in the cottonwood for a better look I could see no Mother busy preparing our meal. Starting to truly share Nachoga's worry I urged Eagle back to the sky and we continued searching.

Heading up the creek to where I'd last seen Mother digging coussa root I saw only a tipped over basket roots falling out, a scattered tangle of cleaned bandages laying in the grass, but no mother. <<Help me, Brother Eagle. My Nest-Mother where...?>>

We circled, then a little farther up the stream Eagle's keen sight caught a series of violent movements in the rabbit brush. Pushing past my own turbulent emotions, I was at last able to translate the jumble of avian images Eagle's eyes were sending me.

Torn clothing, bruises, blood, Dotsuwa and Mother were struggling. She was fighting him, trying hard to defend herself with her digging stick, not making it easy for him, but she was losing her battle. Then as I watched he jerked the stick out of her hands and smashed his fist into her unprotected belly. Mother sank to the ground, and clutched at her middle. Throwing the digger to one side he loosened his clothing, rolled her over and tried to mount her like a maddened dog.

Rage goading me I conveyed my fear to Eagle. <<Help, Nest Mother, Egg-Layer, Attack enemy, kill, KILL!>>

With a scream of white-hot rage Eagle folded his wings and plunged earthward.

Before Dotsuwa could complete his vile act, a heavy weight slammed into him, knocking him aside. Powerful talons bit deep into his head and neck while a hooked beak tore at his face. Blinded by blood and pain Dotsuwa let out a piercing roar, and batted unsuccessfully at the winged demon trying to kill him.

Rolling out of the way Mother managed with the help of her discarded stick to pull herself out of danger and get to her feet. Wide eyed, and gasping for breath, she added her own shouts to the growing din, begging me to stop.

Eagle and I might have killed the man, and a part of me wished we had for all the trouble he and his son caused us, but the Unseen Ones had other plans for him. And at last Mother's frantic shouting to me to stop penetrated through the haze of white-hot fury clouding my reason. I released Eagle to fly away, leaving the bloody man sobbing and cursing in a crumpled heap on the ground.

Falling back into my body I swallowed my nausea at such a quick transition, staggered to my feet, and lurched for my horse. Once I was mounted I galloped down the path, heading for my injured mother. Already alerted by Eagle's scream and Dotsuwa and Mother's shouting Tuumaz and Nachoga, still by the miners' destroyed campsite, had stopped working and grabbed up weapons.

"Are we being attacked?" Tuumaz shouted as I raced past him.

"No. You come—Mother..."

All the horses were at the creek with Samiqwas and Jenaitsi, but Nachoga needed no further explanation from me. Leaping bareback atop the startled mule, he slapped its rump with his quirt and pounded after me. Still afoot Tuumaz raced along in his wake.

Being closer to the trouble both Samiqwas and Jenaitsi had gotten to the site before us. When Nachoga and I arrived Jenaitsi had helped his father to his feet and was urging him to climb onto his horse and shouting curses and promises of revenge at mother. Still wide eyed and frightened she had retreated a little way up the slope and was trying to pull her torn clothing together while Samiqwas possessed by his snarling wolf stood protectively in front of her with his bow drawn.

I saw with grim satisfaction that though nowhere close to giving him dying wounds, Eagle's attack would leave him hideously scarred for life, and he might lose an eye. Long talon marks scored his head, neck and shoulders, streams of red flowing down his arms, back and chest. Only half conscious Dotsuwa was barely able to stay on the horse unaided. When he saw us coming Jenaitsi took one look at Nachoga's face, leapt onto the horse behind his father and together they galloped off up the creek.

Beating the mule cruelly Nachoga raced after them. Sensing its rider's urgency the mule tried to catch up to the fleeing horse, but even carrying double Jenaitsi's horse soon left the exhausted and struggling mule behind.

At last the war leader gave up and rode the wheezing mule back to us. Sliding off its back he rushed to Mother. The back of his shirt was now stained red; the day's events had indeed opened the wound in his shoulder as Mother had feared.

Pulling her to him he hugged her then held her out to examine her injuries. "How badly are you hurt?"

"I'm all right, war leader, only cuts and bruises—I'm not hurt—truly. He just surprised me when I was digging for coussa. He claimed I'd been teasing him, wanting him to—but I've done nothing to encourage his interest," Mother protested, her eyes moist and pleading for Nachoga to believe her.

Grim-faced Nachoga nodded and stared at the dust cloud that was all that remained of the retreating men. "I believe you, Qwani'Ya Woman, I truly do. Because he has a powerful Puhani for an uncle that weasel piss drinker thinks he can get away with anything. For years he and his family have tried to destroy me, my brother, and all we care about at every opportunity. —But not this time. He has gone too far..." The fist on his uninjured side was clinched tight enough to crush rocks as he struggled to master his emotions.

I said, "His injuries are my doing. Samiqwas and I warned him last night what would happen if either of them bothered her again. I would have killed him this time if she hadn't pleaded for me to stop."

The war leader whirled to glare at me. "What are you talking about—this time?"

"Last night when we were coming back from setting our snares we heard the dog turd threatening her and calling her bad names," Samiqwas said. "I drew my bow and told him I, too, would kill him if he bothered her again."

Shifting his anger to Mother he said, "This has happened before?" When she reluctantly nodded he swore a terrible curse. "Why didn't you tell me, woman?"

Standing up to his ire, she snapped, "And what would you have done, eh? Get into a fight with him—injure your shoulder worse—or get yourself killed? And for what? You would risk your life over the mindless chatter of a scolding jay?

"I didn't tell you, and made the boys promise not to tell you, to avoid what I am seeing in your eyes right now. I thought I could handle him. And I didn't want you to get hurt—again."

He swore once more, his eyes flashing green fire. "And do you always protect your men and try to fight a warrior's battles for him?" he growled.

"Yes I do," she shot back. "If the warrior is injured—and behaving stupidly—like you are now. I did it for Tas's father and now I do it for you."

That gave him pause. Closing his mouth he stared at her, his fierce expression demanding an answer. "What do you mean? If the stories about your son's father being a Spirit warrior from the Unseen World are true how could that be?"

"Because when I found him he had been badly injured. He was still in his seal form—too injured to change." She chuckled reliving the memory. "I thought I was the luckiest woman in my village to find such a big piece of meat unclaimed on the beach. Then he spoke to me and I realized my mistake.

"I dragged him back to my lodge and cared for him until he was well enough and had to leave me. But while he was still with me I twice fought off the evil monsters that were chasing him."

Caught up in her tale, but not sure if he totally believed her, Nachoga snorted. "You, a mere human woman, defeated creatures from Beyond, who hunted a Spirit warrior? I find that hard to believe. How did you do that, Qwani'Ya woman?"

Eyes defiant, she glared at him and the rest of her male audience and dared them to question her account. "I don't really care if you believe me."

"How?"

"I used my woman's magic to defeat them. The first time I was alone when those fearsome creatures found me. They were searching for him. Using my moon blood's power, I made them leave.

"The second time we were together, but he was still too weak to fight them. So, he showed me the glyphs and we painted them in my blood to protect us that terrible night," she said.

Defiant and angry now herself she used a soldier's bad word and folded her arms across her chest. "And I don't care if you men believe me or not. I speak true."

When the two continued to glare at one another Samiqwas diverted them, by saying, "Aunty that is an amazing story." Turning to me, he murmured, "Did you know about this, Tas?"

I did know, but I wasn't going to admit it, because I had found out by spying on her dreams at Chumco's urging, and I was ashamed of my prying. So I just shook my head and gave him an enigmatic smile.

Mounted now with Thunder weapon in hand, Tuumaz returned the topic to the matter of punishing the fleeing Dotsuwa. And asked, "Want me to go after them; kill the mad dog for you, war leader?"

"No. I will do it myself." Nachoga snarled. "Samiqwas get my horse."

Mother clutched his uninjured arm and pleaded. "Nachoga, stop! You have torn open the wound again. Can't you feel the warm blood dripping down your back? Already you have damaged the healing my father gave you. Do you want to be a crippled warrior for the rest of your life?

"Please, stop and think. Take your vengeance—later—if you must but not now while you are so weak."

"Woman, don't try to tell me what to do! I won't let you rule me. A woman's blood Puwa can't resolve what has been festering between me and that weasel dung for far too long. It's time to lance the boil."

"Stupid, stubborn man!" she cried still holding onto his good arm. "How can I marry you if you get yourself killed?"

They have no supplies with them," Samiqwas said, pouring a cup of cool reason onto their heating argument. "Maybe they come back. Better we wait and set a trap for them rather than chasing them now, and riding into an ambush." Nachoga considered and reluctantly agreed.

Then hearing the boom of a thunder weapon in the distance and then the noise of frightened horses running away both Kukiya knew exactly what had happened. Tuumaz took off in pursuit, Nachoga, ignoring his bleeding shoulder snatched up the reigns of my mare, and then he and Samiqwas raced after Tuumaz.

With only the poor tired mule left for us, Mother sighed. We looked at one another then started back to our camp among the cottonwoods. Leading the poor beast between us we paused at the creek for her to wash up, while I collected her fallen belongings and gathered a couple clay jars of water. We were going to need them.

We learned when we returned to our camp that while we had all been busy with other tasks that afternoon, Dotsuwa had packed up his and his son's things and hidden them away elsewhere in case he had needed a quick escape after planning his attack on my mother.

And leaving the horses as they had in such a hurry neither Samiqwas nor Jenaitsi had hobbled them. They had only left them to graze and drink as they pleased by the creek. So it had been easy for the fugitives to circle around, reclaim their things, collect another mount, then scatter the rest.

When the warriors returned later they brought with them most of the missing horses, but Nachoga's gray, that he was growing quite fond of, was not among them. Knowing what a blow that would be to Nachoga's pride, Jenaitsi had managed to steel him away before scattering the rest. And by heading east, to join the raiders into the Chamuqwani claimed lands the fugitives knew we wouldn't follow.

Stronger than Nachoga in speaking mind-to-mind my Gift made contacting Utsiyonti easy for me and that night I entered his dreams and told him what had happened to Mother and Nachoga. I didn't want the fugitives to be spreading lies when they caught up with the rest of the warband.

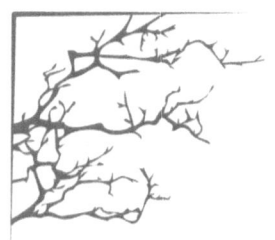

Chapter Five

Fortunately Tuumaz knew where to find Golannah's camp, because by the time we reached Saluuli Lake two days later War Leader Nachoga was burning up with fever and unable to guide us. Over his feeble protests we had strapped him to a pony-drag that morning to keep him from falling off the spare horse again. With only the young Tuumaz and his thunder weapon to protect us I had spent much of the journey tied to my mare, my spirit flying with the winged ones scouting.

Saluuli Lake was a shallow bowl of water in a dry valley surrounded by purple mountains that were often capped with snow in deep winter. Although to the west and southern edges of the lake the land dried out once again, around the eastern and northern edges the lake's shoreline was covered with a thick green mass of cat tails and other edible swamp-growing plants that the Kukiya gathered for food.

When we reached the sprawling camp on the east side of the lake we were met by a delegation of armed warriors and Elders. Though Golannah was away that day, fortunately several men recognized Tuumaz so we had no trouble being welcomed and shown to a grassy ledge where members of Golannah's clan were staying.

The news already spread of our arrival Aunty Ashiqwa and Uncle Tli's new wife were there to greet us as we led our tired horses and the mule into their camp. All smiles her round body seemingly bigger than when I last saw her, Sagila was quivering with excitement until she saw Nachoga on the pony-drag and then realized Uncle wasn't among us as well. But she brightened again when she heard Uncle wasn't dead and then saw Mother, and Samiqwas told her that she was Tli's sister.

"Come, come my new relatives, you come sit my fire I make food, you rest."

We gratefully followed her to a grassy spot where Sagila and other relatives had constructed several cattail mat covered shelters around a central stone hearth. We helped carry Nachoga into the shelter Sagila directed us to, and laid him on a thick mattress of grasses and reed mats. His fever high in spite of Mother's constant efforts to force willow bark tea down his throat, he was mumbling and incoherent by the time we got him settled.

Refusing to leave him to eat or rest, Mother sat down beside him talking to him in a soothing voice and bathing his face with a wet rag from time to time.

Motioning us back outside Sagila directed us to sit by her fire while she brewed up and served us tea and a thick mush made with cattail roots, wild onions and goose grease.

"No worry about mother," Sagila confided to me when I would have argued with Amima about resting. "Me make mother eat and rest soon."

As we rested and ate we were joined from time to time by more Kukiya relatives and other interested people who were staying by the lake for the annual harvest of roots and the big hunt for the migrating wild birds. Each time a new group joined us we had to repeat our story of Nachoga's wounding and Dotsuwa's betrayal and attack again.

I was exhausted and wanting nothing more than to curl up in my blankets and sleep for about a year, when Golannah and a few of his most trusted warriors arrived on dusty horses, demanding answers. Hurrying into the hut he saw his feverish brother, spoke briefly with Mother then backed out to fix Tuumaz and me with the full force of his angry, accusing glare.

Tuumaz quickly stammered through a more detailed account of our journey. Still not satisfied he next turned his ire on me. "I think you have big Puwa, young Puhani, but your family cause Kukiya much trouble."

After the agency rescue that caused his brother's wounding I was afraid he would make us leave—and not sure what Samiqwas, mother and I would do if that happened, I looked him in the eye and boldly said, "A warrior knows he could be wounded, or die at any time he challenges the enemy.

"Yes Nachoga was injured while rescuing members of my family, but my Grandfather used his Puwa to draw the Chamuqwani iron from his shoulder and I gave him some of my power on several occasions on our journey to help him get here safely.

"Before Dotsuwa's betrayal he was doing fine, Betsiya even said so, and that's why she chose to go with her husband instead of staying with us like you wanted."

"That's true," Samiqwas added. "He was doing well until your own Kukiya warrior attacked my aunty, a woman your brother cares for. He chose of his own free will to go after the pair of dog turds who injured her, thus undoing much of the healing that had already begun from his earlier wound."

"Knowing there was already bad blood between them, why did Eqwohi send that particular pair to escort us here, ask yourself that before you blame us for this terrible misfortune," I added.

Golannah grunted then fell silent, taking a moment perhaps to ask himself that very question. Into the silence, I swallowed hard to choke down my fear and quietly said, "I love Nachoga like a father, war leader, I want to see him healed as much as you do—and I will do all in my power to see that happens.

"Before he left us my grandfather recommended we seek a further healing from Iyantsha or another with him who has a strong gift for healing. So maybe instead of blaming someone for this misfortune we should seek out the Prophet. Where is he; can we bring your brother to him now?"

Golannah glared at me for my impudence, then at last nodded and gave orders to a couple warriors to find Iyantsha.

It was our good fortune that Iyantsha was nearby and had planned a ceremony for several others who were injured or sick that had come to him to ask for his healing and to hear the teachings. We were told he would send for us to bring Nachoga to the ceremonial grounds when all was ready.

Barely able to keep my eyes open after Golannah left I took my blankets and crawled into the nearby shelter Sagila directed me to and lay down on the cattail mats and grasses that had been piled up for sleeping upon. Once there, however, my mind wouldn't release me into the oblivion sleep offered. I lay in the darkness, watching the firelight make flickering shadows on the hut's wall, and listening to the quiet talk still going on around the cook fires.

I was worried, about my family's uncertain standing among the outlaws, and most of all what would happen to Nachoga, a man I had truly grown to care for. None of the Kukiya had bothered to tell me what had caused the bad feelings between the war leader and Dotsuwa—though they all seemed to know.

But I couldn't help suspecting that there was more to the war leader's fever than the fact that he had reinjured his shoulder when chasing after Dotsuwa and his son. I feared a malicer's power was at work here and I needed help if I wanted to protect him.

In the Dream I shifted into my half seal half human form and swam to the deep grotto under the Earth where I had last seen my benefactor Kunai. Climbing out of the black pool I sat on a flat rock, composed myself, and sent out a call to him. While I waited Rattlesnake joined me, wrapping her sinuous body around my waist.

<<I am here if you need me,>> she said as I stroked her cool scales.

It is hard to get a sense of time passing within the Dream, but I felt like we waited for a long period before the Great One chose to come to me. And when he did, I was surprised, because he appeared in his true form. I only became aware of his approach when I saw a light shining up from the depths getting larger as he came. Lifting his horned head out of the dark pool at last, I realized that the light's source was a small crystal embedded in the scales of his forehead. Water dripping from his jaw he surveyed me with cool green eyes, dragon eyes with their vertically slit pupils that seemed to look into the very depths of my soul.

Kunai drew from my thoughts without me having to explain in words all that had happened since our last meeting. When he'd finished with me he rumbled a laugh. <<So your mother has finally forsaken her Qwa'Nayhi Seal lover and now wishes to lie with the Cougar and bear his kittens, hmm? And you, Siyatli Boy, do you want to claim the big cat as a new father, as well? Star Swimmer will be crushed when I tell him of your fickle human betrayal.>>

<<I doubt that, Great One, my father wishes only good for my mother—and me. I heard him tell her that when I spied on her dreams. He will not begrudge us the love of another human when he himself can't come to us, I think.>>

Kunai rumbled another laugh. <<You are a bold one, little Siyatli, and that is why I have favored you with my Gifts. You have done well with the tasks I have set for you so far and I am pleased. Perhaps you deserve the

happiness and love that the Cougar will give you—for a time. And so I will give you another Gift to show my favor.>>

Coming closer Kunai laid his massive head on the ledge beside me and once more fixed me with his penetrating dragon stare. The jewel nestled in a cleft between his brows pulsed with white fire, nearly blinding me with its Qwakaiva.

<<You are right to suspect that there is more to the warrior's illness than can be detected in the physical realm. His old enemy has concealed a charm given to him by a powerful malicer among the Cougar's belongings. It was triggered when Nachoga himself tore open his wound and allowed his blood to touch it.

<<I will give you a Gift to help return the evil to its source and aid in his recovery, but you will have to earn it.>>

In my mind Rattlesnake whirred a warning, reminding me that Kunai's favor was not given lightly. A gift of power would demand a sacrifice on my part in return. All the thoughts about our place among the outlaws, my mother's happiness, and my overwhelming desire to know a father's love and approval, all these feelings tumbled around in my mind as I considered Kunai's offer.

Deciding I had no other choice I accepted. <<What must I do, Honored One to receive your blessings?>>

Kunai smiled showing his fangs. <<You will have to use your wits and your Qwakaiva to take the crystal that you see lying in the cleft on my forehead. If you can obtain it, keep it in a pouch and wear it always. It will speak to you and guide you on how to use its power. You will find it useful—for many things in future.>> Kunai rumbled another laugh. <<But first you have to take it, little Siyatli. Come let's see how clever you are.>> and without another word of warning the Great One disappeared into the black water.

<<Quickly now,>> Rattlesnake cried. <<Or you will lose him.>>

With her still wrapped about my body I assumed my seal form and dived into the pool, swimming after him. Through my whiskers I could sense the disturbance in the water ahead as the massive bulk of the dragon sped through the blackness. Occasionally I caught glimpses of light as he navigated the twists of the channel and the crystal's glow reflected off the cavern walls.

It seemed like I had been chasing him for days and getting no closer to catching up to him, but I knew that was only a figment of my human imagination. I was tiring, but I refused to give in to the temptation to stop—rest. If I did that I would lose the trail and might as well just return with nothing to my sleeping body.

At Rattlesnake's urging to hurry I heedlessly sped around a bend in the channel and then suddenly became entangled in a mass of slimy black weeds, stinking of mold and rot. As I tried to push my way through, the gluey mass came alive, stems wrapping themselves around my flippers to pull me under the water's surface.

<<Keep going they are but an illusion,>> Rattlesnake counseled.

Illusion they might be, but the vegetation was a very "real illusion," and it seemed their intent was definitely to trap and smother me. Every time I tried to wriggle my way through, sinuous branches grabbed for me and flat black leaves clung to my face covering my nose and mouth. Thorns raked my flesh and I choked on a foul tasting slime that clogged my throat when I tried freeing myself by biting them.

Even within the realm of the Dream the instinct of my spirit body to breathe was undeniable. I growled a bad Chamuqwani word, and shifted into a half-human form. With my Qwakaiva I created a long knife and slashed my way through the clinging mass until I reached open water again.

But somewhere in my struggle I had lost Rattlesnake. Panicked I started back to look for her, calling out, and fearing that once again I had been careless and taken the life of a guide sent to aid me.

Then I paused, the war leader's words coming into my mind, Spirit Helpers can take care of themselves. If I went back among those lethal plants to look for her, I would surely die. I must continue—alone if necessary. At that point I wasn't sure if she was dead, or alive and had retreated on her own, the vegetation just another illusion sent by my Benefactor to test me.

Back at the corral with the cai I could have died when I foolishly wanted to rescue the snake that didn't need my help, and now I was being tempted to risk myself again. Not this time, I would keep going.

Still in my half seal half human shape, with knife in hand I continued swimming through the blackness, my senses straining to catch the first sign of danger. On my own for the first time in the underground watery world of the Dream's unpredictable inhabitants I was cautious, cringing at any unfamiliar sound.

Then up a head light reflected on the rock wall of the passage—surely it was Kunai. Maybe at last I was nearing the end of my quest... But fearing another trick I preceded slowly. When I swam around the next bend I saw to my dismay that the channel split into three passages, each glowing with their own source of radiance.

I stopped to contemplate my options. Three passages, three sources of light, did that mean that there were three dragons waiting to attack, and maybe eat me? And when I swam down one passage the others would come at me from behind? Or were two glowing beacons only illusions meant to divert me from my true goal.

Feeling the first signs of panic knotting in my gut I hesitated, but knew I must master my fear and do something—the Great One wouldn't wait forever. Doing nothing could be as deadly as making the wrong choice.

At last choosing not to play his game I decided to change the rules and win the prize on my terms. I wasn't going to swim into any glowing passage where I could be ambushed if I chose wrong. I would make him come to me.

Diving to the bottom of the channel I collected several fist-size rocks and placed them in a net I created with my Qwakaiva. Returning to the surface I took in a great lungful of air and roared my challenge. At the same time I started hurling my rocks into each passage, hoping to flush out my true adversary.

It didn't take long. Suddenly three angry dragons came charging at me out of the darkness, the crystals on their foreheads blinding me with their brilliance. Throwing one last missile at the advancing beasts I backed up till I had solid rock at my back. Forming a war spear I shouted my defiance and thrust it forward in my defense.

The three images of the Great One mocked me, their thunderous laughter echoing off the cavern walls, causing small rocks to fall from the ceiling.

<<Puny human you can't scare us with your little stick. Come, little Siyatli, choose and quickly now or become our next meal.>>

Oh, which one of the three monsters advancing on me was my Benefactor, the only one who wouldn't kill me. Rattlesnake was no longer there for me to rely upon her advice. I was on my own. Studying the images before me in the narrow passage my first instinct was to choose the dragon looming in the middle, but that might be too easy of a choice, and one Kunai might have figured I might choose.

While I pondered, trying to determine if the image seemed a little blurred and unformed at the edges, the dragon monster on my right had crept closer and now took a swipe at me with his lethal claws extended.

I saw the blow just before it would have taken my head from my body, and dodged, so that only the tip of one talon scraped down my cheek. The smell of fresh blood perfumed the moist air and the dragon images roared in triumph and charged me.

Back in my seal shape I barked a war cry of my own, and then using my Qwakaiva I spat a fiery bolt at the nearest clawed foot coming at me again. As the missile struck, the image exploded in a burst of white-hot fire. Diving under water I swam for the bottom hoping to elude my pursuers for a time in the murk the dragons had churned up during our combat.

I hoped the fiery explosion meant that I had eliminated one of my adversaries, but even if that was so, Kunai and another still pursued me—and I would need to come up for air soon. Staying down till I thought my lungs would burst, I swam as fast as my strength would allow, not to escape them, but to go beneath them so I could attack from behind.

Surfacing at last I found myself, not behind them as I'd hoped, but between them. Before one could turn to bite me, or slap me with its mighty tail I became human again. I chose the nearest solid body at random, and began climbing up his scaled shoulder. I grabbed onto one of his horns and swung out of reach as he swiveled around to snap at me. The dragon roared and shook his head violently, trying to dislodge me, but like a leech holding fast to a healthy white fish I wouldn't let go.

When he next tried to dislodge me by scraping his horns against the rock wall I slithered down to their base and then crawled up to the bony plates between his eyes.

A smile of triumph curving my lips I reached out and grasped the glowing crystal. My Benefactor had one more surprise to test me, however. As my hands closed around the crystal, the force of its Qwakaiva shot a wave of blinding pain up my arm that continued to spread throughout my body. Though it felt like I held Sun's living fire between my fingers I refused to let go.

I opened my mouth wide and screamed, singing the pain, letting my agony explode in a kaleidoscope of color and sound. I was trembling like a leaf in the wind, but I refused to release my hold. I was determined to endure his trials and survive or die in the attempt. Too many I loved were counting on me needing me to help push away the evil threatening my people—my world.

My fingers like bloody claws I pulled and at last he allowed me to take it. With one last stab of fiery pain the crystal loosened and with it still held tight in my hand I fell backwards into oblivion.

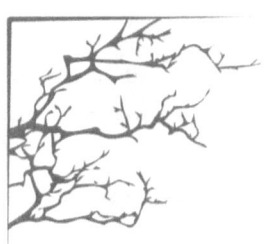

Chapter Six

When I took in a deep breath and opened my eyes I could make out the bundled forms of several people sleeping around me in the gloom. It must be nearing dawn, I reasoned, and then I also became aware of the throbbing pain radiating from my clinched fist. I sat up slowly so as not to alarm Rattlesnake, who I was relieved to see had joined me again under my blankets.

There on my blood-crusted palm when I opened my hand, a clear crystal being with points on both ends lay. Though it didn't glow in the Physical world as it had in the Dream, I could still feel its power. It had already been coated with my blood but to make the connection between us stronger I took it into my mouth, covered it with my spit, and savored its bitter mineral flavor upon my tongue.

<<Greetings, Honored Elder, touch my memories and savor my Spirit as you get to know me—as I will you. Thank you for coming to be my guide and protector.>>

At first the crystal I had taken from Kunai still claimed much Qwakaiva from the Great One, but beneath his presence I could feel the connection beginning between us. At last placing the crystal being in a small pouch that I wore around my neck I gathered up the sleepy snake and stepped outside to find the privy.

By this time there was a rosy glow in the east. Fog had crept in silently during the night and now hid all but the closest bunches of cattails in its heavy mass. Out on the lake a few ducks called a sleepy greeting to the day. Somewhere further away a horse nickered and a couple women chatted with one another as they tended the fires under the drying racks. The air was moist, smelling of smoke, frying wild onions, old blood and rotting swamp weed.

Heading to the shore I soaked my sore hand for a time in Lake's cool soothing water. Finally washing off some of the blood that had begun to dry on my arms and face I walked to the shelter where I knew we had laid Nachoga and entered.

Mother had fallen asleep, curled up near him in the cocoon of her blanket, snoring softly, one hand reaching out for him even in her slumber. There were others sleeping in the shadows of the lodge, but when I came near his bed, Nachoga himself was awake. He was lying on his side so as not to put pressure on his shoulder. He didn't speak, but his feverish green eyes followed me as I approached and knelt beside him.

<<Rattlesnake, help me. What should I do now?>>

Poking her head out of my shirt she touched her tongue to my ear, and said, <<Take out the crystal you won from Kunai and look through it with your left eye. It will show you where the evil is lodged.>>

Nachoga had noticed my companion, but said nothing and showed no fear. "Don't be afraid; we are here to help you," I murmured to assure both him and myself." Taking out the crystal being from its pouch I showed it to him. "I travelled into the Dream tonight for you, and my Benefactor, the Great Kunai, gave this one to me."

I wasn't sure how much of what I was telling him he could understand in his fever, but as I held the crystal to my eye, I explained, "Using it I may be able to see the bad Puwa a malicer has placed on you. That is the first step towards your healing."

Through the lens of the crystal I scanned Nachoga from the top of his head to his feet. I found it difficult to interpret what I was seeing at first, but between Crystal Being and Rattlesnake I was able to understand.

On his back and down the afflicted arm I could see muddy swirls of a sticky gray substance that was growing larger as it fed off his injured flesh. I hissed and dropped the stone from my eye. Taking a deep breath I replace the lens and asked my guides, <<Will this evil kill him?>>

<<Maybe. If the evil isn't removed soon then that is a true possibility.>>

<<How can we stop this evil?>>

Mother had awakened and was watching me. Before my guides could answer she asked me what I was doing and I turned to her with the crystal still held to my eye. Looking at her through the crystal without thinking I saw that she, too had been infected by the malicer's Puwa. On her, there were only faint traces of the gray substance, but in time she too would sicken if not treated.

<<Rattlesnake, are all of us who traveled with the war leader infected by this evil one's malice,>> I cried.

<<All but you, yes, to some degree, but I have, at the Great One's command, protected you. Now you must find the source of the evil and burn it so that your relatives can be healed.>>

When Mother repeated her question I returned my attention to her and the other people awake and watching me. "Nachoga has been witched by a malicer's charm that someone, probably Dotsuwa or his son, placed among Nachoga's belongings. We must find it and destroy it or he may not survive, my helpers tell me."

Mother gasped, looking at me wide eyed. "Oh, Tas that is so terrible. What can we do to save him?"

"It's worse than that, Amima, you are infected with the evil and maybe Samiqwas and Tuumaz as well. We must search through Nachoga's things until we find the talisman—"

"Don't bother searching just burn everything, my clothes, my bedding my saddle weapons—everything," Nachoga growled and swore in the Chamuqwani language. "I should have killed that lying weasel Dotsuwa years ago, instead of giving way to the wishes of—others." He had been listening and surprised everyone when he spoke.

"Burning everything may be too extreme, warrior, but all of you are right that the evil must be found and destroyed, before it does more harm."

I turned at the sound of a strange voice and saw that someone unknown to me had entered the lodge while I had been busy. He was a slim dark-skinned Kukiya man with luminous brown eyes and full lips. He wore a headband braided with colored yarns across his forehead, his black hair tied back to fall in a long tail down his back.

When he had everyone's attention he came forward to crouch in front of Nachoga. "I am Tiwari, I have been sent to bring you to the ceremonial ground and help prepare you—all of you for the ceremony."

Over Tiwari and Mother's protests, being the stubborn man that he was, Nachoga refused a litter and insisted he would walk to the ceremonial grounds, which turned out to be some distance to the south on the lakeshore.

With Tiwari leading the way and mother and I walking beside him he made his slow, shuffling way to the gravel beach where the ground had been cleared for the Prophet's gathering. Nearly at the end of his great strength by the time Golannah and his warrior's met us Nachoga didn't argue with his brother and allowed himself to be placed on a litter and carried the rest of the way to the center of the circle. Ignoring the glares given us by some of the Kukiya, I took Mother's hand and followed Golannah into the inner circle.

Directed by the Prophet's helpers, all wearing similar headbands to Tiwari, the warriors set Nachoga's litter down in the southern arm of a four armed cross with a fire wafting sweet smoke at its middle. Three other litters with severely injured or sick people laid upon them formed the east, west, and north arms of the cross.

At the outer perimeter of the circle people were gathering, waiting for the ceremony to begin. Off to one side, just outside the circle several men stood around a small fire warming their hand drums.

As I pulled mother down to sit opposite Golannah at Nachoga's side, she got a good look at me in the morning light. Her eyes widened and she murmured, "Tas, what happened to your face? There's a bloody wound on your cheek. How?"

Sometime along our journey to that place the claw wound on my cheek had begun to bleed again. I smiled to reassure her and patted her hand. "It's nothing, Amima, it's only a gift from my Benefactor to remind me not to be stupid in future." She looked at me as if she wanted to ask for more information, but decided this wasn't the time.

Now that she had drawn my attention back to my own injuries I became aware of the rivulet of red dripping down inside my shirt and made an ineffectual swipe at my face that probably only made it worse. Rattlesnake solved my problem by lifting her head from my shirt and licked my face clean with her forked tongue. Well if the people giving us angry glares weren't aware of my companion before then, they were now, I thought to myself and ducked my head to hide my smile.

Suddenly aware of someone near me I looked up. Standing among his four helpers, a short squarely-built man with a weathered face and his gray hair twisted into long braids with colored yarns woven into them watched me with mismatched eyes. One eye was a deep brown, almost black, while the other was covered with a film that caused that one to appear gray or blue depending on the light.

I learned later from Tiwari that with his brown eye he saw the normal things of our Physical World, while with his other, the one covered with a veil, Iyantsha could see into the Unseen world of Spirit. And at that moment I knew he was studying me with all his powers.

When he'd finished his exam, he said, "I sense that you are the one Wind has been telling me about. Welcome, young Puhani, I am glad you have come." Then switching to the mind speech he addressed my companion, <<Welcome, Sister, I am most honored that you have chosen to come with this one to aid my People.>>

He held out his hands to her inviting her to leave me and go to him. Rattlesnake drew her head back and hissed a warning. <<When you have need of me tonight I will come to you, but I will stay with this one for now,>> she informed him.

Iyantsha bowed his head in acknowledgement and returned his attention to me. "I sense that you have also brought with you a talisman of great Puwa from the Unseen World. May I see it?"

Reaching into my shirt I lifted out the little bag and poured out the shining crystal onto my palm. Catching the sunlight it glowed bright with power. Iyantsha and his helpers gasped, marveling at its brilliance and Puwa. "This being has only recently been gifted to me by my Benefactor," I explained and pointed to the claw wound on my cheek.

"We are still getting acquainted with each other, but when I looked through it, Crystal showed me the gray patches of the evil on Nachoga—and on my mother, who has been caring for him. Rattlesnake assures me that I don't carry the taint, but my cousin and the Kukiya warrior who came with us may also have traces of the evil."

"Thank you for telling me. All will be taken care of as we pray during the next five days. I may need to call upon you later as well." With a nod to Golannah, Iyantsha and his followers left us to continue with their preparations.

After Iyantsha left us Golannah's first wife brought us some tea and roasted strips of goose meat folded between flat seed cakes. More exhausted than hungry I drank the tea and ate a wrap to please her then lay down in a clump of trampled grass near the lake shore, covered my head with my blanket and fell into exhausted sleep. Rattlesnake dozed in the sun at my back; she would wake me when I was needed.

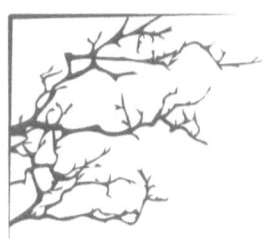

Chapter Seven

It was late afternoon when the sound of the drums and people singing woke me. I sat up and looked around. Sun's fire was golden as he neared the end of his journey for the day. In the south dark clouds were massing in the far mountains beyond the lake. They were still too far away to hear Thunder's growl, but I could see flashes of purple lightning stabbing the gray mass from time to time.

I shivered as a cold wind blew across the lake and touched me. Rattlesnake felt it, too, and slithered back into my lap for warmth. I lifted my shirt and let her crawl inside next to my skin, then through my blanket around my shoulders and walked down to the lake where I saw the Prophet and his helpers bringing the sick ones.

Besides Nachoga there was an old woman nearly bent in half with age and some wasting disease. I learned later that she was a well-loved Elder and lore keeper. There was also another wounded warrior, and a young mother coughing up blood. Those were the four that would need the greatest power to heal, but others, like Mother and Samiqwas were also invited to receive a brushing with the sacred boughs and enter the lake for a cleansing bath.

Amidst the drumming and singing Iyantsha prayed over each person as they were led into the water. When they were led out again the sick ones who could walk were taken back to the central fire where other helpers painted their naked bodies with white and red paint, covered them with blankets and directed them to sit or lie down in a circle to one side of the central fire.

I followed Nachoga back to his pallet, but instead of lying upon it he chose to sit cross-legged upon the cattail mats. Studying him carefully with my Spirit Sight I was reassured that Death's Emissary was no longer near him. There was however the ghost of a Kukiya woman and two children hovering. When she noticed that I could see her she floated closer to me, the children trailing in her wake.

Her features were blurred, but still I could tell she had been a beautiful young woman in life. Beside her a boy of about six stood tall and protective of his mother and younger sister. The ghost glanced at Nachoga and then at Mother and a sad smile curved her lips. <<Tell my husband that we still love him and don't blame him for what happened to us. Tell him Githa says that it's time to stop blaming himself, too, and to let go of the bitterness. Tell him I want him to be happy with the one beside him who I will welcome as my sister wife when we all come together again someday.>>

<<I will tell him, Honored Mother, I will tell him that His sorrow is keeping you and the children from continuing your journey.>>

I felt a cool moist hand touch my face. <<Thank you, My New Son.>>

When I leaned over and relayed her message to Nachoga his stony expression didn't change, but he had heard me and knew I spoke true—and that was all I could do for him at that time. But over the next four days of the ceremony I sensed him change and was glad of it.

As Sun sank below the horizon the drums and one of Iyantsha's apprentices called for quiet. The Prophet stepped into the center of the circle as Tiwari tossed a bundle of sage onto the fire, its fragrant smoke drifting skyward as the Prophet raised his hands and began to pray.

When he had finished, Tiwari place more fragrant herbs in the flames. In the silence that followed Iyantsha finally lowered his arms and began to speak again. "Each of us who has journeyed here has come with a heart filled with sorrow and loss. We have all suffered cruelly, lost loved ones to hunger, sickness and war.

"We have been beaten, raped and starved, driven from our homes and watched them burn as the invaders of our land carried us away so they could claim what our ancestors and beautiful Mother Earth gave us.

"Forcing us to try and survive on land they didn't want the invaders have broken every promise made to us. They took away our weapons, starved us, and then call us outlaws when our warriors take back what was stolen from us to try and feed their families. We have suffered so much and so many have given up hope, swallowed up by misery and despair.

"We grieve for our dead relatives and our dead way of life. And in our suffering it is so easy to turn to the invaders waskyja and forget the sorrows of our lives. The fiery drink promises an end to sadness. It is a tempting lure but a false one.

"I was such a man once. I drank, I gambled, I left my family to starve while I tried to drown my suffering in the oblivion the invader's fiery drink offers. But its promise of peace and happiness is a false promise. To go down that path there is only death—for you—and for all our people if we continue that way. That is what the Spirits of our Ancestors and the Sky Beings that bring the rain have told me."

As if to add emphases to his words thunder rumbled from the approaching storm. "When I became so ill from the drink and my evil ways that I was near death I crawled away into the mountains to die, but I didn't die. The Sky Beings had pity on me. They sent Eagle to grab me in his talons and bring me to their home among the clouds.

"There I was given two choices. I could die and join my relatives in the Beyond Place, or I could live, and pledge myself to their service and do Good in my world, and work to end suffering and bring back the Renewal.

"During the time I stayed with them they gave me many gifts of Puwa, which I was instructed to use for healing and prophesy. They showed me glimpses of our future and it was a terrible revelation. They told me that in order to prevent disaster they would teach me five songs, five songs that would bring about the renewal of the world. I was to return and teach these five songs to all who would learn them.

"If we danced and sang at the new and full moon the power would build, and someday, when there were many, many people dancing and singing these sacred songs, and our Puwa was mighty, the world would change. Our dead relatives would return and our land would be ours again all the invaders with evil hearts gone—forever.

"That's what the Sky Beings promised me, that's what we can achieve if we dance, sing and pray. Warring against the invaders isn't the answer, no killing, no death, no enemy can stop us if our Puwa is strong. I tell you now that this cycle of anger, bitterness and war must end. It is not the way to get back all that we have lost."

As he ended Iyantsha raised his cupped hands to the sky. Thunder boomed overhead, and, for just a moment, a bolt of lightning seemed to come down to form a ball of fire between his fingers.

People cried out and someone ululated a praise call. Opening his hand the Prophet released the Puwa and Tiwari began to sing, he was joined almost immediately by other followers who already knew the songs.

I joined the dancers for a time, falling into a light trance, feeling the mournful ghosts of our dead hovering around the circle. Other Spirits gathered as well offering love and healing Qwakaiva to their living descendants. The faces of so many we left behind on our terrible march appeared before my inner eye. Seicu with a red and white striped candy stick in her mouth her eyes alight with mischief, as well as so many others left in shallow graves along the trail south to the Preserve.

Like Grandfather, I so desperately wanted Iyantsha's vision to be true and like the people around me I added my voice to our prayer. With my Spirit Sight I could see Eagle and many other powerful beings gathering our Qwakaiva. Someday I truly hoped we could store up enough to send the invaders away and return our land and our loved ones to us as the Prophet foresaw.

With the Prophet's Puwa surrounding and protecting me I called Grandmother's ghost to me and was able to release her from the evil Specter's snare, so that she could go home and find peace among our ancestors.

Sometime during that long night Iyantsha looked up and found me in the dancing circle. Our eyes met. Leaving the dancers I walked over to where he knelt next to Nachoga. Crouching beside him I opened my shirt and lifted Rattlesnake out of her warm nest and held her out to him. This time she went willingly into his outstretched hands. Like with me she wound herself around his chest her head resting on his shoulder next to his ear.

Body covered in white and red sacred glyphs, the war leader was lying on his stomach the wound in his shoulder an angry red blemish on his white painted skin. "What can I do to help, Elder?" I asked the Prophet.

"Take out your special crystal and show me where he has been marked by the malicer's spite."

Holding the crystal being to my eye once again I pointed to the places where the gray film clung to his body. In several places in, and around the wound itself, I showed him where the evil was burrowing into Nachoga's flesh.

Like me, when she had helped me send the ghosts of Lynx Hunting's band home Rattlesnake bit into Iyantsha's flesh to give him her Qwakaiva. But unlike me, he didn't sicken from her bite, not then, or later. I watched as he channeled her added power into the wound to burn out the malicer's taint. The Spirit Fire flowed through his body searching and finding every tiny crevice where the evil tried to hide. Though Nachoga made not a sound I could tell by how his body spasmed at times that it was a painful process for both of them.

Done at last Nachoga sat up, his fever was gone and the wound looked healthy and clean. Tiwari wrapped him in a fresh blanket and handed him a cup of willow bark tea, which he gratefully drank. The taint already removed by another of Iyantsha's helpers Mother joined him by the fire with her own cup.

After a short rest Iyantsha moved on to the old woman's litter, but there was little for me to do No malicer had caused her trouble. Hunger and old age were the problems that only rest, good food and Puwa of the Spirit could cure.

The young warrior's wound though serious—worse than Nachoga's, had only a simple cause. He needed only Puwa to aid in his healing. The young mother, however, was another matter and I told the Prophet so.

Using the mind speech, so as not to alarm her and her relatives further I told him what the crystal showed me. <<She has been infected with the sickness that the invaders brought with them. It is deep in her lungs. I can see Death's Emissary hovering.>>

<<I know; I can see the Emissary, too. But she is young with small children still to care for. I will pray to the Thunder Beings to help her. We will sing and dance for her for the next four nights and we'll see if we can heal her.>>

<<I will leave you now,>> Rattlesnake said as she unwound herself and came back to me. <<I must hunt and renew myself soon,>> she explained.

The Prophet thanked her then rising from his place he laid fragrant bows on the fire and raised his arms to the night sky. Over the lake thunder rumbled in answer to his song. As he prayed Tiwari spoke to the drummers and the dancers and explained what they were going to do for the young mother.

After releasing Rattlesnake in the grass by the lakeshore I joined the dancers again. Thunder rolled and crashed about us, bringing with it a pelting cold rain. Iyantsha caught the fire of the lightning once more, and then placing his glowing hands upon the woman's chest, he directed the storm's power to enter her lungs, find, and burn away the evil disease.

She cried out with the pain several times, but at last it was over, and he rolled her on her side so she could cough up a foul dark liquid. And through it all we kept singing the sacred songs we were taught and dancing the circle dance.

After the healing the rain moved on to the west leaving the sweet smell of pine and sage in its wake. Feeling suddenly the call of the lake to my Spirit I left the drumming and dancing and walked down to the shore. Laying aside my blanket and clothes I stepped into the cool water. Far out lightning flashed in the dark sky, the growl of thunder echoing off far mountainsides. I went deeper, savoring its sensual coolness on my skin, overheated by my dance and Fire's breath.

Plunging under the surface I swam, my body undulating with legs and feet together, mimicking the movements I assumed when I took my seal form while in the Dream. A school of small fish surrounded me, darting in to nip me whenever they thought they could. I growled at them for their disrespect and chased them away, threatening to eat them if I caught them.

I couldn't, of course, my human body was too clumsy and slow, but if I could change into my seal form in the Physical World...

<<If the Great One continues to favor you, some day you will have the Qwakaiva to do that—and much more, my son.>>

Startled I suddenly realized that I was no longer swimming alone. The glowing form of a seal now swam beside me. Father? Was my Seal father truly here with me, or was this just another illusion sent to test me? I stopped swimming, opened my mouth to ask that question, choked on a mouthful of water and sank below the surface again.

In the next moment he shape-shifted and strong human arms grabbed my braid and pulled me choking and spluttering to the surface. He laughed, his sharp white teeth gleaming in a distant flash of lightning. "I said someday, but you aren't ready for that shift in your world yet."

I stared, drinking in the sight of his brindle colored long hair, and high cheek boned face with its full lips and violet eyes. This was the first time I had felt his solid physical substance enfolding me and I shamelessly snuggled next to him like a young child. A torrent of emotions and words wanted to pour out of me, but couldn't get past the lump clogging my throat. Finally I managed to murmur the first stupid question that came into my mind, "How did you get here?"

He chuckled again. "This lake is fed by a spring deep in those mountains." He motioned to the peaks on the northern horizon. "I swam the black water to come see you, but I can't stay long. The Evil Ones watchers mustn't know that I am here, or there will be bad trouble for me, and your people. Kunai teases me with talk of you, but I wanted to see you for myself."

Still cradling me in one arm he extended the other and drew upon his power. Three small blue shell pendants appeared in his palm. "Keep one of these with your crystal so that our bond will be strengthened in future. Give one to your mother and the other to the Cougar for me. Tell them I wish them well."

You could come to the ceremony and tell them yourself," I suggested. "The Prophet would welcome your aid with the healings."

"Yes, I know he would. Though I believe he strives for only good in your world his Qwakaiva comes from a different source, which may not be compatible with mine. But he will have to do what is needed with only you and his own Spirit Helpers to guide him."

As I opened my mouth to argue Star Swimmer shook his head. "No, it would be too dangerous for me to be seen over there. There are watchers everywhere. I could come to you in the dark, only because you heeded Lake's call and swam out to me."

As he made to leave me, I blurted, the pain in my voice clear even to my own ears. "I tried to tell you—back at Drown Canoe Rapids that the Chamuqwani made us leave and we were never coming back to our home. I wish you had listened to me—saved us from all this."

His luminous deep violet eyes, so like my own moistened with sadness. "I know you did, and I wish truly that things were different for us. I wish I had the power to have stopped them from forcing your people to leave the lake—truly I do. But I will promise you this, my son, you will see your home on the Big Ice Lake again in your physical lifetime. And to bring that about is why I, and the others like me, must keep fighting the Evil that has invaded this and other worlds."

"Take me with you," I pleaded and held onto his arm as he started to shift back into his seal form. "I have pledged my life and my Qwakaiva to that end as well.

He placed his other hand over mine and gently removed it. Shaking his head, he said, "Though I would like nothing better, Tasimu, the Pattern won't allow it at this time. But Kunai has foreseen a day when I will return."

Star Swimmer looked towards the lakeshore where Samiqwas and one of Iyantsha's helpers were standing peering into the darkness and calling for me. "I must go, before those who hunt me become aware of my presence in your world. And you too are needed, my son. Give my love to your mother and tell her and the Cougar I wish them all the happiness your world has to offer."

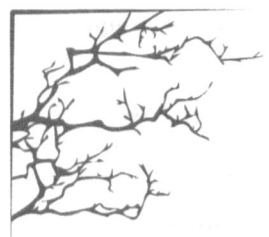

Chapter Eight

B y the time the prophet's ceremony ended War Leader Nachoga was truly on the mend. His fever was gone and his shoulder finally healing. Mother and I had already been made welcome by Sagila and her family, so we stayed with our new Kukiya relatives throughout the rest of the summer season. The women and girls gathered cattail leaves and roots while men and boys organized community hunts and did other camp chores. It was a happy time for me, giving me strength for what was to come, I now believe.

During this time as well the Prophet's message had been spreading among the people on the Preserve thanks to Grandfather and Iyantsha's other followers. Broken and despairing people arrived in small groups every few days, bringing their sick and hungry to ingest the prayers and the message of hope he offered. When Iyantsha needed me I went to him and added the aid of my Gift to help with a particularly difficult healing, but otherwise I worked alongside Samiqwas at whatever work the war leader and our women relatives thought up for us.

During this time as well the growing attraction between Mother and Nachoga flowered and bore fruit. Those who loved them both shared in their happiness. Not long after I gave them Star Swimmer's shell charms Mother and Sagila made a pole and cattail mat-covered hut at the edge of Sagila's family circle and the couple moved in together. Uncle Tli and the warband had yet to return so to give them some privacy Samiqwas and I stayed with Sagila to help her as the time for her baby's birth drew near, and then we continued to stay after the baby came to help out until Uncle returned.

As the warm moons gave way to the cooler days leading into autumn, Uncle Tli and the rest of Eqwohi's warband finally joined us on a grassy plateau that was part of the tribe's traditional hunting lands, where we had gathered in preparation for the annual rabbit hunt. Past disagreements forgotten everyone was happy to see them. The war band brought with them a small herd of cai and other plunder of great value the People would need in the cold moons.

As the camp crier announced their return I rushed outside Sagila's shelter with everyone else, but in my heart I worried about what might happen when the nearly healed Nachoga caught sight of Dotsuwa and his son. Dotsuwa and his son had been sent to protect us when we were returning to the People with a wounded Nachoga earlier in the summer.

Taking advantage of Nachoga's injuries amidst the glad shouts of the people gathering I scanned the arriving war band for familiar faces. Uncle was there and Utsiyonti, as well as Eqwohi and his wife Betsiya, but I saw no sign of the treacherous father and son.

As I scanned the arriving warriors no one I knew and cared about seemed to be missing. The boys from back home were there and to my relief, Thonna, or should I now say Xyilaha, was among them. Dusty and smiling she rode her spotted pony with ease and confidence, helping Matoqwa, Cohasi and the rest of the young men herd the bawling Cai into a roped off area hastily set aside for them.

Knowing that Tuumaz was away hunting that day I hurried over to help Utsiyonti with his horses. He was riding a newly acquired fine black gelding and holding the lead rope for a pack mare piled high with blanketed bundles.

Taking the lead rope of the pack horse I followed him down to the stream to water the horses and here the news. As we brushed the horses down before turning them loose up the meadow with the others I looked over the brown mare's back, stared into his eyes, and in the mind speech asked the question I could no longer keep inside. <<Where are they?>>

I had no need to explain further; he knew exactly what and who I meant. He chuckled and giving the gelding one last swipe with his horse broom, he knelt to check the beast's hooves, making me wait. I folded my arms across my chest, determined to wait him out.

Finishing one hoof he moved on to the next one on that side. At last he took pity on me and still holding up the nearly finished hoof he smiled up at me. "It's a good thing for the War Leader that the weasel-piss stole the gray horse Nachoga liked so much."

"Oh, why is that?"

He finished the hoof and moved onto the next before answering. "That horse was bad luck—maybe had a malicer's curse on him. Might have got the war leader killed—like Dotsuwa—if Nachoga had kept him."

Dotsuwa and his son dead—and not my fault, I couldn't help it, I breathed out a sigh of relief at the news. "The wounds Eagle and I gave him were bad, but not bad enough to kill. What happened?"

Utsiyonti laughed. "He did look terrible, and probably was going to be blind in one eye, but you are right, his wounds weren't dangerous. Too bad for him I had told Eqwohi what had happened before he caught up to us. And though he tried to deny it, Eqwohi wouldn't listen to his excuses and let him join us—so he left again.

"But instead of going back to the Preserve, or going to the lake where he knew Golannah and the rest of our people were, and maybe wanting to take vengeance on him, he decided to do a little raiding on his own with a couple cousins, before he returned to the People."

He snorted another laugh. "I guess he thought going back to camp with horses and gifts might sweeten his reception, but a Chamuqwani among the rancha-men searching for their stolen cai must have recognized that gray horse when they ran into the war party.

"Assuming the warriors were the band that took their cai the Chamuqwani pursued them, took back the horse, and killed them. Following the trail of the carrion birds two days later we found what was left of their bodies—and no horses."

Taking a long moment to absorb the news I finally said, "I must admit your news comes as a relief to me. I was worried that my new father might take it into his head to fight the pair if they had dared show their faces here right now. Though his shoulder is coming along nicely my Mother says his wound still needs time to finish healing properly. If Dotsuwa had been with you..." I left the rest of my thought unvoiced, but Utsiyonti knew and understood what I left unsaid.

Then absorbing what else I had said his head shot up at my unexpected news. Eyes wide he whistled softly. "New father, eh? I never thought to see that day. Your mother must have great woman's Puwa to make the war leader set aside his loss and want to live again. And how do you like having this 'new father' of yours?"

I couldn't help grinning. "I like it just fine."

When we got back to camp, Uncle and several members of the returning war band were sitting around Sagila's family fire smoking as the women handed out cups of tea, while slices of antelope meat roasted on a rack over the fire. At the other end of the fire trench Mother pressed balls of coussa dough into flat cakes to cook on a stone griddle set among the coals.

Sagila had had her baby only a half moon earlier and so Uncle Tli got a big surprise when a cry from her shelter caused everyone to smile and look in that direction. Sagila abandoned her cooking and hurried inside and in a moment the crying stopped. A while later she reappeared with the baby tucked into a sling on her hip. Coming over to Uncle Tli she sat down beside him and showed him his new son.

Uncle studied the little brown face with its mop of thick black hair without speaking. The baby's dark eyes were open, and maybe trying to focus on his father's solemn face. His red bow of a mouth made a sucking motion with his lips then broadened into what might have been a smile.

Tli grinned in answer, and to the Kukiya warriors' sitting around the fire surprise, he held out his hands to take the baby.

Almost as startled as the men, Sagila hesitated for a moment then lifting the baby out of her sling she placed him in his father's waiting arms.

Cradling him expertly in the crook of one arm Tli continued to smile down at the child tickling him under the chin with a finger and making soft cooing noises to the little one.

Watching the two lost in their own private communication for a long moment Nachoga at last turned to Mother and asked, "I can see that your brother has had lots of practice taking care of little ones. Is it a Qwani'Ya custom for your men to take such an interest in womanly things?"

Mother chuckled and touched his hand with an affectionate gesture. Looking deep into his eyes, she said with a playful note in her voice, "Maybe." Then at his horrified look she chuckled again to let him know she was just teasing him. "You might not think it such a burden to hold and play with your own little one, mighty warrior, when she is born to us in the early spring."

Nachoga snorted, but a smile played around the corners of his mouth, so I could tell he wasn't horrified by the idea. Letting Tli know by his next words that there was no bad feelings left between them, he pointed with his lips to the baby still in Tli's arms and said, "I can see that I will need to learn much from you Qwani'Ya brother-in-law, about your people's child rearing customs in the coming moons before my own child is born."

Tli's eyes widened and he glanced at his sister for confirmation. When Mother nodded he grinned. "Gladly, Brother-in-law."

After the meal I finally understood Samiqwas's unsubtle hints, grabbed my bedding from Sagila's lodge and followed my cousin out of camp to where the unmarried young men and boys had set up their own camp near the horse herd and the penned cai.

With a small thunder weapon in a holster on her hip Xyilaha was with us for a time laughing and joking and telling war stories with the others, but as the night deepened and everyone thought about our blankets and the night guards for the horses were assigned she left with her new uncle Talulsit when he came to fetch her.

My coshelah cousin had truly changed during her time away with the war band. I was happy for her and couldn't wait till I had a chance to talk to her and hear more about her adventures.

A few days later as we were preparing for the great rabbit drive to begin, Golannah received word that the commander at Black Rock Fort was calling for a big meeting of all the leaders to talk about the trouble that had arisen between the tribal peoples on the Preserve and the nearby settlements of Chamuqwani. The messenger to us gave Golannah a large white cloth and told him that the soldier's chief promised no harm would come to any who came to the fort displaying the white banner.

After arguing back and forth for a day and night it was decided that Golannah and Eqwohi would go from our combined Qwani'Ya and Kukiya band. And though Nachoga argued that he should go to help translate, Golannah said no, and left him and Uncle Tli in charge of the rabbit hunt, and all those left behind to prepare for winter instead.

To my surprise it was suggested that I be included in the party preparing to go. "I will take the young Puhani with me," Golannah said and laid a heavy hand on my shoulder. He beamed down at me with a toothy smile and then added when he saw Nachoga's scowl, "I know you want to go and protect me, but the soldiers might arrest you like last time if they know you have come back to us. Is better you stay here with the People—and your new woman, eh?"

"After our rescue at the agency the soldiers may already know I have returned," he argued.

"Then all the more reason for you to stay away from them," his brother countered. "Besides, your new son can pass on messages between us if I need your advice, and he can see with his Puwa if these men are telling us the truth. He will be a great help to me in your absence."

I had mixed feelings about the trip. I wanted to stay with Nachoga and Mother, but I also was excited by the honor given me to be included in the party. Then Nachoga's next words soured my enthusiasm.

"It might be as dangerous for my son as for me," Nachoga said. "As a Puhani who helped prisoners escape from the agency jail he isn't unknown to our enemies, either."

Golannah thought about his brother's argument for a moment as he studied me. Then he waved his hand in dismissal. "Maybe they know a little Qwani'Ya boy who lived with some convert turds, but they not know the young Kukiya warrior that I will bring with me to care for my horses. We make him dress and look like Kukiya. We adopt him—like you. Give him tattoos and paint his face with Puwa magic designs. No enemy will know him—even his traitorous convert kin."

Golannah turned to me and smiled. "Would you like that, young Puhani, want your new father adopt you? Want to be a Kukiya warrior?"

Suddenly everything was happening so fast. Like the Chamuqwani the Kukiya people claimed their descent through their father's lineage not their mother's line as my Qwani'Ya people did. I loved Nachoga and was happy to be named his son. His presence filled a gaping hole in my life—and yet I still considered myself my mother's child and a part of her Qwani'Ya lineage. What to do?

As if divining my dilemma Nachoga said into my mind, <<I would be honored to make you my son for all to see and know, but that doesn't mean you need forsake your Qwani'Ya people. You can be a person of two peoples if you agree to this adoption my brother suggests.>>

And so, I agreed, and the ceremony, a simple affair under the circumstances, was arranged for the next day.

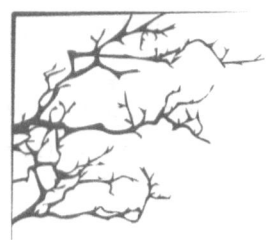

Chapter Nine

During the usual prayer ceremony next day, Iyantsha was asked to conduct the adoption proceedings. When it was time the two brothers stepped into the center of the big circle with me walking along between them. Going to the fire Nachoga placed an offering bundle in the flames as Iyantsha raised his hands in a prayer song.

When he finished, he said, "I have been asked by these two war leaders to welcome this fine young man into their family." He placed a hand on Nachoga's arm bringing him forward to stand by him. Our brother here, a fine hunter and brave war leader among the People has remarried and wishes to adopt his new woman's son as his own."

Motioning me forward to stand by Nachoga, he continued. "This young Puhani has willingly shared his Puwa with me when I have called upon him to help with a healing. I have asked the Thunder Beings and all the helpful Spirits of our land to bless this family, Shkii'a! Let it be so."

There was a chorus of agreement from the people gathered around us, then Golannah came forward, and said, "As our chief I approve of my brother's wish to adopt this young warrior. He is brave and generous. He and his skills as warrior and Puhani will be a true gift to our People."

Then going to the fire he placed his own offering to the Unseen Ones within the flames. "As his new uncle, with this offering I pledge to be this one and his mother's protector and provider if a time should come when my brother is no longer able to do so."

As Iyantsha and his followers prayed and sang around us I sat near the fire so that Nachoga could see to put the tattoos of adoption on my face. Sticking a sharpened reed into a heated pot of grease mixed with charcoal my new father pricked my skin in a series of dots that traced a pattern across my cheeks similar to his own. With my eyes closed I held perfectly still and made no sound as Golannah wiped away my blood with a clean rag and Nachoga created the symbol that would always bind us.

Then he surprised me by making a curving line near the point of my jaw near the base of my left ear. My eyes flew open as I felt the first prick in that unexpected place. I dared not move my mouth to ask what he was doing, so I asked him in the mind speech.

He chuckled and said in the same manner, <<Iyantsha suggested I create a new sign, one that combines our symbol for a rattlesnake with the horns on its head of the mighty being from the Dream that is the source of your Puwa. Since the spirit of rattlesnake and the dragon deep in the Earth who is your benefactor favor you, it is a sign of great power>>

His lips twitched in a ghost of a smile. <<It will also let your enemies know that you have powerful allies in the Other World, eh?>>

When my part of the ceremony was completed, and I took my place besides Nachoga and Mother in the outer circle, I suddenly realized that I wasn't the only one being singled out that day.

Xyilaha was being formally adopted by her aunty and her Kukiya husband Talulsit as well. Stepping to the central fire with my cousin by his side he sang her praises to the People. "On our raid into enemy lands my new daughter showed bravery and skill, both when she helped capture new horses and when she had to use her weapons to protect others. She can also cook and sew like any woman. She will make a fine wife for some lucky man—someday—when I find a warrior worthy of her."

That brought a laugh from some of the people listening. I saw Xyilaha scowl at the mention of another father-planned marriage, but I doubted she had anything to worry about. Her aunty, who ran away from her own forced marriage wasn't going to let her get married off to a bad person.

And besides, she now had that thunder weapon on her hip to scare off any undesirable suitors. When I caught her eye, I motioned with my lips to the holstered weapon. She understood my meaning and her lips twitched as if she wanted to smile.

The pattern of dots on her cheeks was slightly different than mine, Talulsit being of a different lineage, and she being a girl, but like me, she bore the ordeal in silence and showing no pain. I was happy for her. The old bitter angry girl that was a convert's daughter named Thonna was gone.

Self-assured and strong, this new person named Xyilaha had bloomed in the atmosphere of freedom among the outlaws.

Later the women folk of our combined families cooked a feast in our honor to which all were welcome.

Not in any hurry to come like dogs to this Chamuqwani war chief's command we took our time about leaving the big combined camp on the plateau. After many council sessions in the evenings it was decided that along with Golannah and me, Eqwohi and his wife Betsiya were going as well as Utsiyonti, Tuumaz and an escort of ten warriors.

Much to their disgust Xyilaha, Samiqwas, Matoqwa and Cohasi were not included in the party. Lots of willing young hands would be needed to help kill and dress the meat when the food-beasts were driven into the nets. They would also be needed for setting up drying racks and preparing the rabbit skins for the women to weave into warm blankets and other clothing over the coming winter.

Finally all the preparations had been made and we left at dawn next morning. We traveled light, bringing with us only our weapons, some food, blankets and some rolled-up cattail mats that we could tie together to make a lean-to shelter if needed.

At the last moment two of Iyantsha's followers asked to go with us as far as the destroyed miners' camp on Sandy Bottom Creek. They were worried that the land was still disturbed because of the Chamuqwani diggings. They wanted to offer more prayers in that evil place to bring it back into harmony.

The warriors hadn't planned on going that way on their journey to Black Rock Fort, but agreed to the detour. "I want to see for myself what those Chamuqwani did on our land," Golannah said when he told the others of our slight change of plans. And so with Tuumaz and me leading, we headed across the grassy plateau towards Red Rock Butte on the eastern horizon.

Traveling with the war band our journey to that disrupted place was much quicker than I expected. Without a sick and injured man in tow, or the need for stealth, we could travel much faster and so arrived at the miners' camp by the creek in less than two days.

The place was much as we'd left it, with the smashed in pit house and mounds of garbage barely covered over with dirt. Golannah took his time looking around, even having me show him up the slope to one of the half-filled in holes where the men had been digging for the yellow rock the Chamuqwani prize so highly.

The prophet's followers were right to come, I thought as we headed down the narrow valley made by the creek to show Iyantsha's followers a safe place to camp if they planned to stay here for a while. The land in this whole area was not a restful place anymore. I sensed the miners angry ghosts had returned and I told the older of the two who were staying to conduct the ceremony that fact.

"Yes, I sense them, too," he told me. "We will try to help them leave for a better place."

"I hope they will listen and agree to leave, because I sense they are very angry," I said. He patted my arm and told me not to worry, but I couldn't totally put aside my fears for them. Overconfident, arrogant maybe, I hoped they had the Puwa to banish the evil lurking in this valley as they thought, and not become a victim of its malice.

Finally Golannah called for the rest of the war band to gather their horses. He had seen enough and we were leaving, and that suited me just fine. I was happy to get on my little mare and lead the way out of that terrible place.

It took us three more days of hard riding to reach Black Rock Fort by the next full moon. The fort was perched like a hungry vulture on a rocky outcrop of land overlooking the Bahas River. On the grassy slopes below the fort sprawled a large encampment made up of white soldier tents and hide and brush shelters. Further to the south a herd of horses grazed, guarded by mounted riders.

We were spotted by soldiers posted atop the fort's log and earthen walls when we rode our horses over the hill crest and headed down to the ford by the river, waving the white banner on a war spear. As we reached the other side five soldiers and two of our own people from other clans left the fort and rode up to meet us.

Their leader was an older Chamuqwani with strands of gray threaded through his short hair and beard and golden stripes sewn onto the shoulders of his uniform. These soldiers wore dark blue, but like the others I had seen before wearing brown or grey, these blue warriors had their emperor's lightning bolt patch sewn onto the front of their coats.

Golannah seemed to recognize the Kukiya man wearing soldier clothing with them, and he wasn't happy to see him. The other was a Convert man I'd seen before at Chief Eagan's settlement, but didn't know his name. He too was wearing the soldiers' blue.

Golannah stopped his horse and waited for the soldiers to come to him. Eqwohi rode up beside him with the rest of the warriors fanning out around them. Betsiya, as the only woman in the group stayed near the back of the warriors. With Rattlesnake whirring a warning in my mind and hoping the convert man wouldn't recognize me, I tried to hide myself behind the taller men, because I suddenly knew he was looking for something, or someone.

Stopping in front of us the older Chamuqwani spoke and then the Kukiya man translated his words for us. "Commander Rossman welcomes the great Kukiya chief Golannah to his fort. We have been waiting on you. Now that you have come we can begin the council tomorrow."

Golannah made a slight nod in the soldier's direction, then spoke to the Kukiya warrior with them. "I see you, Ahaz, so, you have left your own people and become a Chamuqwani now. I wondered why you disappeared from your parents' lodge. Do you also pray to their thunder god? Why don't you paint your face white if you want to be like them so much."

Ahaz scowled and glared at his tormentor. "I am as much a Kukiya as you. I have forsaken no one. I send script and food back to my parents like any good son they are doing well. It is you who clings to the ways of our ancestors so completely that you can't feel the winds of change sweeping across our land. Your raiding and fighting helps no one. It only angers the Chamuqwani and they are too many to fight. We must bend like the willow or be broken and die."

Golannah snorted and looked down his nose at the man in the soldier's shirt. "Die? It is always a good day to die if it means being true to the teachings of our ancestors and our land."

Before the Kukiya soldier could reply the soldiers' leader spoke, demanding he translate what was being said. Reluctantly Ahaz started to answer, but the leader made an angry hand gesture to cut him off. He motioned up the trail to the grassy slope near the fort.

"Enough! I've heard all this before," the soldier said in his own language. He said more but I was finding it hard to follow, so I waited for Ahaz to translate the rest for us.

"This soldier says that we can talk more about such things later in the council meeting. Now it is time to come set up camp and rest."

We followed the soldiers back up the slope towards the fort. But when we were directed to a fine white soldier's tent in the middle of the encampment Golannah surveyed the close-packed tents all around it and shook his head. "No we will camp over there." He told the interpreter and pointed with his lips to an open area near the edge of the encampment.

This seemed to annoy our hosts, but after a heated discussion among themselves the soldier in charge agreed. He issued orders and several soldiers hurried to take down the big tent and move it to the place that Golannah wanted.

As we were unloading, and our warriors were leading the horses away to join the horse herd Golannah motioned for Utsiyonti and me to join him. When we were near enough to hear him he said in a low voice, "I don't trust these soldiers. And the one who translates for them is a liar and a traitor. Stake the horses on long ropes when you release them to graze in case we need to leave quickly."

Utsiyonti gave him a nod, the scar on his chin shifting as his mouth hardened into a thin line. "I hear you, Cousin, and share your concern. I will tell the others. We will be watchful."

As I started to follow Utsiyonti to the horses Golannah stopped me with a gesture. "And what do you see with your Puwa, Nephew? Tell me about these men."

What did I know...? "I see muddy colors in their Spirit Fires, true enough. They are concealing something, but I don't know yet what it is. I will keep on guard and tell you or Utsiyonti when I know something for certain."

Then deciding to voice my personal concern I added, "I don't know his name but I know the Convert man who came with the soldiers just now. I have seen him at the convert settlement where I was living. I sensed that he is looking for someone, maybe your brother, or my Uncle—or maybe even me. And when he finds the one he seeks he will want to kill him."

Golannah gave me a wolfish smile. "Then it's a good thing my brother and your uncle are with the People—hunting, eh?" he stroked his jaw thoughtfully for a moment, then said, "And as for you, as I told you and your new father it is unlikely that anyone will recognize you now, but as my nephew I plan to keep you close by me anyway, so not to worry."

Sun was nearing the western horizon by the time we had the big tent erected and our few belongings and beds laid out inside. Tuumaz and I and a couple of the younger warriors went to the river for water, and then to the fort for other rations and a supply of firewood.

But when we got to the trading post we found to our disgust, that what the trader offered was the same kind of rations given to us on our long march to the Preserve. Reluctantly we collected oat-mush, white flour, lasses and grease, but no one was overly excited about the food. We could smell roasting Cai beast from somewhere inside the fort, but was told the meat was being fixed for the feast planned for tomorrow after the council, so we would have to wait.

When we returned I saw that Golannah and the others had been joined by men they knew from other clans. They were all sipping tea and talking among themselves about the soldiers and the reason they had been called to this council. Betsiya crouched by the fire watching the last of our deer meat roasting on long sticks leaning over the coals. Though she pretended to have her attention focused solely on her cooking, I knew she was listening carefully to the men's talk and observing the newcomers with her own Gift.

After placing my share of the supplies I'd carried inside the tent I returned to the fire and squatting beside her asked, "Aunty, what can I do to help you?"

Betsiya tossed one of her braids back over her shoulder and smiled at me. "Thank you, Nephew, for asking, but there's nothing I need at the moment. Sit and have some mint tea. The meat will be done soon."

I took the cup from the pouch at my waist and poured myself some tea from the nearly empty pot. Then I sat where I could watch what was going on around me, but still be far enough into the shadows that my face wouldn't be recognized.

I barely listened to the talk by our fire, being more interested in the activity going on in the camp around us. Soldiers came and went on unknown errands among the tents and out to the horse corrals. Often the newer soldiers stopped to just stare at a family while some of the older soldiers that had been among us for a while might pause to talk to a Kukiya or Qwani'Ya person they knew.

After we had eaten I was thinking about checking on the horses then crawling under my blankets to sleep when Kunai's crystal moved within the little pouch around my neck and a colorless voice in my mind warned me to pay attention.

Suddenly I became aware of a group of Chamuqwani heading our way. These Chamuqwani weren't soldiers. They were dressed in the black jackets and trousers like Jombonni the trader back home always wore. They also wore wide brimmed black hats and they were talking loudly to one another and rudely staring wide eyed at everyone and everything they saw. The Kukiya interpreter who was with the soldiers earlier was with them as well as someone I knew all too well Charlic's father Samith.

I resolved to use my special string and look for Charlic in the Seer's Pool the first chance I got. If he was here, too, my life was going to become very—complicated.

Ignoring the icy shiver sliding down my spine, I paid attention to the next message the crystal was giving me. I was too far away to pass it on to Golannah directly, but I could speak to Utsiyonti mind-to-mind and maybe Betsiya, though I'd never tried with her. They were much closer to the war leader and could give him my message.

Calling to Utsiyonti with the mind speech I said when I had his attention, <<The Chamuqwani coming want to ask our war leader something. My crystal helper says he should answer them courteously and agree to what the man with the black box wants of him. I've been told that in the future what they do and learn here will be important for our people. Tell him that for me.

<<If I go to him myself I will attract the attention of someone with them who knows me well and that might cause trouble for all of us.>>

Utsiyonti gave me a slight nod, to tell me he understood then stood to refill his cup. As he took his place again he leaned toward Golannah and relayed my message.

Betsiya had obviously sensed my use of the power and looked at me curiously, the question plain in her eyes, so I tried repeating my message for her. I think she got most of it and I would tell her more, later. And then there was no more time, because these loud-talking Chamuqwani were there among us and Golannah was rising to greet them.

Much to the surprise of most of his warriors he welcomed these strange Chamuqwani solemnly and invited them to sit by our fire. Startled the Chamuqwani looked at one another then asked their guides a few questions. When they received only shrugs as answers they walked forward and awkwardly sat on the cattail mats Betsiya placed on the ground for them.

"You want tea?" Golannah said in their language, which surprised them. "This woman," Golannah pointed with his lips to Betsiya, "she make."

Altogether there were five of them, the two interpreters and three unknown Chamuqwani. The thin man with bushy orange hair on his upper lip and sky blue eyes alight with curiosity seemed to be their leader. He smiled and said, "You speak our language?"

"I speak little," Golannah replied. Then turning to the army man to translate he asked in his own language, "Who are these men? I can see they aren't soldiers and they don't look like traders either. What are they doing here, and what do they want?"

When Ahaz translated the one with the orange hair on his lip said, "My name is Lord Yon Bronworthy and I come from the Emperor's capital city far to the east of your land.

"These are my colleagues Collin Golbraith and Willum Bruner." Collin, the younger of the two, had sparkling brown eyes and no hair on his face. He wore his long dark hair tied back in a knot at the nape of his neck. The other, a square-built man with curly yellow hair on his head and face, was Willum.

"We have heard about the trouble between our peoples and we wanted to come see for ourselves so we can tell the people back east the true story of what is happening out here on the Preserve and the surrounding imperial settlements. We want to tell our readers your side of the story, not just what the soldiers and Djoven's missionaries say."

Golannah rudely looked him in the eye. "I have been counseled by one of my people with strong Puwa to talk to you and answer your questions, so I will tell you truth. But will you believe me?"

"Possibly. I want to believe you; tell me."

Golannah grunted and sat back. "My people are starving. We were promised many things when we agreed to live on your Tribal Preserve. We stay there, but last winter we starve. Your agents and soldiers steal the food and other things promised us. They try to take away our weapons so we can't hunt, but then they say they have no food to feed our hungry women and children."

The outlaw war leader folded his arms across his chest and glared, daring them to deny his words. "So we take back the cai beasts that the fat agent at Willow Creek sold to rancha-men because the cai are ours by right. Father Emperor say so. We don't want make war. We only want to feed and take care our hungry relatives."

When Golannah's words were translated for him the one called Bronworthy talked excitedly with the dark haired man who had been writing down Golannah's words in his book as they were translated for him.

Addressing Samith directly Eqwohi said, "And what about you, Convert Man, you know what we say is true—your own family starve, too. Why you no tell them, eh?"

"I think maybe you one who go Black Rock Fort with no pass, eh?" Utsiyonti said in Chamuqwani. "You want show soldier war chief boxes have no food, no farm tools, only good-for-nothing pieces glass inside."

Once again my people surprised these foreigners with their ability to understand and speak their language.

Samith's paler skin flushed a deep red when Bronworthy and the others turned to look at him. "What is Chief Golannah and these warriors talking about?" Bronworthy asked.

"Were some of their treaty goods stolen from them? Are women and children starving on the Preserve?" the dark haired one named Collin wanted to know.

Samith looked bleak, glancing at the other interpreter, and then finally admitted, "Maybe agent take, and some people hungry, but Commander say it my job to help translate not to tell my own story. He be angry I tell you, maybe."

Bronworthy waved away his concerns about future punishment with a dismissive gesture. "Never mind that; I will speak to your Commander later.

You won't be punished if you tell me. We have been sent here on a fact finding mission, so if you have information to tell us then it is important you do so."

While Samith took a moment to consider his position Betsiya refilled the men's cups. Samith glared at the warriors and Golannah for putting him in such a dangerous position. Golannah's face remained expressionless, but I could see colors of mischief dancing in his Spirit Fire. He knew exactly what he was doing, and how uncomfortable he was making his convert adversary.

At last Samith sighed and told them about the stolen boxes of food and tools and the substitution of farm tools with useless mirrors and broken pieces of glass. When the agent or the priest wouldn't give the starving people any food, some of the men defied the agent and went to Black Rock Fort without a pass to plead for help for their starving families."

Turning round he lifted up his soldier shirt and showed the Chamuqwani the scars from the whipping he and the others received when they returned to the Preserve after Commander Rossman refused to give them food or help them.

"Now maybe you understand a little why we fight," Golannah said. We have no choice. So, my question to you, Chamuqwani, is if we talk to you and you write on your paper our words to tell the Father Emperor's men in the east, will it make a difference for us? Will they listen; will things on this Preserve change?"

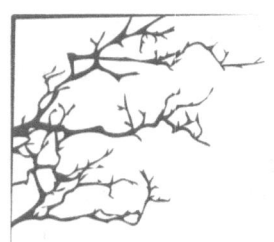

Chapter Ten

Joined by other headmen and warriors from nearby tents Golannah and the others talked to the strangers until the soldier atop the fort's wall blew his horn to let people know they would be closing the gate soon. As Bronworthy and his companions rose to leave, I sent Utsiyonti another warning and Golannah stopped them.

Looking Bronworthy straight in the eye, in the Chamuqwani way, he said in the man's language, "Be careful, Chamuqwani who want to be friend, Golannah. Like fox by mouse hole, you watch, you listen, but no talk."

His eyes raking over both the army interpreters and the rest of the strangers, he added, "No tell anyone at fort what we say, what you know. Commander, agent, priest, be angry you. No like Golannah tell you truth. Maybe you no leave here alive you tell, eh? You go far away from here then you tell."

Bronworthy's eyes widened and his mouth dropped open in shock, then his eyes narrowed as he thought about it and understood Golannah's warning. "Thank you, Chief Golannah. It has been a pleasure talking with you this evening. May I come talk to you again?"

When Golannah nodded Bronworthy pointed to the short square man and said, "My friend Willum here would like to take everyone's picture in the morning when the light is better."

I wasn't sure why this was so urgent, but both Rattlesnake and Crystal Being commanded me to speak. <<Tell the war leader to say yes. He is the one with the black box I told you about. The Unseen Ones want him to use his Puwa to help us in the future.>>

"Pitcha?" Golannah's eyes searched the shadows for me, finding me at last I gave him a slight nod.

Then Utsiyonti acting on what I'd told him mind-to-mind, said, "I want pitcha, too," he said to Bronworthy. "Puhani say is good," he pointed with his lips to the one named Willum. "Him got much Puwa good for Kukiya people him make pitcha."

Not used to being interrupted Golannah stared at Utsiyonti like he had just grown moose antlers, then he shrugged and agreed. "You come back in morning. You make pitcha. We make tea and talk."

"Puwa, Puhani?" Bronworthy turned to Samith and asked, "Do you know what those words mean—what he is talking about?"

Grim-faced Samith nodded. Finally he said through gritted teeth, "You must understand, Sir, these people are heathens they refuse to hear the words of Mighty Djoven's priests and change their ways. There must be a foul heathen witch among them."

Bronworthy's eyes popped wide at that revelation. "Really?" he glanced round at each of the now expressionless Kukiya faces, hoping to spot the person that had awakened his interest. When no one looked like a malicer to him he shrugged and as the horn sounded again he waved for his party to start back to the fort.

As they turned to go, Golannah switched languages and warned the two interpreters. "Whether you keep the old traditions or not doesn't matter to me, but my Puhani warns that there is danger here for you as well. Don't be stupid. Zaunks are all the same to the soldiers; never forget that. Maybe is good for your families now, but you starved the same as us, and others in your lineage still cry with hunger. If these Chamuqwani can help us—don't betray them to the soldiers. All our children may suffer if you do."

Next day after the morning meal Bronworthy and his companions showed up at our camp again. The council wasn't due to start until later in the day. Tuumaz and I had been taking care of our horses when they arrived, and so I had no time to conceal myself before almost walking into the midst of them. Fortunately for me I decided later, it had been dusty by the horses and I had pulled my neck rag up over my nose, so my face was still partially concealed when we arrived back at our tent.

But in truth my fears about being recognized by Charlic's father were slim. He had never paid much attention to me back at the convert settlement, so I doubt he would recognize me with tattoos on my face, here with the Kukiya, as Golannah assured me. Now his son, on the other hand... But I need not worry about Charlic for the moment. When I looked for him with my string last evening I saw that he was still far away at the convert settlement.

Betsiya didn't need me to get water for her or do other chores so I sat down in the shade of the big tent idly listening to the men's talk until someone needed me. To pass the time I took my special string from around my neck and amused myself by making the string figures that all children learn. Then wanting to check on Mother and Nachoga I twisted the cord into the pattern of the Seer's pool.

There were no soldiers nearby and everyone seemed well on the plateau. Mother was cooking coussa cakes on the family's shared stone griddle. Sitting companionably nearby Nachoga was carving something out of a long piece of wood, but he had just started his work and I couldn't tell what he was making yet. Maybe I would go to him in the Dream tonight and tell him all was well with us, so far. I smiled watching Uncle playing with his new son. The baby was a fine healthy boy who delighted his father and smiled a lot like his mother.

And Samiqwas and our friends were guarding the horses and throwing mud balls and horse dung at one another until an Elder made them stop. I laughed as Samiqwas hit Cohasi in the chest with a wet one.

"What are you doing?"

I jerked as if stung by a bee. Would I ever learn? The question had been asked in Chamuqwani. I looked up to see the dark haired man named Collin who was always writing in his little book standing over me. He pointed with his finger to my string, now laying looped in my lap and repeated his question.

I dropped my eyes and said in a voice barely above a whisper. "Bored me, so play with string like child. Make picture, tell story."

He smiled and crouched down beside me. "That's fascinating. I used to do that, too, when I was young. Taking off the long leather cord that bound his hair off his face, he tied it into a loop and then formed a pattern that I'd never seen before. He leaned over and showed it to me.

"We called this one, the kitten's nest."

I studied the pattern carefully, wondering if I could recreate it. I wasn't sure what kind of bird a kitten was, but I wondered if the pattern might have a magical use as well as just a game to amuse children. I would have to ask my Benefactor sometime.

"You show how make?" I pointed to the pattern he still held in his cord. "Me want make, maybe."

He pretended to think about my request for a moment then smiled. "I will show you, if you show me how to make something, too."

I hesitated. Was he asking me to show him how to make magical patterns like he had just seen me doing? I shifted my perception to study him with my Puwa...

He didn't appear to have power enough to see into the pattern of the Seer's Pool, but I knew so little about the Chamuqwani; they were a strange people. Nachoga had been born Chamuqwani and he had Puha—how could I know for sure this man didn't as well?

Then a horrible thought came to me, was he trying to trap me into revealing myself as the witch these strangers were curious about and wanted to find. Deciding to teach him a simple pattern like the raven's wing, and maybe sled dog/horse running that I knew were just string patterns with no Qwakaiva, I agreed.

Engrossed in our mutual game I was surprised when someone nearby called to us and we both looked up straight into the eye of Willum's little black box. I hadn't meant to be a part of the picture making that morning, but it would seem that the Unseen Ones had other ideas about the matter.

I learned later that Willum and his black box set on sticks was taking pictures of anyone who would stand or sit still and let him. Utsiyonti told me he'd heard that Willum planned to put them in a book about our land and show it to lots of Chamuqwani in his homeland.

Not long after that, the pictures were done for the day as the men would be called to the council soon. Betsiya asked me to get water for tea while she finished cooking our meal, so I said good bye to my new friend and headed for the little creek that ran with clear water farther up the slope away from the fort. When I returned the Chamuqwani were gone and the meal was ready to eat.

About the time we finished one of the soldiers came around to each tent and told the chiefs to prepare for the council. Golannah had already decided to take Eqwohi and two warriors with him to this meeting. Utsiyonti and the others would stay at the camp or with the horses in case of trouble. I was going with Golannah to watch the Chamuqwani—and maybe some of the other headmen. I could also talk to Utsiyonti or Betsiya, using the mind speech in case of trouble.

Golannah had already been warned not to bring weapons into the council, so the men left their bows and spears at the tent, and their thunder weapons were already hidden in a thicket near the horse corral. Belt knives they kept with them, concealed under their long vests.

Both men had dressed for the meeting, wearing clean shirts, loin cloths and leggings, hair neatly braided and bright red cloths wrapped around their foreheads. Shell earrings hung from their ear lobes and blue rock necklaces and trade silver pendants covered their chests.

Betsiya told them they looked very handsome. "And don't come back tonight with a new wife I will have to train," she playfully warned her husband. Neither man smiled at her comment, but I could see in the swirling patterns of their Spirit Fires that they were amused.

Trailing along in the warriors' wake I headed up the slope toward the open gate of the fort. As Golannah had expected everyone was checked at the entrance to make sure no one was carrying a thunder weapon. With grim amusement Eqwohi commented, loud enough for the soldiers to hear, that the rule didn't seem to apply to the soldiers who openly wore their holstered weapons on their belts.

As we came near the tempting smells of roasting meat wafted out to greet us from a far corner of the open space inside where a large pit had been dug to hold a fire. Two great spits hung over the coals on which whole quarters of roasting cai were being turned by soldiers assigned the task of cooking the meat for the coming feast.

There were too many people coming to this meeting to fit in one of the rooms in the soldiers' wooden houses, so the commander had erected a large canvas tent in the fort's parade ground to shelter the people invited. Though the day was sunny the wind when it blew up from the river had an autumn bite so the shelter might be welcome if the council went over long.

In the center of the tent was a large table behind which some blue coated soldiers with lightning bolts on their shoulders and gold disks and ribbons on their chests were just taking their seats. To my surprise there were also two black coated men at the table. One was fat with folds of extra pink flesh under his chin. The other was taller with hard blue eyes and brown hair covering his jaw and none on his head.

When they were introduced later I learned that they were imperial government men from the Office of Tribal Affairs who had been sent to check on the agents and discover the truth behind the rumors of violence on and off the Preserve. Sitting next to the government men was a blue-robed priest with a pointed white hat, his mouth set in a hard line.

Standing by the wall behind the Chamuqwani officials were several soldiers and the two interpreters we had already met, laughing and joking among themselves. On one end of the table near the soldier headman sat a soldier with a big book to write down what was said at the council.

Golannah and Eqwohi were directed to chairs at the end of one side, facing the Chamuqwani. The two men they brought as an escort stood directly behind them while I squatted on the ground by the tent wall. I was close enough to Golannah that I could speak to him, but far enough away to remain unnoticed. As his nephew my presence at the council was explained to the soldiers as being there to run errands for him, such as bringing tea if any was needed.

Twelve leaders of the combined Qwani'Ya and Kukiya clans were being seated around the table as I watched. They were a mix of Traditionals and a few Convert leaders. The headmen and their escorts were all men of middle years. Most of our wise men and Elders were either dead or too weak to travel such a long way. Besides Golannah and the old hunter who had helped me at Lynx Hunting's camp after the attack, I didn't know the rest by more than sight, though I'm sure many were relatives of one kind or another.

I was surprised that Chief Eagan wasn't present. Though I was relieved, I was also curious. Because of the demon that clung to his spirit I'd never dared to check on him for fear of falling victim to another trap. Maybe Grandfather had killed him after all. Uncle Royston had survived his wounds, though he was still in poor health, I did know, when I checked on him in the Seer's Pool.

Aware of my reason for being included in this gathering I studied all the participants with my Spirit Sight. A few among the clans were aware of my probe, like the old hunter, but most were not. When the man from Lynx Hunting's camp named Gay'u felt my touch he glanced around and when he found me his eyes widened for a moment, then he ignored me. I would talk to him later, I decided.

Uncertainty, anger, fear, those were the emotions I saw mostly swirling about in the peoples' Spirit Fires, understandable considering everything happening on the Preserve. Touching my hand to the hidden pouch under my shirt I called upon Crystal to help me as I next considered the Chamuqwani at the table.

They were an interesting bunch, but I could detect no hidden Chamuqwani magic, even with the Crystal Being's added Gift, there was no malicer among them, but they definitely wanted to hide something from the headmen called to the table. My skills didn't include forcing my way into another's mind to hear their thoughts, so I could only gather a vague impression of deceit and some kind of planned treachery.

"There is no malicer in this tent, but all here isn't what it seems, war leader. Have a care," I told him when I poured Golannah and Eqwohi water from the water-skin I'd brought with me. I'd been aware of Golannah giving me side-long glances earlier, but he'd been raised beside a man with power. He knew the signs when someone was using their Gift and knew better than to interrupt.

When I finished he grunted his understanding and I took my place by the tent wall again as the fort's commander signaled that the council was about to begin.

To my surprise, just as a soldier was about to close the tent flap my new Chamuqwani friend Collin slipped in. Spying me he smiled and came over to sit on the ground beside me and took out his little book and writing stick. "I will take notes as well he told me, so later those government men can't change what is said here today," he confided.

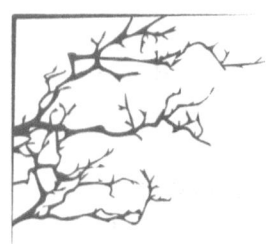

Chapter Eleven

At last all were settled and the commander nodded to the priest who rose and in a deep booming voice began a long prayer to his god. All the converts put their hands together and bowed their heads. Golannah and the other Traditionals at the table held their heads high and their faces remained expressionless as the priest droned on.

When the priest finally finished there was a moment of silence then the fort's headman, Commander Rossman rose to speak. He was a big man, both tall and broad of shoulder, and starting to grow a belly. His brown hair was threaded with white above his ears and the curly hair on his chin showed even more gray. When he began speaking Ahaz and Samith translated his words into the Kukiya and Qwani'Ya languages.

"I have asked you here today because the Father Emperor has heard about all the fighting and raiding that has been happening between your people and his imperial settlers. He is very disappointed in his tribal children for behaving so badly. All this raiding and steeling must stop—now or the army will be forced to come onto the Preserve and if that happens there will be more bloodshed and many people will die."

Though the men's expressions remained calm and unreadable throughout his talk, when he finished and sat down I could see the swirling colors of anger and frustration in the Spirit Fires of every headman and warrior inside the big tent, but no one spoke.

At last when the Chamuqwani were becoming uncomfortable with our silence a Convert headman named Rogarson from another settlement nearer to the Willow Creek Agency rose to speak.

"When Mighty Djoven's priests and the Father Emperor's men came to our northern villages with their treaties we were promised many good things if we signed the paper and agreed to leave our beautiful northern home and move to this Tribal Preserve. They told us if we abandoned the graves of our ancestors our children would have a bright future in this new land. Our people would be able to build fine houses and we would get herd beast to eat, and tools to tear up the land to plant new foods so that our children would never go hungry."

Leaning forward he placed his hands flat upon the table and looked the government men in the eye. "We signed those papers in good faith, but did you, Chamuqwani? No food, no tools, no schools for our children, or wooden houses for our families. Where are these good things you promised us if we gave you our homelands?"

As he sat down another Elder rose to complain about our treatment and how the agent was lying and steeling the cai beasts and other food we were supposed to receive, but were not.

"And when the agent does give us some rations there are bugs in the flour and oat-mush, and the salt meat is rotten. When hungry people eat they get sick—maybe die," a Kukiya warrior grumbled.

The council continued with each headman and war leader having a chance to speak as they went around the table.

At last it was Golannah's tern. In no hurry he took his time, making them wait. Finally he rose slowly and looked into the eye of each man at the table in the Chamuqwani fashion, his Spirit Fire bright with his controlled rage.

"Father Emperor promised that this Preserve land is our land, and only our land forever. No Chamuqwani allowed to live with us. You make go away even our adopted relatives. You say they not our relatives but Chamuqwani like you. You send our relatives away, but you don't stop bad Chamuqwani from trespassing on our land. Miners come look for yellow rocks, traders come to sell waskyja and fat agent steals our treaty goods and soldiers do nothing—Father Emperor's man do nothing.

"Our women and children are starving and sick. Then when warriors take back what treaty say is ours to feed hungry relatives you be angry. If we are all children of the Father Emperor why you no protect us like any good father do with children, eh?"

When Golannah finished and sat down there were murmurs of agreement from even some of the convert leaders at the table. Adding to what his war leader had to say Eqwohi rose and said, "You do nothing to stop the Chamuqwani who come on our land and cheat us. Why do you chase and kill us why don't you protect us from these bad Chamuqwani?"

The Chamuqwani shuffled papers and refused to meet the angry warriors' eyes. Finally Commander Rossman cleared his throat. "This is a difficult problem. The preserve is a big place and I have only a hundred and fifty soldiers to patrol it. My men and I can't be everywhere. We are doing our best."

"Then give us back our weapons and we will help you," a headman further up the table said. "We will send away bad Chamuqwani who steel and cheat us."

Commander Rossman's mouth hardened into a thin line. "I cannot do that. It's against my orders to arm you."

The anger in his voice barely controlled another headman said, "Who give you those orders, who? We need weapons to hunt and feed our families. If agent and Father Emperor's men not feed us then give us weapons to hunt. We can't survive another winter like last one. We will all be dead of hunger and Chamuqwani diseases if we have no food."

"I am Lord Donwood, and the commander is right," the imperial government man with no hair on his head and cold eyes said. "It is against the law to give you weapons. If you wish to make bows and arrows for yourselves we will not stop you. You can hunt and feed your families with them. But I am here to investigate your claims about agent Daglish cheating you out of your treaty goods."

He motioned to the red-faced man with the heavy chins sitting next to him. "This man is Lord Baskin. He will be your new agent at the Willow Creek agency. He will not cheat you out of your treaty goods. You will have plenty of food for the coming winter and farming tools to plant your crops in the spring. The Father Emperor has promised it."

"What about the cai and the other things stolen from us; will we get them back?" A warrior asked.

"There will be an investigation," the imperial man assured us.

"And what about fat agent will he go to jail for what he do?" another wanted to know.

"There will be an investigation," he repeated.

Investigation. I wasn't exactly sure what that word meant, the interpreter had difficulty translating it, but it didn't matter, because when I looked at Lord Donwood with my gift I could see he was lying.

Evidently others in the tent didn't believe him either, because a man from one of the convert settlements stood, turned and showed the imperial man the whip scars on his back. "I get these for going off Preserve to tell priest in Chamuqwani settlement about sickness and no food. When I come back fat agent put me in jail and have soldiers whip me because I tell. Will agent be whipped and put in jail for stealing from us, eh?"

As I said there will be an investigation. Agent Daglish will be reprimanded—if he is found guilty,"

"What it mean, re-pre-manda?" the hunter named Gay'u from Lynx Hunting's camp asked.

"It means that Agent Daglish will be removed from his post. He will go with us and we will investigate the accusations made against him. If he is found guilty of the crime he will be punished. I assure you."

"Will he be whipped?"

"I don't know."

"Lot people die because hungry. Will fat agent go to jail?"

"I don't know—maybe."

"Why you take him away? Why you no invest-tigate here so we can tell truth about what he do. You go back east maybe nobody speak for us and tell truth."

"There will be an investigation and we will discover the truth," both imperial men insisted.

"Maybe me not believe you. If you take him far away and no one of the people see maybe you do nothing, eh? If we all children of Father Emperor then why we not all treated same? You whip fat agent and put in jail, let everybody see. Then we know Father Emperor speak true," Golannah countered.

The soldiers and the Emperor's men looked at one another but they had little to say after that to assure us. It was growing late and the men were saved more questioning when a soldier entered to announce that the feast was ready. Gratefully the commander stood and said the council would resume next day after breakfast.

The delicious smells of roasting meat making my mouth water I followed my war leader out into the parade ground where long tables with meat, pots of white beans and flat breads and big pots of steaming kafa with sweet lasses had been set out for all to enjoy.

Golannah and Eqwohi seemed more interested in talking with some of the other chiefs invited to this council than eating, much to my disappointment. Still worried about being noticed I dutifully trailed after them in case I was needed. But every chance I got my eyes looked hungrily at the platters of rich meat, noticing they were growing smaller as the line of hungry people grew longer. At last he had pity on me and told me to go get myself something to eat. He wouldn't need me for a while.

Still keeping a wary eye out for Samith and any other convert that might recognize me I got in line and picked up my share of flat bread, meat, beans, and filled my cup with hot kafa.

As I was just walking away from the table and looking for a hidden away spot to devour my meal, Gay'u and the men from his camp saw me and motioned for me to join them. Coming over to them they smiled and made room for me, remembering, no doubt how I had helped their ghosts depart for the north after the converts attacked their peaceful camp.

As I sat down Gay'u said, "I was surprised to see you here, grandson. Is your Grandfather here as well? I haven't seen him if he is."

"No, I think the soldiers might still be looking for him. It would be dangerous for him to come after we got him out of the fat agent's jail."

Gay'u chuckled and bit off a large chunk of bloody meat. When he had chewed and swallowed, he said, "Yes, I heard about his escape and how he tried to kill that old malicer of a convert chief."

"Is chief Eagan really dead then?"

One of the others snorted his mouth curling up into a grim smile. "Might as well be. It's said that he has gone completely crazy. Babbles nonsense and soils his clothes like a baby, so they say."

"Serves him right," another said, "after what he ordered done to us."

Inwardly I breathed a sigh of relief. And like my relative I couldn't say I felt sorry for him and his situation.

Bringing me back out of my musings, Gay'u said, "Grandson, I hadn't heard that you were a part of that. We thought it was only your Uncle Tli and some of his men that were responsible."

"Uncle was there with some others, true enough, but they needed me to use my Gift to open the jail door, so I came, too."

"Hmm, yes, I can see that someone with your Qwakaiva could be of great use to those people who resist the soldiers and try to feed the hungry ones. Your uncle has sent cai meat our way several times over the summer. I noticed you with that Kukiya outlaw, Golannah today. Does your uncle know you are with the dust eaters?"

There was that bad name again. I frowned, but I wasn't about to correct an Elder. "He knows,' I explained. "But I'm not staying with Uncle Tli. He has a wife now and she has just given him a new baby, too."

I pointed to the tribal tattoos on my face. "My mother has married and I live with her and my new Kukiya father."

Gay'u's eyes widened at that bit of news. "Well that would explain why you are traveling with the Kukiya. Does your uncle approve?"

Though his words weren't unkind I could tell by his tone of voice and the shifting colors in his Spirit Fire that even though both our peoples had been thrown together on the Tribal Preserve the Chamuqwani created, he didn't agree with the idea of Mother's marriage and a Qwani'Ya boy being adopted by someone from outside our clans.

"Yes, his wife is Kukiya, too."

"And where is your grandfather then?" one of the warriors asked, changing the subject. "My wife has a bad cough that won't go away. Our camp could use his healing skills."

"I don't know exactly where he is," I said. "I haven't seen him for some time now. The last I knew he was traveling with some of the Prophet's followers, heading back to encampments of our people to teach. Later I will look for him using my Gift and tell you tomorrow what I find out."

Realizing that I knew about the Prophet they asked me many more questions about him and his teachings. I told the man with a sick wife that if Grandfather couldn't be found he could leave the preserve and seek out Iyantsha on the desert plateaus to the west.

The meal was long over and it was growing late when Tuumaz found me and told me I was to come with him back to our tent. It had been good to visit with Qwani'Ya people from back home, but I wasn't sorry to go with my Kukiya relative either. I missed Mother and Nachoga. I hoped we would leave this place of lies and treachery soon.

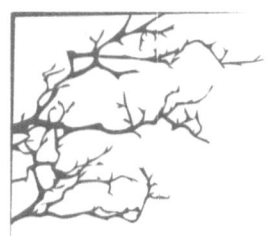

Chapter Twelve

Next day after breakfast the council continued. For nearly the whole morning the headmen and the Chamuqwani just repeated what had been said the day before, so I was bored and barely listening. My Chamuqwani friend Collin joined me again on the ground by the tent wall as the meeting started, but even he was bored and wrote little in his book.

Nearing midday the talk became interesting again when Gay'u rose and glaring directly at Samith accused him and other converts of attacking his camp and killing innocent women and children.

"None of my people were responsible for burning down your god's house. Yet your malicer chief sent your young warriors to kill us. Many women and children also died that terrible night."

Turning to look at the fort commander, and unable to keep the anger out of his voice, he demanded, "Instead of protecting us you let this man join you Chamuqwani army. You give him thunder weapon. You make him traitor to his own Qwani'Ya people once again. Why you no punish this man and the others for killing us? How can we trust you to keep your word and punish bad agent if you can't even punish a treacherous zaunk who betrays his own once again?"

"You are not my kin and I didn't kill your relatives, you filthy heathen!" Samith snarled in our language.

"Hah, but you knew what your chief had ordered and your brother was the one who led the raid. We know; he was recognized even wearing his paint." Gay'u shot back.

As the meeting erupted into chaos, Collin turned to me. "What are they saying?"

When I told him in the best Chamuqwani I could manage, his mouth dropped open in shock. "If I understand you correctly, you are telling me that some of your people who have converted to one of our religions attacked and killed people who were not baptized to Djoven's worship?"

When I nodded, he said a Chamuqwani bad word, then muttered, as much to himself as me, "This is terrible. We had no idea..." focusing his attention back on me again, he continued, "Tas, there is something you and your people need to know. I hope you can understand enough of my language to tell your chief what I will say to you now.

"If you didn't already know the Empire is made up of many different groups of people, each with their own customs, religions and way of thinking. Some of us don't like how the government and Djoven's priests are treating the primitive tribal peoples the Empire has encountered as we've moved our boundaries westward. That's why Lord Bronworthy and the rest of us came here along with the imperial representatives from the capital. We are part of a group that is trying to change things.

"Oh, like other nations in the past who joined the Empire there is great opportunities for your people available, but Yon and I don't believe that the harsh ways of Djoven's priests should ever have been allowed to play such a major role in the government's dealings with your people—any primitive people."

I hadn't understood the meaning of everything the earnest young man was trying to tell me, but with the aid of my spirit helpers I understood enough. "Me tell what you say, Chamuqwani friend," I told him. "Me pray for you. Me ask Unseen Ones protect."

"Thank you. I think we will need all the help we can get."

I patted his hand to reassure him. "Spirits tell me you good man, someday you be great man among your people. They help you—you will see."

Collin nodded, but his attention had returned to what was happening in the tent around us. Commander Rossman had risen to his feet and was bellowing for quiet.

When silence returned, he said, "These accusations will also be investigated by me and these imperial men. But now it is time to talk about other important things." Motioning for the imperial man with the hard blue eyes to stand and speak, he took his seat once more at the table.

Lord Donwood rose and clearing his throat he began. "Our Father Emperor is sorry he gave you such bad land so he wants to buy some of it back. This land he wants to buy is no good for farming or raising the cai beasts either. It is no good. It is too dry—no water to grow food there."

"If it is so bad then why do they want it?" I heard Eqwohi murmur under his breath.

Golannah grunted. "For miners; they know about yellow rocks and they want," he said in the same low voice.

Removing a rolled-up leather scroll from its case on the table, the imperial man opened it part way to show us. "On this document is a new treaty—a better treaty for all the primitive tribal peoples on the Preserve. In this new treaty the Father Emperor promises to give you back all the things stolen from you and much more as well.

"You will get your wooden houses and herds of cai, better rations and farm tools of your own to plow and grow your food in future. We will build a school for your children so they can learn our ways. All this we will do for you.

"But to have all these good things you must do something good for the Empire, too. You must sign the new treaty and give us some of the vacant land to the west that is no good for farming.

"The Preserve we set aside for you in the old treaty is too big for people wanting to be farmers and cai herders. Much of the land to the western mountains isn't suitable. It will be no good for you and your children in the future. So we will pay you for it and give you lots of good things in return for this bad land."

Trembling with outrage Golannah rose to his feet when the imperial man finished, raking them with his hard black stare. "Kukiya land is not bad, is good to us. We lived here for many, many generations before you invaded our land and took it by force away from us.

"You allow us to keep only small part of our land after war with us, a part you say you don't want. A part we now have to share with others—strangers. Peoples you make come here when you steal their land as well. But when we agree and sign treaty you say it is ours forever. Now you want more Kukiya land. So you lie before? Forever is no more? How can we trust you to keep your word this time, eh? Will you want more Kukiya land next year as well?"

"In the past you were barely able to survive in such a difficult environment—even with all that land," Agent Baskin said, interrupting. "But that was in the past when you were savages without the blessings of Mighty Djoven's teachings. With education and training your children won't have to live in such primitive conditions.

"With this new treaty you will be freed from your primitive past so that you can become happy and productive citizens of the empire. Please understand the Great God and the Father Emperor know what is best for you. They want only good things for you and your children

Glaring at the ignorant new agent for his lack of understanding of our protocol and his rudeness Golannah snarled, "Our ancestors are buried in this land. Creator give it to us—not you. And now you make us share our land with other peoples when you Chamuqwani steal their land, too. We say is all right because northern people like Kukiya—little bit.

"But we no want Chamuqwani—especially Chamuqwani miners on the land that is left to us."

Golannah made an angry cutting gesture with his hand. "I will sign no treaty that gives away more Kukiya land. Give me no more empty promises, promises that we all know you don't intend to keep. You start by keeping promises made in treaty we did sign and then talk to me about new treaty. And make soldiers keep bad Chamuqwani out of the Preserve—especially ones who tear up our land looking for yellow rocks."

I heard no more after that because Golannah stormed out of the council, the rest of us hastily following.

The morning session broke up after that for a midday meal. When Golannah returned to our tent and had cooled down enough to think, he told Betsiya and the warriors to discretely begin packing. We were planning to leave that very afternoon, but then Bronworthy and his two companions arrived and our plans changed once again.

Eyes bright and bodies quivering with excitement our new friends were bursting with their news. "I think this is the solution we have been hoping for," Bronworthy announced when he sat by our fire. "If you accept the offer that the tribal officials plan to give you I think it will be good for your people. Please, Chief Golannah, come back to the council and at least listen to what Lord Donwood and Agent Baskin have to say to all of you."

Bronworthy's child-like excitement was contagious and made Golannah hesitate about leaving, and then with a little more persuasion, he agreed to go back to the council and at least listen.

He liked the man and because of my earlier urging, maybe he even trusted him a little. I studied them carefully with my Spirit Sight again, but I could detect no treachery in their enthusiasm, but something "felt" wrong about the matter.

When the strangers finally left us, Golannah turned to me and asked my opinion. "I detect no deceit in Bronworthy. He believes whatever the soldiers and imperial man told him."

"I too believe he isn't lying," Betsiya said. "I see no treachery in his Spirit Fire, either. But that doesn't mean there isn't treachery—somewhere."

"The man has a child-like nature," Utsiyonti mused. "It would be easy enough for someone to use him for a darker purpose without him being aware of it."

"Mm, but who is trying to play games with us, the fort's commander, the agent, or the imperial man?" Golannah said as he pondered the matter.

"You won't know unless you men go and find out, eh?" Betsiya said and folded her arms across her chest. When Golannah still hesitated, she added, "We can still pack, and the men can take a few things we won't need tonight out to our hidden site by the horses just in case."

"Is a good idea to hear what they want," Utsiyonti said, his expression thoughtful. "If the Chamuqwani are planning some kind of trap, better not to let them know we suspect them."

"Hmm, you have a point, Brother," Eqwohi said. If we leave now maybe soldiers come after us. Maybe they try to kill us or take us prisoner. Better we play their game for now, eh?"

The warriors all agreed, and so I once more trailed after the Kukiya back to the council tent within the fort.

When all were once more seated and the priest had opened the council with another long prayer, the imperial man, Lord Donwood, rose to speak. "In the past couple days I have listened to all your concerns. I was sent here to make a new treaty with both the Kukiya and the northern tribes, and that is all. I am not authorized to punish Agent Daglish, mediate squabbles between one faction or another who are fighting on the Preserve, or deal with your many other complaints.

"So, I propose that you come back east with me and speak to the Father Emperor and his Parliament yourselves. Tell him in person what you want and how you think the Imperial Government isn't keeping their promises to you."

As he waited to hear the headmen's answer another Kukiya chief named Ocoa, rose and spoke, "Is too far to ride, it would take many moons to go and come back. Who will feed our families and hunt for them if we are gone so long, eh?"

"It wouldn't take long at all if you go with me," Lord Donwood countered. "We will arrange for you to ride a train that is the way we ourselves will travel. It is perfectly safe. Come with us, and then you can speak to all our great lords' at once, and tell them your concerns. If you come to our great capital city with me you can get to know them, and they you. In the east you will see better how we live and the wonderful opportunities we are offering you and your children with this new treaty."

The discussion dragged on throughout the long afternoon. From my place against the tent wall I could see that the convert headmen and some of the traditional chiefs were seriously considering his offer—Gay'u among them to my dismay. Golannah remained stubbornly unwilling to commit himself until just before the meeting broke up for the day when he too agreed to go.

"I will not sign new treaty, but I will go on Train to see Chamuqwani Father Emperor and tell him how fat agent cheat us and soldiers no protect us" Looking the imperial man straight in the eye, he said, "If Father Emperor agree to punish bad men who cheat us, and give us what is promised in treaty, then I sign."

Ignoring the startled looks he was getting from Eqwohi and his warriors, he folded his arms across his chest, and asked, "When we go?"

Lord Donwood's eyes widened for a moment then he mastered his surprise and nodded. "Soon. We will go soon."

Commander Rossman wasn't so trusting, however, and glared at Golannah with narrowed eyes, probably not believing a word of it. I knew we were going to have trouble with that one.

Eqwohi could barely wait till we returned to our tent, before he exploded. "Why did you agree to such a foolish and dangerous plan? Those Chamuqwani weasels aren't going to let you get anywhere near their Father Emperor. They will probably put you in their jail house as soon as you leave our protection and go on Train with them."

"I know they will which is why I'm not going to go with them," Golannah said calmly as he reached for the cup of tea Betsiya was handing him.

Eqwohi opened his mouth several times, but no words came out. Betsiya smiled and put a cup of tea in his hand. He took a long swallow of the hot liquid before he could bring himself back under control.

Glaring at all of us gathered round our fire, Golannah said, "I have no intention of leaving with the lying malicer, but if he and the fort commander think I am going, then maybe they don't watch us so closely, eh?"

"I heard soldiers talking about taking new agent to Willow Creek and bringing fat agent back with them," Utsiyonti said. "I think nobody will leave for place where Train lives, until they bring prisoner back, so we can see they keep their promise to punish him."

"So, we too, have time to make our own plans," Eqwohi said and smiled.

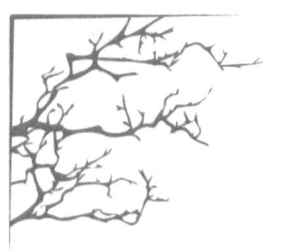

Chapter Thirteen

The soldiers assigned to collect the fat agent, and bring the new one to Willow Creek, left the very next morning. That meant there wasn't much time before the party going on Train would leave as well. Though there was more discussion about the new treaty and who would go in the delegation that day, all the leaders seemed distracted—different factions keeping to themselves. Though nothing had been declared officially, everyone seemed to know who was going to sign the new treaty now and who would wait until the people traveling east returned, and so, to my relief, the session broke up early.

We collected the rations due us from the post and went back to our encampment for tea and a meal. The atmosphere was relaxed men and women gossiped and joked, visiting from one tent to another. Some of the men suggested a race and several warriors trooped off to get their best horses. From somewhere in the middle of the encampment a drum beat out a lively rhythm and people began to sing.

Soon after we finished our meal several men who were friends with our warriors joined us for tea and a smoke at our fire. The talk was light, but I suspected some were curious why Golannah had agreed to travel east with the Chamuqwani. He told them the same story he told at the council. Though no one was rude enough to come right out and say he was lying, I suspected that not everyone believed him.

Golannah was well-known among the clans for his skill in out maneuvering the enemy in battle. They probably were thinking that he must be playing some clever game with the Chamuqwani. They were curious to know what it was, but dared not openly ask.

Bronworthy and his friends joined us early in the evening after the light was too bad for Willum's black box. He had been taking pictures of the people dancing and singing earlier and had just come from the warriors showing off their horses.

Ahaz was with them this time, not Samith, which is why, much to my discomfort Bronworthy brought up the subject of magic and witches again. Utsiyonti had told me that, though no one among our people liked him much, because he had chosen to join the army as a scout for the soldiers, Ahaz still was a Traditional and hadn't converted to the new Chamuqwani religion. Which also meant that he already knew who among us was the Puhani. He would have recognized the tattoo on my jaw, and what it meant.

Staring him boldly in the eye, I made him drop his eyes and look away first. I was sure he knew it was me Bronworthy was looking for, but for his own reasons he was keeping my secret. Had he heard gossip about me from others? Was he afraid of me and what I might do to him or his family if he crossed me? I didn't know, and the thought of it made me uncomfortable.

I didn't want people to fear me—except maybe Charlic and his pack of carrion eaters—well, maybe not even them. I wanted to be good, and do only good with my Gift, but sometimes it was so hard to know what good really was.

Just as before Golannah and the others were vague about the witch when answering the Chamuqwani's questions. They told him about things a Puhani could do, like healing sick people and talking to ghosts, but no names were ever spoken. And then someone was stupid enough to mention Iyantsha.

"Yes, I have heard about him," Bronworthy said, his blue eyes alight with excitement. "Some call him a prophet. Do you know him?"

Golannah's expression was unreadable, but he answered the man willingly enough. "I know Prophet; he is good man powerful Puhani."

"Some of the people I've talked to say this prophet of yours can call down lightning from the sky to heal the sick and injured. I'm sorry, but I find that hard to believe."

"Is true," one of the warriors said. "My sister have coughing sickness. Iyantsha make better when he touch her with lightning in hands."

"Hmm, maybe this prophet make a trick to fool you, and your sister just got better on her own," Bronworthy offered.

"No, Prophet heal," the man insisted, his expression stubborn.

"Prophet heal my brother, too," Golannah said, before the warrior could take more offence.

"Really, and did he call upon the lightning for that miracle, too?" Bronworthy asked. Though he had asked politely, I saw the disbelief in his Spirit Fire.

Though unable to see what I could, Golannah was aware of the Chamuqwani's disbelief when he continued, "No. Him call Rattlesnake for Puwa that time."

Bronworthy was about to take another drink of his tea when Golannah revealed that. He choked and sat down his cup. Willum patted him on the back when he began coughing. "When he had his voice back under control, he drank more tea then said, "Rattlesnakes healing people. I still find this all hard to believe. You seem like a very intelligent man to me, Chief Golannah; are you sure it wasn't trickery?"

Golannah snorted with disgust. "You also seem like an intelligent man. You ask, so we tell. You no want listen we stop talk now."

Willum mumbled something I couldn't hear. Flushing with irritation Bronworthy snapped something back to him in the same low voice and Willum's expression soured. Then he smiled and apologized to Golannah. "No, no, please continue. I want to hear this."

Golannah took a moment to consider his words, then gave the Chamuqwani a short version of the ceremony he had witnessed, and took part in by Saluuli Lake. I was grateful that he was careful only to refer to me as one of Iyantsha's helpers when he explained my part in the ceremony.

Ahaz and most of the others sitting round our fire hadn't heard the story and were far more impressed with his telling than the Chamuqwani seemed to be. The strangers were too polite to say so, but I doubted if they believed him.

When he finished, Bronworthy also took a moment before speaking, at last he said, "Thank you for trusting me enough to share that story with me."

Still feeling annoyed with his friend, Willum lashed out, "The soldiers say that this prophet of yours is stirring up your people to make war again," Willum said, changing the subject.

Golannah's eyes flashed in anger and Willum shrank back. "Soldiers lie. Prophet don't want warriors kill anyone. He want people only pray."

"Pray for what?" Bronworthy asked. "Please tell us, Chief Golannah. What does the Prophet pray for?"

Golannah sighed. I guessed he was wondering how to explain to these ignorant strangers the Puwa and visions of a man so alien to their own way of thinking. "Prophet have dream," Golannah began. "In dream Spirits give him much Puwa. Spirits tell him how to change world and make things better for Kukiya—and all tribal people who invaders take away land and kill relatives. Someday will come a Renewal and it will be like before—and good for us again."

Looking up from his book where he had been writing down our words, a puzzled frown wrinkled Collin's forehead, as he thought about the war chief's answer. Leaning forward he finally asked, "Return your land and bring back the old good life, but how can you accomplish that without going to war? The soldiers and imperial settlers aren't going to just walk away."

"Iyantsha say Thunder Beings tell him if we dance and pray hard, someday our Puwa will be strong enough to make all Chamuqwani leave our land," Utsiyonti said, a wistful expression coming over his face. Several of the others grunted their agreement to his words.

The three Chamuqwani exchanged looks, astonished. "Pray? Am I understanding you correctly? You believe that if you dance and pray we will all leave and give you back your land?" Bronworthy asked.

"That's what Prophet say," Golannah said.

"And what do you say, Chief Golannah?" Willum asked.

"Golannah say that Prophet have much Puwa, so we pray."

Bronworthy chuckled. "And that, Friend Golannah is a very diplomatic answer, one worthy of the most experienced politician in the Emperor's court."

Two days passed with no news from Willow Creek and little to say in the council meetings, either. The wrongness in the air was growing; many could sense it and were uneasy, though unsure of its cause. I knew the source, the imperial man and the commander, but I couldn't detect what treachery they were planning.

On the day before we finally made our escape Golannah told me to remain just inside the gate of the fort in a quiet place where I could watch the soldiers while he went back to our tent to rest and see how our plans to leave were going. I was squatting in the shade, watching a group of new soldiers being drilled by their sergeant when Collin found me and wanted me to teach him another pattern with my string.

Having nothing better to do, I took the cord from around my neck and looped it over my hands. "Maybe today I show you how make pattern of Kunai's teeth."

"Kunai? What is a Kunai?"

I grinned showing lots of my own teeth. "Him big, got lot Puwa. Him live in bottom of lake back home." I could tell he still didn't understand, and I had no Chamuqwani words to explain, so I took out my knife and drew a simple picture of Kunai's true form on the ground between us.

Collin's eyes widened. "Ah, a dragon! Do you mean this Kunai is a dragon? Is he a monster that lives at the bottom of a lake near here?"

"Kunai no live round here. Live up north, but him no monster," I insisted. Well, maybe he was to some of my people, but this Chamuqwani didn't need to know that.

"That's fascinating. I have read of other peoples in the Empire having such stories—about dragons. I would love to see a real dragon someday. Yes, please teach me the pattern."

See a dragon—Kunai! I nearly choked on my laughter. Oh, Chamuqwani, you have no idea. Be careful what you wish for, I thought. To hide my amusement, I lowered my head and began looping my string in the familiar pattern of triangles that was Kunai's teeth to show him.

He watched me and tried to copy my actions, but I could tell he had something else on his mind. Finally he gave up, unbound his loop and tied it back around his hair. Then he just sat staring down into his lap.

We stayed that way for a long moment before he next spoke. "Since I agreed to become Yon's scribe for this trip I have seen many strange things, some beautiful, others horrifying, frightening and a lot more I just don't understand.

"Most of my people think your people are lazy or backward, but you aren't that way at all. Different, yes, but not stupid or child-like, just different."

Not looking at me he began drawing meaningless designs in the dirt with his pen, then erasing them with his other palm. At last as if thinking out loud, he said, "I think the difference lies in what you call your Puwa. I don't understand it, but I think whatever it is it has given your people the power to survive terrible hardships that would have totally destroyed other people—especially my people.

"You probably don't have the right words in my language to explain, but I want to know, what is Puwa? Where does it come from?"

When I looked at him with my spirit sight I could see his sincerity. He truly wanted to know—and not to share with his friends. "Puwa is a gift given to all children. It come from Earth Mother. All people that live close to Earth Mother can touch Puwa. Chamuqwani born with Puwa, but forget when older, because priests say Puwa is bad, so they forget."

Putting a hand on his arm, I looked deep into his eyes, and said, "you good man, Friend Collin. You have Puwa, you can learn again to touch Puwa. Look in dreams and pray, ask Earth Mother and Unseen Ones to help you find you Puwa. They will answer—you pray."

Collin sighed, put his hand over mine, and dropped his eyes. When he spoke again there was such a tone of longing in his voice that I pitied him and wished him well on his quest.

"Pray, I wish it were that simple. Is that what a Puhani does, help people find their Puwa?"

I shrugged. "It one thing Puhani do, sometimes."

"Is the Prophet what you call a Puhani?"

"Yes, him Puhani—strong Puhani. All people have gifts, but Puhani, him special. Unseen One make strong so can help people not strong.

"Thank you for telling me. I hope someday to be lucky enough to find such a Puhani among my own people."

"You pray to Earth mother and Unseen Ones with a good heart, and spirits help you. Show you teacher, help protect and guide you. This me believe."

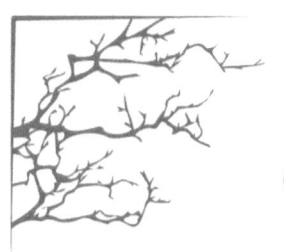

Chapter Fourteen

That evening Tuumaz came back from caring for our horses with disturbing news. "It seems that Commander Rossman is now posting soldiers at the river to guard the ford at night," he announced and flopped down upon his blankets with a discouraged sigh.

Golannah grunted to show he had heard him, but his face remained expressionless as he smoked his pipe and digested this obstacle to his plan. It was clear to everyone in our tent that he was in danger of losing this skirmish before the battle with the Chamuqwani began. We had to leave, soon, or be trapped and arrested. But how to leave without risking a fight that might get most of us killed? That was the question on everyone's mind.

Four or five of the warriors who wouldn't be missed, because they spent little time in the main camp, being assigned mostly to guard the horses and our secret cash of thunder weapons, had already slipped across the river on the excuse of going hunting.

When they never returned with meat, maybe the Commander got suspicious. Fearing imprisonment if we just tried to leave in daylight now that guards were posted, no final plans were in place before I crawled under my blankets that night.

I'm not sure how long I'd been sleeping when I heard Rattlesnake's whirr in my mind's ear. She had just coiled around me when a strong wind sucked me into the dream, plopping me down on the ledge above the black pool where I'd encountered my Benefactor, Kunai, on earlier occasions.

Taking on Chumco's form again he was waiting for me. I cringed and stepped back when I saw his angry face. <<Stupid, ignorant humans!>> he snarled. <<Damned Kukiya they have waited too long. Your enemies are ready to close the jaws of their trap now. If the warriors are there in the morning they will be imprisoned as Golannah suspects.>>

He suddenly roared loud enough to loosen tiny rocks in the darkness above. I could hear them splashing into the water somewhere out in the blackness. When the echoes died away he was still growling an impressive variety of Chamuqwani and other beings curses as he fought to bring his rage under control.

Quieting at last he turned back to me and grumbled, <<And as for you, my little Siyatli, if they are captured the priest with the emperor's man will put you in the special prison they have designed for children they call a live-away school. If the soldiers capture you with the outlaws he will be very pleased.

<<But I will not be pleased—not pleased at all.>> Kunai rumbled a menacing growl, and flexed fingers, that suddenly grew sharp claws. <<Meddling priest he will pay for his insolence, he and those carrion eaters that whisper to him in his dreams. You are far too important to the future we plan, to be lost to us in such a trivial manner.>>

I shivered. I had heard about those schools. My former mentor Chumco had predicted that I would be placed in one of the Chamuqwani prisons for children just before I turned away from him and his teachings. Then later on the Preserve ignorant convert parents also talked about the schools the priests promised.

Unlike my former mentor, however, they wanted their children to be locked away in those terrible places. I guess they were hoping by learning Chamuqwani ways their children would have a better future, but how could anybody have a better future after being locked up?

I feared the prisons made for children—always had—ever since Chumco warned me about them. I prayed Kunai would save me from ever being forced into one.

<<Have a care, Siyatli Boy,>> Rattlesnake whispered near my ear. <<Dragons are capricious creatures, best not to put all your hopes in a nest of their making. You must keep your inner power strong. Learn to rely on your own clever wits and Puwa, as well, if you want to protect yourself and survive.>>

I trembled with the power of foretelling at her words. <<Yes, Honored One, thank you for reminding me.>>

Returning his attention to me at last, Kunai fixed me with his green dragon eyes. I could tell he had come to some conclusion about our dilemma, and I wasn't sure I was going to like it. Motioning for Rattlesnake to uncoil herself from me, he stepped closer.

<<In order to see you don't fall into the enemy's clutches right now, I will be forced to help these stupid Kukiya or lose you as well in the Chamuqwani's trap, damn them....

<<I didn't want my enemies to know that I was taking an interest in your world, and your time, right now.>>

Once more he growled a curse, his claws flexing. <<Golannah should have left the very afternoon he stormed out of their council. He should have known the meeting was a trick and never left the plateau at all, for that matter. So, you tell those ignorant, stupid warriors they will owe me for this. And I will expect 'payment' for my aid, a big payment, when this is over. You tell them!

<<Now come here. I will need to share with you some of my power if you and those men are to make your escape tonight. You aren't strong enough, or skilled enough to do this on your own.>>

<<I will tell them, Great Kunai, I will tell them and they will be thankful for your aid, truly,>> I murmured as his clawed hands gripped my shoulders. <<Hold still now!>>

He gave me no more warning than that, because suddenly I had no voice to make more promises on behalf of the Kukiya, or me. I had only voice enough for screaming as his power surged into me like molten fire. From the crown of my head to the soles of my feet I was burning, burning up with joy, and pain. The crystal around my neck blazed white hot, like a star fallen from the night sky.

Too much, it was all too much. I was drowning; I was burning. I screamed again and I felt my knees buckle and then I was falling.

<<I said, hold still,>> he snarled and tightened his grip, continuing to fill me with his magic.

<<If you gift him with too much of your power, Great One, he may die,>> Rattlesnake warned. <<He will do what you require of him, never fear. I will help him if he needs it.>>

Kunai growled another angry curse, but did slow the flood. When he finished with me I crumpled to the stone in a boneless heap. Rattlesnake crawled to me and wrapped herself around my chest again. Her cool presence helped to sooth the fire burning inside.

He was about to dismiss me back to my world to wake the warriors when a new thought came to him and it made him smile. <<Perhaps there is a way that won't reveal my involvement so openly.>> He chuckled to himself, still considering his plan.

A mirthless smile still curving his lips he turned to me and finally said, <<So, you have a new friend who wishes he could meet a dragon.>> He laughed, seemingly pleased with himself. <<Maybe someday soon I will grant him his wish. But for now I will send you to him instead. Rattlesnake will help you enter his dream, and then you can give him my message.

<<If he is clever, and remembers your words when he wakes, and then carries out the task I tell you to give him, maybe he will be worthy of my regard in future.>>

When Rattlesnake and I entered his dream Collin was sitting in one of two comfortable-looking chairs that squatted near a large stone fireplace, a book laid across his lap. He was lost in thought, as I'd often seen him in the Waking World. Unaware of me yet, he watched the flames dance upon the sooty hearth, ignoring his book.

<<He is troubled by what he has seen while among your people,>> Rattlesnake confided.

<<I sensed that, too. Our ways are so different than what he has known in his Chamuqwani world.>>

<<And yet like a moth drawn to the lantern's flame, he is attracted to your people and their teachings.>>

Collin most have caught a whisper of our private communication, or sensed our presence in some other way, because he looked towards the doorway at that moment and saw us.

A tattooed young savage with Rattlesnake wrapped about my waist and Crystal Being's radiance shining like a star upon my chest, I must have looked quite the strange sight to him standing in the doorway of his Dream-created sanctuary. Putting Crystal back inside my shirt so he could see me better I smiled at him. <<Greetings, Friend Collin.>>

<<T-Tas?>> he stammered.

I laughed softly at his open mouthed stare and stepped further into the room, <<Yes, it's me, Tas.>> I looked around me, curious to see this unfamiliar Chamuqwani place for the first time.

A tall wooden bookshelf containing many books took up most of one wall. Next to a window several plants with flat leaves of a bright green nested their roots in brightly colored clay pots. On the opposite wall a long desk piled high with books and papers stood waiting for him to resume his seat on the wooden chair in front of it.

I smiled and sat in the other chair near him. <<This is a very nice place. You have created a warm, peaceful feeling in here. It must be a great comfort to imagine yourself here when you are troubled.>>

<<Ye-s-s it is... Who are you really?>>

I laughed again. <<I am Tas, as I said. Haven't you and your friends been looking for me? Haven't you figured it out yet? I am the Puhani, the heathen witch Praiser Samith was trying to warn you about.

<<Only the Converts have it wrong. I am no evil malicer like they claim. I have pledged my life to do only good with my power.>>

Having no skill to shield his thoughts from me, I heard him mutter to himself, <<A witch? No impossible, he is so young. I'm dreaming just imagining all this. I need to wake up... Why am I imagining this?>>

<<No, Collin, you aren't imagining me. I am here in your dream, true enough, but I and my companions,>> I pointed to Rattlesnake coiled about my middle and the crystal being tucked under my shirt, <<are separate from your dreaming mind. We are quite real, truly,>> I said, breaking in on his talk with himself.

<<Rattlesnake?>> Collin's eyes opened wide, becoming aware of the Spirit Being coiled around me for the first time. Raising her head, she looked him in the eye. He shivered and dropped his eyes.

Focusing on me again, as if he was finally understanding some of what we had been trying to tell him and his friends, he said, <<You're the one that Chief Golannah was telling us about—the Prophet's assistant with the snake.>>

When I nodded, he rubbed a hand across his face and shook his head. <<This is all so hard to believe. I don't understand all this.>>

<<I'm sorry, I know this is your first encounter with the Unseen World in which Spirits and Puhani walk. And, as a Chamuqwani unused to these things it is perfectly natural to be unsettled in your mind, but trust me, we are not something dreamed up by your imagination.>>

He wasn't sure he totally believed me, but when I didn't disappear when he told me to go, he finally asked, <<W-what do you want?>>

He was trying to hide from me his growing fear, but it glowed with a light of its own in the swirling currents of his Spirit Fire. <<Don't be afraid of me, Collin, I'm not here to hurt you. As I said I try to do only good with my Puwa, my power. I am here in your dream, because I came to give you a message from my Benefactor, Kunai, and warn you. And if you are willing, maybe ask a personal favor of you.>>

<<Give me a message—message from who? Warn me—about what?>>

I stroked Rattlesnake's sinuous coils as she slithered up to wind herself around my neck. <<At the bequest of my Benefactor this one came to warn me of treachery. The imperial man has given the fort's commander orders not to allow my people to go and speak to your great lords back east. When they board the train they will be put in chains and arrested as soon as they are gone from here.

<<No one will have the chance to speak. Some will go to prison far away, so they won't make trouble for the soldiers and your headmen ever again. Others, like my uncle Golannah, they plan to hang. They want to punish the warriors for the raids on the ranchas and the imperial settlements when they get food for starving relatives.>>

His eyes widened at my words, I smiled, showing lots of teeth. <<But that will not happen. By the time you wake in the morning we will be far away from here. And no soldiers will catch us. I will use mine and my Benefactor's Puwa, to see to that.>>

<<But I thought Agent Baskin and Lord Donwood wanted your people to tell their story to parliament. Why would they do such a terrible thing?>>

I looked at him with pity in my eyes, so young, so innocent of the true ways of the world. <<I think in years you be at least twice my age, but in other ways you are as innocent as a babe at his mother's breast. The only thing that hard eyed man you call Lord Donwood wants is Kukiya gold. And he will do everything in his power to get it,>> I growled.

<<I see. Then there is gold in the western desert as some claim.>>

<<Yes, and there are many more among your people who would like to see all of us dead—or at least unable to make more trouble for them, so they can claim the last of Kukiya land as they did my Qwani'Ya People's home in the north.

<<If Golannah and the warriors are gone there will be no one left to challenge Chamuqwani might. No one left to fight against injustice. That is why they want us dead or in prison—far away from the land that gives us strength and power.>>

<<But that's terrible! They can't do that—>>

<<They can and they will. Don't underestimate them, Collin, or you will be seen as an enemy and die, too. They want the gold in our mountains, and will do all in their power to get it. Many have already died for their greed—never forget that.>>

He thought about my words for a time, then said, <<Yes, maybe you have the right of it. Lord Donwood is an ambitious man, but Yon and I never imagined...What do you want me and my companions to do?>>

<<First of all I want you, and your friends, to survive. You and those with you have learned many things during your stay among us. It is important for the future of both our peoples that you tell what you know.

<<You have your writing, Willum has his pictures and I've been told by Rattlesnake that Lord Bronworthy has the wealth and connections at court to make things change.

<<You three have been chosen by Spirit Warriors who work for the good of all living beings, to do great things in your time, but first of all you must stay alive. And if that means playing along with Lord Donwood's evil plan until you can get somewhere safe—do it.>>

<<I see, and maybe there is some truth in what you suggest, but I don't think we can do much about it.>>

<<You can, if you choose to. There is power in your writing, and in Willum's pictures. Go home tell your people what you've learned. Make us and our sufferings real for them. If you choose to join us we will send you teachers who will guide you on your path.>>

I chuckled. <<But a Puhani's path is never easy, but if you are found worthy, as a Chamuqwani Puhani you might even get to see a dragon one day, eh?>>

<<Me? A witch, dressed in buckskins like a savage drumming and dancing at the Emperor's court?>> He laughed. <<Now I know you are joking with me.>>

<<Do you think so?>> I didn't explain further I only smiled, showing lots of teeth. He frowned, not sure now if I was teasing or not and I saw the fear come back into his eyes.

Deciding to change the subject he said, <<Come to think of it, how are you here in the first place, and how come you can speak my language so clearly now, when before you couldn't. Did you know our language all along and were just concealing it from us?>>

I laughed and shook my head with my amusement. He was so innocent of Spirit Ways. <<I am not speaking your language. In the Dream, where we are now, all beings speak mind-to-mind. There are no barriers here as in the Waking World.>>

I waved a hand in a cutting motion and Rattlesnake whirred a warning. This childish Chamuqwani was distracting me with his foolish questions. <<Enough. I have no time to teach you the ways of the Dream. You will have to find someone among your own people to instruct you, if you are interested. I came to tell you we are leaving and to warn you and your friends that when you go with the imperial man and the soldiers, be on your guard against treachery or you may be put in jail, too.>>

Collin nodded. <<Thank you for the warning. I will tell Lord Bronworthy and Willum.>> Recalling what I had said earlier, he said, <<you told me you came with a message for me. What is it?>>

<<Yes, my Benefactor, the one guides me and shares his Puwa with me. He wants you to find someone for him.>>

<<The Empire is a big place with millions of people. I will try, but I don't know if I will be able to do it. Who do you want me to find?>>

<<There is one of Djoven's priests, a man called Intercessor Raymonel. My Benefactor wants you to contact him and let him know how the agent and the soldiers have treated us, and how Djoven's priests here are aiding them cheat and starve us.>>

<<A priest? I thought all Djoven's dedicates want to kill people like you. I heard what the army scout said about the heathens among them, and I heard what Elder Gay'u said about his people being attacked by Djoven's followers. Why should I contact him?>>

<<Because he is a young man who truly knows what it means to be an intercessor. He tries to follow the teachings of his god in the manner in which those teachings were originally meant to be practiced and taught.

<<Intercessor Raymonel traveled with us and defended us when he could, on the long march from our home in the north to this harsh Tribal Preserve. In spite of hunger and bitter winter cold, he stayed with us, helped tend our sick and suffered with us until he became too ill himself to go any further. He of all the Chamuqwani we met on that terrible journey tried to help us.

<<I have been told that he is better now and could be a powerful ally if he knows what has happened to us. He has been assigned other duties by his superiors, but he still dreams of his mission among us. Find him, show him Willum's pictures, tell him what is happening here, and ask him to use his power and influence in the church to help us.>>

<<Being a priest may make him easier to find, I guess,>> he mused. <<But I know little of such things— >>

<<But Bronworthy does. Persuade him to help you. Give him a focus for the good he wishes to do. You are a sensitive and caring man, Collin, searching for a deeper meaning in your life. With my Puwa I can see that in you. We can give you that purpose if you choose to accept the opportunity we are offering you. Find the Intercessor and tell our story to the world.>>

As I turned to go, he said, <<You've given me lots to think about, I thank you. You also said you wanted me to do you a favor, what is it?>>

I smiled. <<Yes, I almost forgot. Among the people who are going to tell the Father Emperor their story are some relatives of mine who will need you and your friends' protection. The Converts going I leave to Djoven's priests, but the Traditionals, like my Elder Gay'u, will be at the mercy of convert and soldier alike on this journey.

<<You and your friends must do the best you can to protect them and see they are returned unharmed to their families on the Preserve. They are

innocent of any crime—except wanting to keep faith with our old ways—and Djoven's priests and their followers hate them for it.>>

Reaching up with one hand I pointed to the tattoo on my jaw. It was a mirror image of the horned, snake-like dragon I had drawn in the dirt for him that afternoon. Then with my other hand I placed a flat gray stone in his Palm, on which I had carved the same design.

Closing his fingers around it tightly I stepped back and said. <<Rattlesnake has worked a conjuring so you can't wake until morning, and by then we will be far from here, so this is good bye, Friend Collin. Keep the stone and remember me and what I have told you.

<<It is unlikely we will see each other again in the flesh, but I am glad I got to know you and your friends a little. You have taught me that some Chamuqwani are good people, too.>>

And with those words I faded out of his dream. As Rattlesnake was quick to remind me, we had much to do before the dawn.

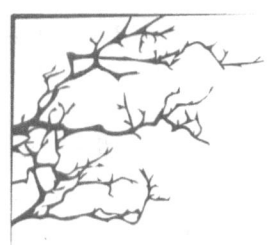

Chapter Fifteen

As Rattlesnake left me I woke to blackness within the tent. Taking in a deep breath, I listened to the sounds of people snoring softly and turning restlessly in their sleep. Outside the tent the night seemed quiet except for a few men in low conversation somewhere on the other end of the encampment. They were far enough away that I could only hear the faint murmur of their voices and smell the sacred herb they were smoking.

Rising, I crossed the short distance to Golannah's blankets and bent to touch his shoulder. "Get up, War Leader, we need to go now—tonight."

To my surprise Golannah hadn't been asleep; he sat up the moment I touched him. "How do you know this, Puhani?"

"My Benefactor came to me in my dreams. The imperial man has been lying to us. Kunai warned me that if we are still in this tent in the morning the soldiers will make us their prisoners."

By the time I finished talking everyone in the tent was awake and listening. No one rekindled the fire or questioned my words; I think we all had been expecting such treachery—just maybe not this soon. Without being told Betsiya and the warriors folded their blankets and finished packing the last of our things back into their saddlebags in the dim light cast by the coals in the fire pit.

"I knew we shouldn't have trusted that hard-eyed Chamuqwani," Eqwohi grumbled to Golannah. Muttering a few angry curses he tightened the straps on his rawhide pack.

He stood and flung his blanket around his shoulders to conceal his identity as he crossed to the entrance. "Shliwa, hurry up," he growled at his nephew. "You and Utsiyonti come and help me gather the horses."

As more warriors started to follow, Golannah stopped them. "Only one or two at a time, like maybe you have to pee, so nobody get suspicious."

"There may also be soldiers posted among the tents as well, My Husband, so have a care," Betsiya warned. "They will know we will have noticed the guards, so they will be expecting us to run tonight, maybe."

"I agree we have to go, but what about the guards posted at the ford that I told you about," Utsiyonti worried as he wrapped his own blanket around himself and his pack. "How will we cross at the ford with them waiting for us? We will have to fight and most of our weapons are with the ones already across the river."

"I will take care of the watchers at the ford," I said, and felt Kunai's power surging through my being. "My Benefactor has gifted me with some of his Puwa. Through me he will help you, but he also expects a great payment for his gift in return." I told them, my voice grim.

Just in case a curious person peeked inside during the night, the last of us mounded up our bedding to resemble sleeping men then covered the mounds with our oldest patched blankets before we crept from the army's tent to follow Eqwohi and the others.

I was able to conjure the mists, already collecting by the river to rise further up the slope and blanket the camp before the first of the warriors crept out into the night. We became only dim shapes moving through the fog. If there were soldiers posted among the tents we managed to evade them, as well as any of our own people still awake and moving around in the darkness.

The first sign of trouble came when we arrived at the place where our horses should have been waiting for us still staked out to graze. I had allowed much of the mists to sink back to the low land by the river once everyone was safely out of the encampment. In the sliver of moonlight that penetrated the fog I left in place, Golannah had led us without difficulty to the tiny meadow where we found the stakes still pounded into the ground, but there were no horses or other warriors there to greet us.

All we found was a wounded Tuumaz and Shliwa tending to him.

"Who did this?" Golannah snarled, crouching down beside them.

"Soldier scouts," Tuumaz said through gritted teeth as Betsiya crouched down to take over from Eqwohi's nephew. "We thought they were just come to help guard the horses like always before, but when it got dark they jumped us and then scattered our horses..."

"Where is O'hika?" Golannah demanded.

"Don't know, dead maybe."

"No horses, no escape, so that is their plan," one of the other men grumbled from the darkness behind me and cursed.

"Was Ahaz with them?" Golannah asked. "If he was I will kill him for this!" Muttering several Chamuqwani curses under his breath he clutched the sheathed knife riding on his hip.

"No, I don't think so just convert army scouts. They called us heathen dogs and laughed. Then I hear them say, can't run away if have no horses before everything get dark for me. When I wake up again horses gone—everybody gone."

Golannah stood. "Where are your uncle and Utsiyonti?" he demanded of Shliwa.

The young man shrugged. "Gone with the others to get our scattered horses... Maybe kill convert traitors. I didn't see I was trying to stop the bleeding on this one's head."

Glancing at me, he sensed my urgent need to hurry, and turned to the two men who had come with us, who were just standing around, and growled, "Find a horse—any horse and get on it. Stop acting like stupid children; dawn will be here soon. We need to get out of here before those murdering converts, or some other soldiers find us!"

"No, I am not leaving before I kill the convert malicer who did this" Utsiyonti growled, materializing suddenly out of a cloud of mist. He was already on a fine new black horse and leading my little mare and another for Tuumaz. Also riding out of the mist was Eqwohi with Betsiya's spotted mount and another horse for Shliwa.

"So take Shliwa with you, find and go kill them, if you must, but kill them quietly," Golannah snarled. "We don't want to alert the soldiers at the fort to our plan. Do what your honor demands you do, then catch up to us."

"Will he be able to ride?" Eqwohi murmured to Betsiya as he brought her horse over for her.

Betsiya looked up from bandaging the young man's head. "Not on his own, but you can put him up in front of me."

I was happy to see my little mare when Utsiyonti gave me her lead rope. I still lacked the skill of a Kukiya rider, so I hadn't been looking forward to catching and riding a strange animal.

"Young Puhani you and Betsiya head to the river," Golannah ordered. "Use your Puwa to conjure whatever it is you plan for our escape. We will meet you there soon."

Like ghosts Golannah and the warriors with no horses yet, moved silently away into the darkness, slipping in among the restless herd as Betsiya, the wounded Tuumaz and I headed down the slope towards the waiting soldiers by the ford.

Some men I knew had trained their mounts to come to a low call or whistle, others probably just through their ropes on the most likely horse they encountered. Either way, I knew they would soon be coming to join us, so I would have to be ready for them.

As we headed down towards the river the nightly fog that often clung to the low places by water this time of year thickened. I could hear impatient horses stamping their discomfort in the cold somewhere ahead. No men were talking, but the light from a partially hidden fire on the beach made a blurred red glow through the mist, giving their presence away.

Closing one hand around the pouch under my shirt that held my crystal helper, I prayed, <<Shining One, I need you. We must get across this river and escape the trap our enemy has laid for us. Help Me, please. Show me the way to save my people.>>

<<Tell the woman to wait here,>> Crystal Being said into my mind.

"Aunty, you must wait here for the warriors, I whispered to Betsiya as I climbed down off my mare and tied her to a sturdy bush. "I will come back for you and the others when it is safe."

In a light trance by then I walked into the fog without hesitation, the mists closing around me as I headed towards the soldiers' fire.

<<Feel the presence of the unseen hunters eager to rise from the ground to wander in the mists, and do your bidding. They are hungry for warm flesh. Feed them, little Siyatli Boy,>> Crystal said. <<Sing to them of your offering, your gift. Sing to them about the tender sweet horse flesh waiting for them by the river. Sing, Little Siyatli, of the enemy blood needing to be spilled. Sing, sing.>>

Concealed by the darkness and the fog I reached the sandy beach without the soldiers' notice. Where Water met Earth, I sank down and buried my hands like claws deep in the muddy soup. Feeling Kunai's power well up to engulf me, I opened my mouth and sang, calling the creatures that dwell within the Black Waters deep in Earth and Stone to come to me and do my bidding.

<<Come to me, Hungry Ones,>> I chanted.

<<Come feast on my enemies,

<<I seek protection from the Evil surrounding me and mine. Come.

<<The souls of my dead cry out for vengeance, come.

<<With the Great One's Qwakaiva I call you, Come!>>

And they came...

Rising up through the layers of stone and Black Water from the depths of the Earth they came, snarling and hungry. Dark lumbering monsters, phosphorescent foam dripping from scaly bodies, claws and fanged mouths, they rose out of the water to feed on the tempting prey I offered them in the Surface World.

Remaining as still as stone I felt them pass by me, but I caught only fragmented images of their shadowy bulk through the swirling fog. Nostrils flared wide they headed for the hobbled horses nearby. It wasn't long before I heard the panicked screams of the frightened animals. I smelled fresh blood and heard the crunch, crunch of shattering bones as my monsters began to feed.

The animal's screams were answered soon enough by the shouts of angry men. Thinking that we had them under attack, but unable to see much in the dark and the mist, they called to one another as they raced to discover who, or what was happening to their mounts.

They found out soon enough...

I shivered, recalling the fearsome monster Waluukba who had tried to eat me once when I was searching for my Benefactor within the deep caverns under the Earth.

<<Show no fear, Siyatli Boy, or you will become a meal for them, too,>> Crystal Being warned. <<You conjured them to come. You hold them in the power gifted you by the Great Kunai, never forget that. Be strong and

fearless. Create a shield around those whom you wish to protect and lead them across River to safety while the creatures feed.>>

When I walked back to where I'd left Betsiya and Tuumaz I breathed a sigh of relief. Golannah and the rest of the warriors had joined her; I wouldn't have to waste time searching for anyone. Unable to see any better than the soldiers, and barely able to control their own mounts, they had formed a circle with bows and spears facing outward to ward off any attack from this terrifying unknown enemy.

The disturbance was starting to attract the attention of men posted as sentries up at the fort. It wouldn't be long before their commander would be sending more men down to the river to investigate, but I knew the monsters I'd summoned would only go as far as the river fog lingered, and by morning they would fade away like the cold mist. No one of the people sheltering in the tents or the fort would be harmed—as long as they stayed out of the mist.

Stepping like a ghost myself out of the fog I called to Golannah. "Don't be afraid, war leader. The creatures I summoned won't harm us."

Placing a calming hand on my trembling mare's flank I soothed her then mounted. Riding over to the wide-eyed men I motioned for them to follow me down the slope leading to the ford. "Quickly now," I urged them. "We haven't much time. Dawn will be upon us soon—and we must be far from here when the sun rises or the men at the fort will find us."

"What is happening?" Golannah demanded as he mastered his fear and rode up to me. "I can't see anything through this thick fog."

I gave him a mirthless laugh. "Trust me, you don't want to see. Now come—all of you. Have no fear. I told you my Benefactor gifted me with great Puwa to save us from the soldiers trap. Through me he is shielding us from all evil this night. Now come!" I growled impatiently, "or run back to the fort and let them imprison you."

Without turning back to see if they followed, I guided my mare into the clinging fog. I led my band across the ford. Behind us I could hear the muffled cries of men and beast alike. From somewhere behind us a thunder weapon boomed and was answered by a mighty roar from one of the monsters I had conjured.

When we were all safely across, I waved them to continue and started back to the ford. "Where are you going, Puhani," Golannah cried.

"I'll catch up to you, keep going. I'm just going to erase our tracks, so the ones that follow will have a harder time of it, that's all."

On the slope on this side of the river ford I tied my mare to a tree and sat down in the tall grass. I wanted to lie down and sleep for a moon, but dared not even close my eyes. Taking my special string off my neck I looped it over my hands and quickly formed the pattern of the Aseutl's Gift.

In the center diamond I formed a picture of the ford and our muddy trail leading off into the sage brush. Urging Water to flow up the bank and wipe out our passing I thanked the Spirit and released it. Getting back on my horse I called on Wind to blow away our tracks in the dry sand for a time as I hurried to catch up with the Kukiya.

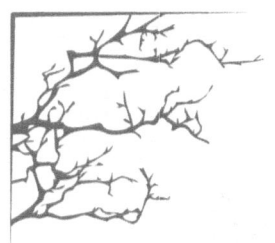

Chapter Sixteen

By the time I caught up with Golannah and the warriors Sun had poked his fiery head above the horizon to bathe the world in soft golden light. Doves cooed in the aspens and rabbits and other small creatures scurried through the underbrush.

They were waiting for me with concerned expressions in a thicket just off the trail as I descended a steep path from the crest of a pine covered ridge. I knew the mare was thirsty, so I'd been heading for the noisy creek in the gulley below when Utsiyonti rode out of the brush to greet me.

It was a good thing he'd come to fetch me, because I was so exhausted by then I had lost all sense of where I was going. Guiding me back to the junipers I nearly fell off my horse when I tried to dismount.

Strong arms catching me Eqwohi steadied me and guided me to the fire where someone pressed a warm cup of tea into my hand.

"Thank you," I murmured and buried my nose in the cup, breathing in its warm fragrance as I sipped.

When I finished, somewhat revived, Betsiya refilled it and handed me a strip of dry-meat dipped in bear fat. I was too tired to think and didn't feel like talking, so I chewed the meat and watched the smoke rising lazily from the dying fire.

"We should go soon," Golannah said, breaking in on my reverie at last. "We are too close to the soldiers' fort to rest for long."

Looking up I met his eye and nodded. "I know we are still too near the soldiers for safety. When the imperial man and the commander realize we have escaped their trap they will be furious and come after us with many soldiers."

"Can you ride if we leave soon?" Golannah asked.

I laughed, but there was no mirth in the sound. "If you tie me to my mare—maybe."

"You can ride with me for a time so you can rest and maybe sleep a little," Betsiya announced. "With my Spirit Sight I can tell how drained of Puwa and strength you are right now. Someone can lead the mare till you are renewed."

"Thank you; that would be best. I truly need sleep." Then recalling Tuumaz's wounds I hesitated. "But what about the wounded one? Shouldn't he—"

"He can ride with Shliwa or one of the others. His dizziness is nearly passed now."

Leaning forward Eqwohi stared me in the eye and demanded, "What happened at the ford, Puhani? We heard—terrible noises, but could see nothing, because of the darkness and the fog."

"I heard shouting—men and horses—screaming. Are the soldiers all dead?" another man asked.

"All dead? I don't know." Inwardly I groaned I was too tired to explain in detail to these frightened yet curious people. But in spite of my fatigue I'd become aware of my companions' fearful side-long glances and I knew I owed them some kind of explanation.

Sighing I held out my cup for another refill of the pine and mint tea. "As I explained last night, my Benefactor, a being of great power among the Unseen Ones, came to me in my dream to warn me of our danger. "He was angry at first that we had been so foolish, but eventually agreed to help us. He gave me some of his great Puwa so I could work a conjuring to save us from being captured and then hung, or send away to a Chamuqwani prison.

"With his gift I called from the stone and black waters deep in Mother Earth great monsters to distract and feed upon our enemies while we made our escape."

My eyes raking over each man coldly to impress them with the seriousness of my next words, I also told them, "The Great One wants me to tell you—all of you that for his favor there is a price. For the gift of your lives last night he will expect an offering—a great sacrifice in return."

"What kind of offering would be suitable?" Utsiyonti wanted to know.

I shrugged. "It is up to you, the Great One didn't say more."

"Enough," Golannah said and rose to his feet. "We can ask the advice of the Prophet later, but now we ride. Our young Puhani is too tired to help us further now. We must rely on our own warriors courage and cunning to bring us safely away from here."

The horse's rhythmic movements lulling me I dozed in Betsiya's strong arms for the rest of that day, as Golannah led us deeper into the broken lands of the Kukiya's desert home. With the soldiers soon to follow no one wanted to lead the enemy to the larger village of our people on the other side of the desert basin, so we struck out for the dry country in the canyons closer to the Big Salt Lake to the south.

I'd heard of this lake, but had never seen it, but I did know that the southern boundary of the Chamuqwani's created Tribal Preserve was by that salt lake. Betsiya told me we had allies living in the hilly country near there. "Maybe we not go as far as the big lake," she said, as like a much younger child, I shamelessly snuggled close to her as we rode. "But there are plenty deep canyons in which to hide, or make ambush for the soldiers in that hot land."

And she was right about having relatives there. News of the trouble at Black Rock had reached even that far, because several young men eager to fight the enemy joined us once we came into the canyon country north of the lake. Golannah and his men lived in the desert further north so we welcomed the local men who knew the land better and could guide us and help scout.

And because of that advantage, it was several days hiding and baking in the desert sun before enemy soldiers chanced upon our trail. We were resting in a sheltered overhang up the slope from a dry creek where we had dug out shallow holes in its sandy bottom to let fill with water so we could fill our gourds and water skins. The horses were watered and staked out to graze, when Mozi, one of Golannah's new scouts found us.

Climbing off his dusty horse to let it graze he trudged up the slope to where we waited. "Enemies are coming," he announced as he greeted the war leader and the rest of us.

Eqwohi scowled and glared at the warrior as if this was somehow his fault. Turning to Golannah, he muttered, "How is that possible? They must have a foul malicer helping them to find our trail this far from the fort."

"Hmm, maybe," Golannah said as he thought about it. Then turning to the warrior, he asked, "Are they the ones from Black Rock Fort?"

"No I don't think so. I could see little through the dust their horses stirred up, but it looked like they wore brown jackets not blue like Black Rock men."

"Agency soldiers then," Golannah mused. "How far behind are they—and are you sure it's us they follow?"

Motioning for the rest of us to pack up and gather our horses, Eqwohi grumbled, "Whether they follow or not we need to go."

"They hunting somebody—can't say if you. Maybe find us before Sun sleeps if we aren't careful," the scout warned.

"Could be soldiers at Black Rock sent runners to all parts of the Preserve. Tell all Chamuqwani look for us, eh?" Utsiyonti offered as he shouldered his pack.

Golannah grunted, still lost in thought.

As the men rose to get their horses I overheard one of our warriors boast to the scout, "Don't matter if soldiers find us. We got Puhani—strong Puhani. He will conjure terrible monster—"

"No!" I shouted. When I had their attention, I said in a quieter voice, "Listen to me—all of you. The monsters I conjured back at the ford I could do only because I had the gift of Puwa from my Benefactor along with his blessing. I myself can't call such creatures. The Puwa that is mine to use can help us survive and escape our enemies, but don't expect me to summon another monster to save you if you are careless or stupid, because I won't—I can't."

"You heard our Puhani," Golannah said as he flung his pack over his shoulder, "Get your horses and don't be stupid."

When I was once more atop my little mare I paused to encourage Wind to blot out our trail while the others headed deeper into a maze of canyons that lead westward away from the Preserve.

For the next two days we played hiding games with the soldiers. In spite of my efforts to mask our trail they continued to follow us through a maze of steep-walled washes and over stony ridgetops. We were running low on food, both for ourselves and the horses, and finding enough water for such a large number of men and ponies this deep into the desert was becoming a real problem.

At night as we rested in dry and fireless camps I heard frightened warriors murmuring about witchcraft, and I too wondered if it could be true. There did seem to be something unnatural about how this enemy always seemed to find our trail in spite of my best efforts to erase our passing with Wind's help. But I wasn't experienced in discovering or combatting this kind of enemy.

I would have liked to seek out my Benefactor, but I knew instinctively that if I did he wouldn't give us any aid and he would be cross with me for asking so soon after he rescued us once before. No, it was up to me and the warriors to escape this new trap. I decided that later I would ask my Spirit Helpers for advice, but at that moment, through the eyes of my hawk helper I noticed that the soldiers had found our trail once again.

That night as I slept Cougar padded into my dreams. Crouching over me he fixed me with his green, cat eyes and said into my mind, <<We expected you and my brother back in camp before now, my son. What has happened—are you safe?>>

A wave of warmth and love filled my heart at his words. My Son, how I'd longed for someone to speak those two words to me... Not allowing my feelings to overwhelm my reason, however, I quickly answered him. <<Everyone is safe for the moment, Father, but we are traveling through the canyon country near the salt lake,>> I explained.

His cougar eyes widened at that piece of news. <<Why is the war band so far south?>>

I rose to sit cross-legged facing him. <<We were betrayed by the Chamuqwani at the fort, and barely escaped death or imprisonment,>> I said. <<Not wanting to lead our enemy to the big camp where the People are preparing food for winter your brother chose to lead the enemy that follows south. We are trying to lose the soldiers in the canyons before we return,>>

Feeling a sudden rush of shame I dropped my eyes. <<It has been several days since we left the land by Black Rock Fort. At first I thought I had lost them when I used my Puwa to mask our trail. But then as we neared the big salt lake another group of soldiers found us—and nothing I do with my Gift seems to stop them—and each day they come closer,>> I whined, hearing the desperation in my voice, and angry at myself for my weakness.

Though wise in the ways of war, Nachoga was several days' ride north of me. Just because I now had a father that didn't mean I could cry like a baby and expect him to rescue me from this evil. It was up to me to figure things out, and help those who counted on me.

Sitting back on his haunches the Cougar wrapped his tail around his forepaws and studied me. <<Be at peace, My Son, I will help you if I can. Start from the beginning and tell me everything.>>

And so I did...

When I finished he was silent for a while then finally said, <<You may be right about a malicer's influence being present, and I can guess who it might be.>>

He fell silent after that, lost in his own musings until I prompted him to tell me more. <<Father, who are you talking about, please tell me, so I can protect the warriors counting on me.>>

Startled out of his thoughts he focused his cougar eyes on me once more. <<There is a man; his name is, Azogi. He is said to be a Man of Power, but many say he is more malicer than Puhani, and that the only good he does is for the benefit of himself and members of his family—like his nephew Dotsuwa.>>

When Nachoga saw that I understood his meaning, he continued, <<The trouble between our families goes back several generations, but now it is getting worse because my father, and then my brother and I, have defied that family's wishes many times over the years. We have worked against their plans for who will be clan leader and war chief—for example. And in the case of Dotsuwa and I, it was over a woman and marriage.>>

<<He wanted to marry your first wife, and she and her parents chose you,>> I guessed.

<<Yes-s-s,>> he snarled. <<And though my brother and several others told me I was a fool to suspect Azogi and his nephew Dotsuwa of using their Puwa to have me imprisoned by the soldiers and then sent far away, I still believe they had a hand in it.

<<It is the usual custom for brothers to take care of each other's women and children when there is a death or other needs, but Githa didn't like my brother's first wife Shinuuta. And with me gone Githa chose to go back to live with her relatives rather than stay with Golannah and his family. And

when the coughing sickness came to those people last winter, there was no one there to hunt for my wife and children and protect them...>>

To distract him from his dark thoughts, I asked, <<But why would this malicer be working against us now? We had nothing to do with Dotsuwa and his son's death. Their own stupidity did that.>>

He growled a laugh. <<Maybe so, but Azogi may not see it that way. He conceals it well in council meetings, but the man and others in his family hate us, and anyone related to us, or who support us. I believe they will do all in their power to destroy our whole family if they can.>>

Thinking of my own situation and the danger posed by the soldiers to all of us in the war band, I asked, <<Do you know where this malicer is right now, Father?>>

<<No, I do not. But Azogi has relatives among the southern clans by the Salt Lake, so he could be down in that dry country. He or one of his younger nephews could be scouting for the soldiers and heard of your escape. Azogi may not be following you in person, but he probably can communicate with his younger relative through the Dream, as we do. And once your trail was discovered...>>

He didn't need to finish his thought I could well imagine the rest.

<<Dawn is coming soon, so I must leave you now. Be on your guard, my son. Shield yourself as best you can and I will send Cougar to watch over you when I can.>> Purring loudly he rubbed his tawny head against my chest, then faded back into the mists of the Dream.

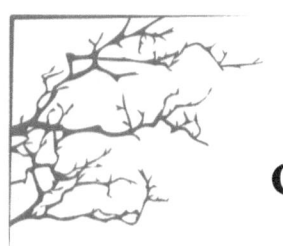

Chapter Seventeen

Over our hasty meal the next evening one of our southern guides named Mozi, told Golannah of a steep narrow-sided canyon about a half day's ride ahead. "Is good place for ambush. If men hide on cliffs while others lure soldiers into trap we can kill them."

"Hmm...Are you thinking of Ghost Creek Wash?" Golannah asked.

Mozi's eyes widened. "How you know about dat?"

Golannah chuckled. "This isn't my first time in this dry land, young warrior. My wife's sister married a man among your clans. My brother and I took the war trail with your great headman Isai a few times before his death found him." Lost in thought he stared off into the distance for a time before he continued. "You are right the wash is a good place to rid ourselves of the troublesome enemy that follows."

"But if it's such a well-known ambush site surely those traitors who ride with the soldiers will know about it, too," Eqwohi objected. "They will warn the soldiers not to fall for our tricks."

Maybe," Utsiyonti said. "But maybe they will think we don't know about Ghost Creek because we come from the land north by Saluuli Lake. I didn't know and I've come here on trading journeys for salt many times."

He glanced at Eqwohi who finally admitted. "I didn't know, either."

Still considering the matter Golannah said, "It is a good idea, but to fool the soldiers and their scouts we would need many of us to bait the trap so they believe we not know about place, and that might be a problem."

"I may be able to help there, War Leader," I said. "If two or three of us fall behind to lure the soldiers I can use my Gift to create an illusion of more men that will make them think for a time there are more of us to easily kill or capture."

Golannah studied me carefully for a long moment, before he said, "I think to do such a great deed will take much Puwa—like back at the ford. Are you rested enough to undertake that?"

Was I rested enough? Did I have a choice? We couldn't keep wandering around this dry desert forever. I longed to go back to my family. I missed Amima, Uncle Tli, Samiqwas—and my new father. "You are right, War Leader, to create such an illusion will take much Puwa, but not like the power I needed to summon the creatures from deep within Earth. With the aid of my Spirit Helpers I can manage the task."

With a little more talk it was decided that Mozi would take Eqwohi, Tuumaz, Betsiya, and those of our men who were the best shots with bow and thunder weapons with him. They would leave before dawn and ride ahead and hide among the rocks above the wash. While Golannah, over many objections, would head up the warriors acting as the decoy party leading our spare horses and the soldiers into the wash.

And as for me, it was decided that I would go with the men setting the ambush. So no one would suspect a trap, I would erase their trail when the warriors left the dry creek bed and headed up into the rocks overlooking the site where Golannah would come with the soldiers. I would position myself as close as I could to the entrance to the wash so I could see and create my illusions and still be out of the way of the fighting.

Things seemed to be going ahead as planned. In the grayness before dawn we rose and made our way to the horses, threw on our saddles and packs and left our silent camp. Far down the valley I saw tiny dots of light and smelled a faint trace of smoke on the light breeze as we crossed a flat sandy area dotted here and there with bunch grass and thorny cacti.

The enemy was near—very near. We would have to hurry to set our trap before they were upon us.

With a slight touch of my power I encouraged Wind to mask our trail across the open place. We were making straight for the wash, but I knew Golannah and his few warriors leading the spare horses would take a winding route to Ghost Creek as if they didn't know the country, were lost and looking for a place to hide.

The warriors left me on a high outcrop of red stone overlooking the dry creek bed at the entrance to the wash. Eqwohi took one group of men with him to the other side while Utsiyonti led his warriors to hide on the rim near me. I was happy that both Tuumaz and Utsiyonti were nearby.

I wasn't sure about some of the new men who had joined us after my talk with Nachoga. Kinship patterns amongst us were a tangled mass of rawhide cordage at the best of times. Any one of them could be related by blood or marriage to this Azogi I'd been warned about.

Feeling a shiver of unease run down my spine I called Wind to blot out their trails as they climbed the cliffs. Sun was awake by this time, rising into the hard blue sky, sending its light down to heat the boulder tops all about me. Putting a pebble in my mouth to save what water I had left in my jar I searched for a friendly bird to help me keep watch on Golannah and the enemy.

While I was scanning likely spots on the ridge above me for a bird helper Rattlesnake wove her way out of the rocks and coiled herself beside me. <<I will keep watch for you,>> she offered. <<Go hunt.>>

I thanked her and continued my search. At last I found a small young Hawk perched on a high boulder and I persuaded him to fly with me to search for my enemy. Soaring high above the canyons we headed for the dust clouds floating above two groups of mounted men.

The first group, as I'd hoped was Golannah, his warriors and the extra horses. Though I was sure they were aware of the bigger cloud of dust catching up to them made by mounted soldiers they acted like they hadn't seen them yet, moving along at the same pace they'd been keeping since I spotted them.

Soon the soldiers would notice that most of the horses were unridden. I would have to get back and conjure my illusions, before the soldiers got close enough to suspect a trap. Golannah was heading straight for Ghost Creek now. Standing up he turned and watched the approaching soldiers for a moment before dropping down and urging his mount to a faster pace.

Suddenly a shadow blocked out the sun and then my little hawk was falling, my view of the riders shattered. As if the attack was happening to me as well, I felt sharp claws bite into flesh, breaking bones and choking out life. Just as darkness and death would have claimed both of us, I broke free of my poor, dying companion and slammed back into my own body.

Gasping for air I rolled over on my side and vomited up the little that was in my stomach. Where was Rattlesnake; why hadn't she warned me? I had no time for such weakness—the soldiers were coming. I had to... I choked and rolled over spewing more precious liquid into the thirsty sand.

When I flopped onto my back again someone was standing over me. Staring up as I gasped for breath he was only a dark shadow against the light. I couldn't see his features, but the war spear aimed at my chest was clear enough even in Sun's glare.

<<Meddling Pup!>> a harsh voice growled in my mind. <<This will put an end to your interference. I will kill you and those pair of treacherous, lying brothers and there is nothing you and your puny snake ally can do to stop what is coming. The conjuring has begun; they promised me my vengeance if I helped them by killing you.>>

<<Not today, Azogi.>>

I heard another voice say as I rolled away from the descending spear. Then a cougar leapt from the rocks and sank his fangs into the back of the man's neck. I scrabbled away from the spasming corpse and sat up taking several deep breaths.

When the unknown warrior was dead the cougar fixed me with glowing eyes and let out a menacing growl. <<Father? It's me, Tasimu; please don't hurt me.>> I held perfectly still unsure if the kill and the stench of fresh blood had shattered Nachoga's control over the beast.

The cat growled once more, placing a protective paw on his kill. "Take him," I breathed, not daring to look the cougar in the eye. "I don't want to fight you for the meat."

The big cat shuddered, his whole body trembling as Nachoga fought to maintain his power over the animal's mind. I dared not move, even though below me I could hear the pounding of horses' hooves and men shouting. I needed to create my illusions of more warriors—now—or all might be yet lost...

The cougar must have heard the men and horses coming, too. He snarled again, then reluctantly let go of his kill and slunk back into the rocks higher up the slope.

As soon as he was no longer in sight, and praying it wasn't too late, I snatched the cord off my neck and quickly formed an image of the riders in the central diamond of the Aseutl's Gift pattern.

There was Golannah bending low over his horse's neck urging him and the others into a gallop as the soldiers' thunder weapons spat fire at their backs. Creating my illusion of other warriors atop our spare horses raising their own thunder weapons and turning to fire at the approaching enemy I saw the soldiers hesitate, then spur their own mounts to go faster. In a cloud of dust and shouting men the two groups of mounted men raced down the dry creek bed towards the waiting men atop the cliffs.

As if sensing where his men had placed themselves among the rocks Golannah leapt to the ground and sprawled behind his now lying down horse. He aimed his thunder weapon at the approaching enemy. At almost the same moment the warriors atop the cliffs loosed their arrows and let go the power of their own thunder weapons.

In the chaos of dust and running horses men and animals screamed and fell to the ground. In the rocks above one of our warriors was shot and tumbled down the slope to risk being trampled in the confusion below.

The sharp coppery taste of blood thick in the air rose up from the creek bed to choke me. As the sadness welled up inside me, I told the big cat still watching and hiding among the rocks, <<Oh, Cougar, be patient. You may have given up one kill, but there will be plenty meat for you to feast upon when we are done.>>

As the last of the soldiers turned their horses, wanting only to escape now, I knew I had one more task to complete, before my strength totally failed me. As a few of the soldiers saw their attack was hopeless and wheeled their mounts around and rode for the canyon's opening, I plucked a string in the pattern and several large boulders rolled down the slopes to partially block their escape. Horses screamed and reared, dropping a couple of the soldiers to the sand where they were trampled by the frightened beasts. The others turned back to be swallowed up in the dust and chaos again.

Totally drained of Puwa by then I left Golannah and the warriors to fight on without me. I let the pattern unravel and the cord fall from my hands. Looking around I found the physical form of my spirit helper Rattlesnake lying on the ground nearby with her head crushed in by a large rock. Sun baking down from the sky overhead and tears rolling down my cheeks I crawled over to the dead warrior. As if directed to do so by the crystal being itself I took Kunai's gift from the bag at my neck and bathed it in the blood still leaking from his torn open throat.

<<Oh Great Kunai, I offer this one's Puwa and those in the wash below to you in partial payment for what is owing for today and back at the ford. My People and I are always grateful for your protection and aid.>>

Its hunger satisfied I put Crystal, back in its bag and laid the dead snake across my lap, now ignoring the body of the man sent to kill me by the malicer, Azogi. We had been saved that day from certain death, but as in all acts of war the innocent had also died in the battle.

Sun was nearing the end of his journey across the Sky Trail, when they found me. Lost in my own dark thoughts I'd heard them coming, but didn't raise my head to greet them. They paused by the body and someone muttered a Chamuqwani curse. I looked up then, Golannah, Utsiyonti and Mozi the southern clan scout were staring down at the dead man with Cougar's claw wounds and drying blood marking his neck and chest.

"Is that one, Azogi?" I asked Golannah.

Startled he stared at me for a searching moment, as if wondering how I knew that name. Then he shook his head. "No, this man is much too young for that old malicer. What happened here?"

I held up the snake I was still cradling. "He—or someone controlling him—killed my helper, and then tried to kill me, too. But Cougar came, and..." I pointed with my lips to the wounds in the man's neck.

Frowning Mozi looked from the dead man back to me and then to Golannah. "There will be trouble over this," he warned and motioned to the dead man at their feet. "Koita was married to the one the People say is Azogi's favorite niece."

Golannah snorted. "Then he should take better care of how he uses his relatives. My brother and I had no quarrel with this man. Without the malicer's urging to do evil he would still be alive."

"Maybe that's true, but those allied with that family will say you had the chance to take your revenge, and ordered your Puhani to kill him because of your brother's recent injury and the old trouble."

Pointing to the snake-like dragon tattoo on my face, I spluttered, "But-but Cougar isn't one of my Spirit Helpers—and-and I would never do anything so evil. He tried to kill me," I repeated, the tone of my words sharp and forceful as I looked from one troubled face to another, focusing at last on the southern man.

Mozi thought about it for a long moment, still shaking his head and unable to hold my gaze. "Maybe I believe you, Puhani, but I think there will still be trouble when the others find out about this man's death. He was well liked among us."

"Men die in war," Utsiyonti said. "There will only be trouble if you tell them how he died, eh? Do you want to cause more bad feelings within our clans? Maybe more people die if you tell. This young Puhani speaks true; he did not kill this man."

"With the aid of his malicer relative, they overpowered and killed Rattlesnake and would have killed me if Cougar hadn't come to save me," I insisted, trying to impress upon him the consequences if the man had succeeded. "This Koita was sent to do murder, a murder that might have gotten you yourself, and more warriors killed if I hadn't been able to create my illusions that fooled the soldiers."

With a deep sigh Mozi finally agreed and he and Utsiyonti dragged the body away to lie among the rocks and boulders in the dusty creek bed, where they would pretend to find him bruised and trampled from his fall off the cliff, after he was wounded.

"If Mozi keeps his word and doesn't tell anyone we may avoid trouble from the other southern clan members for a while," I said to Golannah as he walked with me back to where our people were gathering. "But Azogi knows the truth. He may try again."

Golannah grunted his agreement. "I'm sure he will, but not today. You and my brother have beaten him. He will retreat for a time to lick his wounds and plot a new evil. We will just have to remain vigilant in the meantime."

Though no agency soldiers followed us after the ambush, it still took us nearly two moons to return to our relatives, because on our journey north we discovered miners flaunting the treaty and defiantly digging for yellow rocks on Kukiya land. Unwilling to let such an insult go unpunished over the coming winter we killed as many as we could find, and took the time to destroy their settlement of tents and crude pit-houses, before continuing on to the plateau where the People were finishing up the last of the autumn hunts.

Ice was rimming the edges of the waterholes and creeks when we arrived with our tired ponies weighted down with food and other good things we had taken before we burned the miners' bodies and whatever we couldn't carry away from their camp.

"So you finally come back when I've done all your work and mine too," Samiqwas joked when I was leading my mare to the creek for a drink. "Did you have fun lazing about the fort drinking tea with the soldiers?"

I laughed. "I forgot all about tea when the soldiers were chasing us through the desert. And as for work," I lifted down the heaviest of the packs on my horse and dropped it at his feet.

"I've been working, too—when men weren't trying to kill me, that is. So now—if you're not too tired from all your 'work' you can help carry this back to my lodge for me," I said as I shouldered my own share of the load.

Samiqwas's eyes widened when he realized I wanted him to carry some of the goods we'd taken from the miners' camp. I laughed at his expression. "Yes, I have war plunder to share, too—and maybe I give you some, eh? Are you still staying with Uncle Tli and his family? Is Amima's lodge nearby?" when he nodded, I motioned for him to lead the way.

Samiqwas took me to a cluster of reed-thatched shelters dug into the slope above the little creek. In the clearing between the dwellings a fire burned, sending lazy plumes of blue smoke into the cool air. Mother and several others looked up as we came near. When she recognized me, she rose from her cooking, smiled and held out her arms to me in welcome. My new father Nachoga sat beside his brother smoking and talking to Uncle and Talulsit, his eyes alight with pride as he too smiled at me.

The good smells of cooking meat wafted my way from a bed of hot coals where Xyilaha's aunty Ashiqwa and Golannah's wives tended a carcass of an antelope roasting over the flames. From one of the huts a baby cried and a woman's voice sang a lullaby, trying to sooth him. Farther away down the ravine I heard the shouts of young children at play and saw the smoke of other family cook fires. A lump of gratitude and joy forming in my throat

I barely had enough voice to greet all my smiling relatives. Oh, how I loved them.

<<Unseen Ones,>> I prayed. <<Give me strength and Qwakaiva to use in their protection. Give me strength so that my People will survive whatever the Chamuqwani do to us.>>

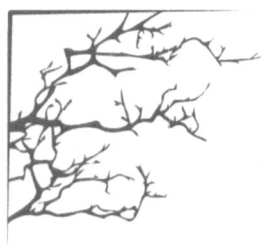

Part Two
Chapter One

THROUGHOUT THE FOLLOWING winter I remained with my Kukiya family tucked away safely in the forested canyons of the Desert Mountains, where the soldiers rarely traveled. The hunting had been good and our plunder from the miner's camp meant that we wouldn't starve during the cold moons, but there still wasn't enough food to hold a winter feast.

Overall we fared much better than my Qwani'Ya relatives who remained near the Willow Creek Agency, however. On the Preserve hungry people still died and the prophet's message spread, helped along by his initiates like Grandfather. People danced, prayed and starved. But the Chamuqwani remained.

Oh the fat agent had been replaced by the new agent, Lord Baskin, the one we had met at the fort, but he wasn't much better. In spite of the imperial man's big talk at the council meetings the promised treaty goods were little more than promises and what did arrive in the way of food and tools was of inferior quality—just like before.

Since most of the outlaw Kukiya families had already left the area for their hidden-away winter lodges there was no big tribal celebration like I had witnessed back in the summer when Eqwohi had returned with Cai and plunder from the Chamuqwani settlements.

So when it came time for the warriors to hand out our gifts to the people left in camp it was a simple affair. I gave Nachoga a fine new thunder weapon that Golannah said was one of the new kind the soldiers were bringing in, a kind that could shoot several iron missiles before it would need to be reloaded.

I gave Mother a nice warm blanket, a Chamuqwani teapot, and a few big cans of the golden fruit called peaches, along with other food stores like oat-mush and dried berries. "The peaches are for you, Amima—and the baby growing inside you," I told her. "I want you and the little one to keep strong this winter."

Tears coming to her eyes she hugged me. "Thank you, my warrior, my little Rock Squirrel." I flushed with pride when she called me a warrior, feeling like a man grown, able to bring home food to feed my People. But I still scowled at her for calling me by my baby use-name, and she laughed, wiping her tears away with a hand.

To Samiqwas I gave a blanket and a used but serviceable axe. "To help you do all the work you will need to do in future when I am away—drinking tea," I joked.

Uncle Tli got a warm blanket coat and Aunty Sagila a real Chamuqwani cooking pot and more food items—including a can of the precious peaches.

To Xyilaha I presented a fine hunting knife and a silver chain with a charm of some kind dangling at its center. The necklace I had found by accident caught in the bottom of one of the miner's torn packs just before I tossed it into the flames.

Later that evening when we had eaten and rested Nachoga brought out the wood I had seen him working on when I had looked into the Seer's Pool to check on the people I loved most, while I was still at the soldiers' camp. It turned out that the wood was to be a bow. He had traded a soft bearskin robe for the seasoned piece of oak.

"This will be for you when it is finished. I am making it for you to replace the one the soldiers made you leave behind in your village," he explained. "You will need it when we go hunting this winter—and next summer when we go to war again as well."

He handed it to me so I could feel its smooth curves. I took it with reverence already able to touch the power he had carved into the sturdy oak with both his Puwa and his love. Feeling tears stinging my own eyes I said, "Thank you, Father. I will treasure it always."

Looking back that winter was one of the happiest in my young life. Though the weather was brutally cold at times I was surrounded by people who loved me and whom I loved in return. I shot my arrows at a rolling hoop and played war games with Samiqwas and the other young warriors when we could be spared from hunting, setting traps, and gathering bark and grasses for the hungry horses.

Though the growing life inside her had only begun to round her belly when I returned from the southern desert, a willow branch cradle board already stood propped up by the far wall in our home. And my lips still curve into a smile when I recall Mother sitting by the pole loom Father made her, weaving the long cordage of twisted rabbit fur and nettle twine into soft warm blankets she made for the coming little one and others needing extra protection from the cold.

Nachoga's shoulder wound healed and the bow completed at last, my new father and I did go hunting whenever the weather permitted. I loved that weapon taking it out of its buckskin case just to feel its smooth texture, trace the fine patterns in the grain of the wood and weave some of my own power into it as I tested its strength and pull. With Nachoga's guidance and lots of target practice I managed to become a reasonably good hunter by the time the weather warmed.

Our food stores were growing low near the end of the Cold Moon, when, bored and tired of hanging around camp, the men decided to go on a long hunting trip. Though still bitterly cold at night there was little snow left on the ground, and the snow high on the peaks hadn't melted yet to make us leave our sheltered spot in the canyons for fear of flooding, so they figured it would be safe for us to be gone for tend days or so.

Our women I think were secretly happy to see us gone for a while, instead of always underfoot. The morning we left the ponies were happy we were leaving, too. Though thin they still had their shaggy winter coats. They were ready to kick up their hooves and search for green shoots on the plateau when we packed our gear and saddled them. We planned to drive deer or other herd beasts over a cliff jump, or into a box canyon, if we could find them also wandering the plateau, eager to taste the promise of Spring grass.

The first few days we were on the flat land we found only a few scrawny deer, with barely enough meat on their bones to be worth our arrows. We killed a couple for our own needs, but didn't bother to set up racks and dry the extra meat. What we didn't use ourselves for our evening meals we left for any wolves or coyotes also hunting nearby.

By our fifth day out, Golannah decided that the larger group should split up, one group staying in the country where we had been hunting, the other heading south and west to search. Knowing that Mother was nearing the time when her baby would be born Nachoga and I had decided to remain with the party staying closer to home while Golannah would head up the band of hunters going further away from camp.

On the seventh day we were sitting around the evening fire, talking about returning to camp with the meat and skins we had collected so far, and then moving further out into the desert to find Golannah when Samiqwas and Matoqwa rode in. Barely able to contain their excitement they hastily hobbled their horses with the rest of the herd and approached the fire.

Uncle Tli looked up and grumbled, "When the work is done you lazy mud turtles turn up."

Ignoring his scowl Samiqwas said to Nachoga, "We have found a small herd of Wapiti, Hunt Leader."

"Where?" Nachoga asked.

"About a half day's ride south, near Eagle Mesa. Your brother says to tell you that if the hunting isn't any better near camp than when he left the rest of the hunters should come to him. He is keeping an eye on the beasts for now. So Matoqwa and I came back to tell you," Samiqwas said.

"Eagle Mesa is near the Preserve border. If we hunt there we might run into other hunters—maybe even soldiers hungry for fresh meat," Uncle Tli warned.

Ignoring his comment, Nachoga asked, "How many animals in the wapiti herd?"

Matoqwa and Samiqwas exchanged looks, finally Matoqwa said, "Maybe as many as thirty, an old bull several cows and the rest yearlings and a few early calves, it's hard to tell exactly. We didn't want to get too close and spook them."

The men talked about it the rest of that evening, weighing the risks against the prospect of killing enough meat to last our families until the warmer weather would put everyone on the move again. They decided to split up the hunt Uncle Tli and a couple young hunters would bring the meat we had back to the women and then they would head south to find the larger party of men hunting the wapiti, bringing with them a few women to help with the butchering.

To his disgust, Uncle Tli said to Samiqwas next morning, "Since you are such a good tracker you will stay with me. Matoqwa can lead the rest of the hunters to Golannah and the elk."

When I smirked, Samiqwas saw my look and glared. Turning to Uncle he said, "Maybe Tas should stay with us, too. He could check on the hunt with his special string so we can find them sooner."

I could tell Uncle was thinking about it. Nachoga must have seen my horrified expression, so before Uncle Tli could open his mouth to ask that I stay, Nachoga laughed and motioned for me to get my horse.

Eagle Mesa was a looming presence on the western horizon when Matoqwa guided us to a willow thicket along a creek where Golannah and his hunters were waiting for us. It had been a long ride that day and I for one was happy to smell the rich odors of roasting meat as Matoqwa led us into a sheltered thicket just as a sleepy Sun disappeared behind a purple ridge to the west.

The men were already sitting around the fire with chunks of meat in hand by the time Matoqwa, Tuumaz and I had finished with the horses and returned to the campfire. Cohasi was just slicing off more meat from the hind quarter of a deer and skewering them on sticks to set over the coals as we crouched down to warm our hands.

Grabbing a couple pieces of the already cooked meat out of the basket beside Cohasi I went to sit by Nachoga. Father smiled and filled my cup for me from the can nesting in the ashes near the edge of the flames. With my belly full I listened to the talk going on around me, but I could feel my eyes trying to close. Not wanting to shame myself by falling asleep like a baby I pinched myself several times determined to keep awake.

Having already been in the area for a few days Golannah and his hunters had had time to scout. They had located a narrow canyon that some of the younger hunters could drive the wapiti into, while others already hidden among the rocks up the slopes would shoot them with their bows and arrows.

This was my first big hunt. I was both excited and nervous. The hunters decided that Nachoga would lead the party driving the wapiti into the canyon and Golannah would lead the hunters hiding in the rocks. I would go with my father, because when the hunters were in place he might want me to create an illusion of hungry wolves attacking the herd if needed, otherwise I would help the other hunters guide the frightened animals into the canyon where most of our men waited.

Rising in the cold of late night, when the new day was only a faint gray line on the eastern horizon, we bathed in the icy water of the shallow creek and rubbed an oil that had been steeped in sage and pine gum on our bodies. Silently we gathered around a tiny fire that Nachoga breathed to life from the ashes of last night's cook fire, but no one placed a can to make tea in the awakened flames. We would all fast this day until the hunt was completed.

Our hunger and thirst would be part of our gift to those who would give us their lives today. Golannah tossed sacred herbs into the flames and everyone held out their hands to draw the rich gray smoke close to face and chest.

"Oh Unseen Ones from Beyond and the Spirit of the Great Wapiti, hear our prayers this day," Golannah prayed. "Our women and children are hungry and will die without the gift of your life's blood, Honored Ones. With respect we ask this of you. And in turn we pledge that when Death comes for us we will nourish the grass on which your descendants will feed. This is the Circle of Life and our gift to you. Shkii'a."

With my rabbit blanket wrapped about my shoulders I saddled my mare, grabbed my bow and quiver and followed Nachoga with Cougar's hide draped across his back down the creek. When he decided we were far enough from our camp Nachoga dismounted, motioning for his men to also dismount and move onto the flats were we could see the shadowy forms of the elk spreading out to feed on the tasty green shoots.

Conjuring an image of more grazing elk to shield our approach and hiding behind the flanks of our horses with the wind in our favor, we moved slowly towards the herd, allowing our mounts to graze as we drew closer and closer. The sun was growing higher in the sky now and I was starting to sweat under my furry covering, but I dared not remove it.

Father and I were nearing the outskirts of the grazing herd when Nachoga pulled cougar's skin over his head and dropped to the ground, still holding on to his horse's reigns. I took in a deep breath and let it out slowly as I felt the moment when he called upon his spirit helper to enter him.

With my own Gift I could see the shimmering image of the Spirit Cougar covering his human body as he flattened himself along the ground. He had his eye on a big yearling and the cow that must be his mother nearby, and patiently crept towards them.

Sensing the Cougar my little mare snorted and tossed her head. Laying a hand on her neck I soothed her with my Puwa, and urged her to keep up with Nachoga's spotted gelding. Invoking my own spirit helpers would do me little good, none having skills to offer me in this type of hunting, so I focused instead on masking our approach as long as possible and keeping my bow ready and arrows to hand.

When he judged he was close enough for a good shot, Nachoga, with Cougar still empowering him, rose in one fluid motion and put an arrow in the big yearling's heart. Cougar roared in triumph and Father shot the cow with his next two arrows. Then leaping atop his horse he raced towards the rest of the frightened and running beasts.

Cougar's scream had been the signal for the other hunters to mount their own horses and drive the wapiti towards the canyon where the rest of our hunters waited. During the chase that followed I managed to shoot a yearling, though my kill wasn't in the heart. It was a decent shot from a running horse that wounded the animal and a grinning Matoqwa finished him for me and teased me later about being as bad a shot with the bow as I was with the stones.

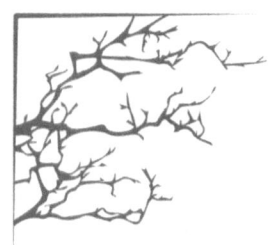

Chapter Two

We managed to kill most of the wapiti before allowing a few to escape down the canyon, and then the real work began. Uncle Tli, Samiqwas, and other men and women in the extended family caught up to us next day, which helped ease the work, but I fell into my blankets exhausted every night for the next several days, stinking of blood.

We had finished all the butchering and the last of the meat on the racks was nearly dry enough for us to pack on the ponies for the trip back to our hidden camp when Cohasi, who with his brothers had been posted as sentries, hurried back to warn the hunters that two wagons and several mounted men were out on the flats and heading in our direction.

"Soldiers?" Golannah asked as he motioned for me to bring his horse.

Cohasi shook his head. "My brother Qwati doesn't think so. They not have clothes like soldiers."

"More greedy miners then," Golannah growled as he took his horse's reigns from me and mounted.

"Maybe not. Tobek always likes to be ahead of the others for the trading," Nachoga said from atop his own horse. "He promised me twenty new thunder weapons when he was here last summer."

Golannah snorted. "That one is more likely to have waskyja than weapons in those wagons—if it is him."

Nachoga's face darkened like a thundercloud. "He had better not have waskyja. I warned him last time not to show his face again on Kukiya land if he brought more of that Chamuqwani poison with him."

Golannah snorted once more and motioned for Cohasi to lead the way. "There are too many thirsty and despairing people among us and too much money to be made for the traders to stop. Tobek may bring the weapons, but he will also have waskyja concealed somewhere among his packs to sell elsewhere on the Preserve." Nachoga grunted and urged his horse to fall into step next to his brother.

"Get your mare and follow us," Nachoga said as he rode past me. "We might need your Puwa if there is trouble."

The men and wagons had slowed close to a rocky outcrop where a small pool of fresh water bubbled up from its base. They had nearly reached the blood-stained ground where we had killed the first of the elk before chasing the rest into the canyon when they saw us. Motioning for Qwati and Matoqwa to join us we rode our horses towards the wagon while still keeping weapons in hand.

The men in the wagons had seen us coming and halted their horses waiting for us. I could see eight men in all, two men on the dusty cloth-covered wagons to manage the teams and four others riding alongside.

"Two Chamuqwani and horses are missing," Qwati warned Golannah as we slowed, "maybe more men inside wagons."

Golannah grunted, but kept his gaze focused on a big man with a silver earring and bushy black beard climbing down from the lead wagon.

Showing brown-stained teeth in a wide smile the big man slowly approached us, another man, equally as tall but much thinner with a brown beard and big nose stepped up to walk alongside him.

"Welcome, welcome, Friends, welcome," the big man said in the Trade Talk used by all the peoples around the Preserve. "I am the honest trader Tobek, and this is my good partner, Lennard."

Climbing down from his horse Nachoga motioned for me to take his mount's reigns as he and Golannah walked forward to meet the men. "Honest trader, eh? Greetings to you as well, Tobek," Nachoga said in the Chamuqwani language. "I see you left your shack in that pest-ridden settlement you call your winter lair early this year. What happened? You cheat the wrong man and the settlers run you out?"

The big man peered closely at Nachoga and the rest of us for a long moment then he began to laugh his paunch jiggling with the sound. "Well if it isn't my old friend, Mathrom Cougarson. Nobody hung you yet?"

Nachoga snorted a laugh. "No, but they keep trying. What are you doing out here on Kukiya land this early, eh?"

Tobek let out his booming laugh again, and motioned towards the wagons. "Hunting fresh meat—same as you buckies. Come, come let us sit by the fire, smoke and talk. Mathrom, you old dog, I see you have come back to live with your savage friends again." He nodded in Golannah's direction. "And this must be your famous brother, Chief Golannah, the zaunk who puts an arrow of fear in the heart of every soldier stationed on the frontier." Tobek gave him a slight bow, then speaking again in our language the trader invited him to come to the fire as well.

Tobek shouted to his men as we approached and by the time we had reached the wagons a younger man with no hair on his face had lit a small fire and brought out a sooty pot that he filled with water and several spoons of powdery kafa, which he set at the edge of the flames to boil.

Though I had stayed with the others holding the horses my father had told me to use my Gift to enter his thoughts, so I was aware of all that was going on by the fire, even though they were some distance away and often speaking in the Chamuqwani language.

<<Tobek's partner isn't happy that you are here,>> I said into Nachoga's mind. <<He hates you, I think, though I don't know why. Did you know him from—before?>>

<<No, I can't remember seeing him before now, but he is probably one of the Chamuqwani that sees my light skin and thinks I am a traitor to my own kind. What of the other men by the wagons will we have trouble with them?>>

<<I can detect no treachery from those I can see, but I wonder about the missing men.>>

<<MM, probably in the rocks with their weapons watching us.>>

As he crouched by the fire Nachoga said, "You said my brother is famous. I know he is a good war leader, but what did you mean by saying that every soldier on the frontier is afraid of him?"

Taking the cup of kafa the young man handed him Tobek saluted Golannah as he said, "Didn't he tell you?"

"Tell me what?"

"It seems that when the Chief and his warriors left the meeting at Black Roc Fort, the priests say that someone conjured some savage witchery. Giant bears of some kind killed several men and horses, and then, while the soldiers were fighting the beasts, the chief and his warriors escaped in a most unnatural fog."

"And what do you say about that?"

Tobek laughed and waved his hand in a dismissive gesture. "I say that soldiers can be a superstitious as any drunken zaunk."

Did you see any of the bodies?"

Tobek shook his head. He opened his mouth as if to add more, but his partner Lennard took up the tale instead. I could see and almost taste the hatred and fear in his Spirit Fire as he said, "I saw them. I was at the fort during the council."

Quivering with the strength of his emotion, he stared into Nachoga's eyes and growled, "That was no bear that killed those men. I don't care what commander Rossman is telling everyone."

Golannah who had been following enough of the Chamuqwani language to know what they had been talking about gave the trader a predatory smile. "You right. No bear." He watched the man carefully as he took another drink of his kafa.

Lennard's skin paled and after another moment he dropped his eyes to the fire. Still seeing the spikes of fear and hatred pulsing in his aura I said, <<I don't trust that one.>>

A mental chuckle, then Nachoga said, <<I don't trust either of them, but they can be useful. We need those weapons—so I have no wish to kill them—yet.>>

Deciding to change the subject before tempers flared Tobek waved for one of the men standing by the wagons to bring out gifts of Smoking mixture, some red cloth, and a pouch of missiles for the men's thunder weapons. "Here are some gifts for the Great Chief—and his 'brother.'"

Golannah motioned for me and Qwati to take the offered goods, all but the pouch of missiles which Nachoga tied to his belt.

"In three moons you come back with family and trade with me on Bahas River," Tobek said in our language. "I got pretty trinkets for your women, kafa, white sugar, nice blankets and sharp knives. I give you good price—best price for your furs and plunder, eh?"

Nachoga fingered the pouch at his waist. "And the weapons I told you to bring when you came this spring?"

Lennard glared, his mouth thinning into a hard line. "No more weapons, you traitorous renegade—the soldiers will—"

"The soldiers will do nothing, compared to what I will do to anyone who breaks their word to me," Nachoga promised. He gave him a predatory cougar smile and had the satisfaction of seeing the trader shrink away.

"Mathrom, Mathrom, my dear friend," Tobek blurted, "you have to understand. It is becoming very dangerous for us to bring you weapons—very dangerous."

Nachoga snorted. "That's never stopped you or the others from bringing weapons before. You turning into an old woman—or a coward? If so, let a real man do the trading and stay home, eh?"

Though his voice never changed I saw the red spikes of anger in Tobek's Spirit Fire as he answered Nachoga's insult. "Things have changed, My Friend. If you had gone back with me to the settlements last fall you would know I speak true.

"The soldiers are angry with all the raiding that has been going on. Cai and horses stolen, innocent people killed, they have become very watchful of anyone wishing to trade with the savages. No matter we are honest traders with government papers they search our wagons—many times if they catch us on the Preserve."

"Mm, so use the hidden compartments built in to the bottom of your wagons to bring us the weapons," Nachoga countered. "Or is the hidy-hole full of liquor?" Then he laughed at the traders' startled expressions. "Didn't think I knew? We need those weapons, Tobek."

"I heard you last time—no liquor. But if you know about the hidden compartments, then maybe the soldiers do, too. We can't bring them—and I know I promised."

"Tobek. Our families are starving."

"If your zaunk friends are hungry tell them to complain to the new agent instead of killing him like that last one," Lennard spat out.

Now it was Golannah and Nachoga's turn to be startled. They tried to hide their shock, but Tobek was a shrewd trader and saw the surprise in the brothers' eyes before they had time to assume stony faces again.

The trader smiled and staring right at Golannah, he said, "Didn't think I knew? Well, the news is all over the settlements. The commander at the fort claims that after you left the fort—so suddenly you ambushed the men bringing back Agent Daglish to the fort. They say you took your own vengeance before he could be tried and found guilty of any crime."

After a long pause Golannah finally said, "We no kill fat agent."

"Neither my brother, nor I killed that greedy pig—though we should have," Nachoga growled. "If the fat agent is truly dead, then other starving people killed him—or the soldiers did it themselves. Blaming my people is just another excuse to hunt us down."

Lennard scowled and waved a hand in a cutting motion. "Don't need an excuse. Some imperial lord has put up reward money for you—both of you, all you outlaw troublemakers."

Nachoga showed him his cougar grin again. "Want to try and collect the reward money—right now? If so, you'll be dead before those men hiding in the rocks can get off a shot."

Lennard's eyes widened and he glanced towards the outcrop, confirming Nachoga's guess.

"Friends, friends, please, let's not spoil a beautiful day by arguing," Tobek soothed. "I'm sure we can come to some agreement. Come to the River in the summer and we can work something out about weapons. Maybe not new kind like I promised, but maybe older ones soldiers don't want—but still good for hunting."

"No come Bahas River," Golannah said in Chamuqwani. "Is too close fort and Chamuqwani settlements. You come with weapons—new kind weapons—to Red Mesa before you go River and maybe we give you more of this for weapons, eh?"

Taking a small pouch from inside his shirt Golannah opened it and pulled out a small lump of yellow rock. The stone gleamed on his brown palm like a tiny sun. The traders gasped and their eyes bugged wide when they recognized what he was holding. Golannah let out a mirthless chuckle and tossed the stone to Tobek.

"Now no more talk about no weapons. You bring Red Mesa and we pay." Golannah pointed with his lips to the gold.

Staring down at the lump in his hand Tobek stammered, "W-where did you get this?"

"From dead miners."

"Is there more of these little stones?"

"Maybe. You bring Red Mesa before summer—in Berry Moon. If we like weapons and missiles to shoot then we make trade for more gold, eh?"

Not long after Golannah showed them his treasure the talk concluded. Eager for the gold in spite of the added risks the traders agreed to bring the required weapons to Red Mesa, so we climbed on our horses and left.

We rode back to our camp in silence, but I was aware of the simmering fury swirling in Nachoga's Spirit Fire. When we arrived back at our temporary camp Golannah sent out scouts both to see where the traders were going and watch for other Chamuqwani intruders.

"It's time we were leaving," Golannah told Uncle Tli and the others. "If one bunch of Chamuqwani is hunting the plateau then others will soon follow. We leave tomorrow."

If we were indeed to leave next day then there was still a lot of work to be done. Drying hides would have to be scraped, soaked and rolled. Meat needed to be packed away in rawhide bags and fires tended all night to finish drying the last of the wapiti still hanging on the racks.

It was late in the night, when Uncle sent me searching for more branches and green sage for the smoky fires. I had had to go far up the canyon so it had taken me a while. When I finally returned the camp was quiet all but a few still awake tending the fires, or out in the dark at the edge of camp as sentries.

I was about to set down my bundle near the fire Golannah was tending and seek my own blankets when I saw Father step out of the darkness with an armful of twigs and leaves for the racks above the same fire. His expression was grim and I could see the anger still simmering in his aura from earlier and didn't want to disturb them.

I should have taken my fuel to one of the other fires, but I was curious what had upset Nachoga back at the traders' wagons, and so I shrank back into the shadows to listen and wait.

Nachoga put down his load, checked the drying meat, and then crouched facing his brother, but didn't speak. The two continued to stare at one another until Nachoga finally dropped his eyes. "I didn't know you had saved some of the miners' gold."

Golannah chuckled and put a twig into the coals while he filled his pipe with some of the traders' smoking mixture. When it glowed with flame he offered the pipe to the four directions, removed the stick and then lit it. Smoke still exhaling from his mouth he said, "You are my brother, and I love you, but as the war leader for our People, I don't need to tell you everything."

Nachoga took the pipe when his brother handed it to him. He offered it to the four directions as Golannah had done, then drew in a great lungful and let it out slowly in a gray plume. "Was it wise to give Tobek the golden stone? He is a greedy weasel. To know that his suspicions about gold on our land are true will make much trouble for us, I believe."

Taking the pipe back Golannah said, "I'm sure you are right about more trouble, but what choice did I have, eh?" he drew in the smoke before going on. "And, you were also right when you told him we needed the weapons. But I could also tell that he wasn't going to give them to us unless I made the extra danger the soldiers represent worth the risk."

Handing Nachoga the pipe, Golannah chuckled again. "Besides, we aren't telling him where to find it, eh? If he wants more he will have to give us what we want. And with more weapons we can keep the miners and the soldiers off our land."

Nachoga relit the pipe and smoked for a while before saying, "I hope you are right, Brother, because I have a bad feeling about all this. Tobek is not to be trusted, and his new partner—that one would sell his own sister to whore for the soldiers if it meant more gold for him. And now that there is a bounty placed on our heads..." Nachoga left the rest of his thought unspoken, but we all knew what danger lurked in the shadows to pounce on us if we weren't careful.

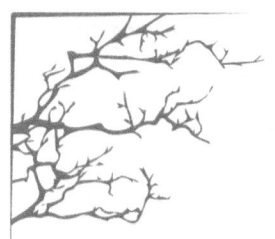

Chapter Three

Drawing near our hidden camp Uncle had sent Samiqwas ahead to let the women know we were coming, so they would have time to get ready for us. Most of the people in our winter village had come out of their lodges to welcome us as we brought our horses with their pony-drags piled high with meat and hides into the central clearing for unloading.

As we were leaving the canyon Nachoga managed to kill a yearling with a wounded leg that had escaped the big hunt, so after leaving a haunch for his Cougar Spirit Helper we returned home with fresh meat for a feast as well.

When I arrived leading my little mare with her pony-drag piled high, a smiling Xyilaha was there to help me unload. "I thought you would have come to help with the butchering. Was that too much work for a warrior woman like you?" I joked.

Xyilaha snorted a laugh, then she punched me hard on the arm. "No, I could have done my share of the butchering, but Betsiya had other work for me to do this time, ptarmigan-brain."

"Ow!" as well as her weapons training with Talulsit I knew she had been training to be a healer with Betsiya, so... "Betsiya? Is someone sick? What kind of work?"

Giving me a mischievous smile she motioned her head towards my lodge. "Go see. I'll take care of your mare for you—this time."

I stared at her confused for a moment, and then my eyes grew wide in understanding. "Amima—the baby?"

"Go see, ptarmigan-brain," she repeated and grinned again.

"Thank you I will." Giving her no time to change her mind I hurried back to the lodge I shared with Amima and Nachoga. As I was about to just rush inside Uncle Tli stopped me and called me over to him. "Sit, Nephew."

"But, Amima—the new baby!" I protested. "Xyilaha told me I—"

He pointed to a place next to him by the fire. In a commanding voice he growled, "Sit!"

When I reluctantly sat, Sagila handed me a cup of pine needle tea. "Mama and new father need time alone first then you can go and see new sister. You sit, drink tea, and eat some my good soup first, eh?"

"Yes, Aunty," I said, feeling like a foolish child myself for not thinking of that. Of course they would need some time alone, before me and other excited relatives barged in to share in their happiness.

Evening's shadows had crept out from their sleep among the trees when Mother and Nachoga came out of their lodge to join the rest of us sharing a meal by the fire. A smiling Amima placed a tiny blanketed bundle in my lap as she sat beside me and accepted the cup of tea and wrap of elk meat Sagila handed her.

Cradling the baby close I looked into the golden cougar eyes of my little sister for the first time and fell in love. She had been born during the time we were hunting so most of the redness that clings to a newborn had faded and I could see she was going to be a pale honey color when she grew older as is common among those of us with a mixed parentage.

"Hello, Baby Girl," I murmured as I touched her cheek. Instinctively she turned towards my finger, her red bow of a mouth making a sucking sound. Her eyes focused on me and I felt the power of the cougar in her Spirit Fire eyeing me thoughtfully as a shiver ran down my spine.

<<And greeting to you as well, Honored One. I hope you will guide and protect this little one, your soul's companion, throughout a long life.>>

When I looked up Nachoga was watching me, smiling. I knew he had also seen the powerful Spirit, akin to his own, who had claimed his daughter. Holding out his hands, I reluctantly handed over the precious bundle into his waiting arms.

Smiling he took her and a little awkwardly settled her in his lap. He brushed back a lock of her thick brown hair and like Uncle Tli with his new son, he gazed down at the baby, making soothing cooing sounds as he rocked her. When she began to fuss he looked up, searching for Mother a panicked gleam in his eye.

Startled to see his brother and so many smiling faces watching him, he assumed a stony expression, as if being found holding a baby was too unmanly for a war leader to be caught doing. The little one was making more insistent sucking noises by then, so he handed her back to Mother.

Golannah chuckled and sat, taking the meat wrap Sagila handed him. "I am happy for you and your new woman," Golannah said when he had finished the wrap. "I can already see that she is going to be a beauty when she grows up. You will have to keep your war spear handy to fight off her many suitors."

Tli smiled and saluted them with his cup. "Maybe I should begin saving up betrothal gifts now, if I want my son to have a chance of winning hers and your favor, eh?"

Everyone laughed and the rest of the evening was spent in pleasant joking talk, ignoring the ominous clouds that might be building on the horizon with the coming summer.

Later that evening when the well-wishers were gone and we were alone in our lodge, I heard Nachoga and Amima talking when they thought me already asleep.

Baby asleep in the blanket cradle swing suspended above their bed, I heard Nachoga say, "She is so beautiful—just like her mother. Thank you, My Heart. You have made me a very happy man, giving me a fine son with gifts to fight at my side and now a beautiful daughter, who has also been blessed with strong Puwa. I shall ask the Prophet how to honor the Unseen Ones with suitable gifts when we travel to the lake country this summer."

I heard soft rustlings in the darkness and the sound of kissing, then just as I was about to drift into my dreams Mother said, "Oh, my Precious love, it is I who should be thanking you. Knowing and loving you has renewed my spirit. I am no longer a half woman stuck in the past, wishing for a dream that could never be.

"I am a new woman—a whole woman, with a handsome husband a son who is growing into a fine young man, and a sweet baby daughter to carry on my Qwani'Ya women's lineage."

Nachoga chuckled and kissed her. "Qwani'Ya Woman's Lineage, eh? And what about her Kukiya father's lineage don't I matter?"

Amima giggled. "Of course you matter, but like you once told Tas there's no reason she can't be taught to be proud of both her ancestral heritages."

"Mm, maybe." She must have poked him, because I heard him grunt and Mother giggled again. There was more rustling in the dark, which quieted when the baby stirred and let out a cry of protest for being disturbed. Still chuckling Mother sat up and lifted the baby from her blanket cradle swing, put her to the breast and settled back into Nachoga's arms.

All was quiet for a while as the baby greedily sucked then finally Nachoga said, "I know it isn't the custom to name a child so young, but this one has a strong spirit companion and she has told me her name already."

"Mm, I have sensed that as well." Mother kissed the baby as she placed her on her chest to burp her. "The name I keep wanting to call her is, Kitahtla, though I'm not sure of its meaning. It's not a word in my Qwani'Ya language."

Nachoga chuckled deep in his throat and kissed both mother and child. "That's because it's a Kukiya word, and cougar told me the same name as you, so it must be a true sending. And, what were you just saying about a woman's lineage, eh?"

Mother leaned forward and kissed him. "So my all wise warrior, what does this Kukiya word mean in my Qwani'Ya tongue, hmm?"

"I'm not sure I can translate the name exactly. I am still learning your language, as you are mine. It has to do with being a keeper of cougar's Puwa and the teachings of our people for future generations."

Mother was silent for a long moment as she thought about his words. The baby finished and asleep once more Mother placed her back in the swing, and snuggled back at Nachoga's side. "That is a very powerful name. Cougar, eh? I can tell she is going to be a, father's girl already."

Next day when I had a free moment to myself I found a shady place down by the creek and searched for Grandfather with my special string. We had hoped that he would have come to join us during the winter, but he chose to stay with our Qwani'Ya relatives and use his healing gift to help the sick and starving survive the cold moons on the Preserve.

When I found him he was sitting alone by a dying fire in a pine thicket. Somewhere behind him I could see the blurred shapes of men and horses preparing for a journey. Older and thinner, I sensed that he was tired, but content to be on the move again, spreading the Prophet's message among the people.

<<Good morning, Grandfather,>> I said into his mind.

He took another drink of his tea before answering. <<Good morning to you as well, Grandson. What news brings you to seek me out today? Is your mother well? No one is injured or sick where you are, I hope.>>

<<No,no we are all well—very well. I'm contacting you to tell you that mother has had the baby. I now have a little sister—and she is beautiful.>>

In the central diamond of the Seer's Pool I saw his image smile. <<That is very good news, Grandson. I would like to come see them.>>

<<Amima would like that, too. She wants you to meet us by Summer Swampy Lake when we come to harvest green cattail shoots and early berries.>>

<<I will be there, my dear one. Give her and the warrior my love and blessings until I get there.>>

Though I was teased mercilessly by Xyilaha and most of my friends for it I spent every free moment I had playing with the new baby, or even just watching her sleeping in her cradleboard, if that was how I found her. Until then I hadn't realized how much I had missed Samiqwas's little sister Seicu, who had died along our terrible journey south to the Preserve. But now I had a baby sister of my own—my very own—and I was so happy. I resolved to protect her, and her children when she had them, as best I could all the days of my life.

Looking back now, I think I must have had a shadowy premonition that our time together would be short lived, and I wanted to absorb as much of her essence as I could in the days allotted us. For this happy period was not without its dire warnings of future events.

Nachoga, too, must have had a foretelling of the trouble, gathering on the horizon for our people. About a moon after we returned from the big hunt, I awoke with a start to find Nachoga crying out in his sleep and the baby screaming. Mother was awake, too, and had snatched the little one out of her cradle swing and was sitting up trying to sooth her with the breast.

"Tasimu, quickly now, get up and put some wood on the fire."

I didn't need to ask her what was wrong; I could feel the evil lurking in the shadows of our lodge. Outside in the night a coyote howled, the sound high-pitched and wild. Down the creek someone's dogs were sounding an alarm as well. We were under attack. In our joy we had been careless, and Azogi had found us.

Scrambling out of my blankets I threw an armful of sticks onto the dozing fire and in the next moment the interior of the entire lodge blazed with golden light. Muttering a hasty prayer I tossed a large handful of sacred herbs onto the hungry flames. As the blue smoke rose into the air I grabbed a feather fan and pushed the sacred smoke into all areas of our home.

During all the commotion Nachoga remained unnaturally asleep, still battling the unseen enemy. Telling mother to sit close to the fire and keep feeding it, I clutched my crystal helper and lay back upon my bed.

"Tasimu, what are you going to do?"

"Father needs my help in the Dream," I hastily explained. "Keep praying and putting wood and herbs on Fire. If we aren't back by dawn take baby and go to Betsiya."

Holding Crystal tight enough for its points to pierce my palm and make it bleed, I slipped into the Dream where the glowing being met me. This was war! Azogi was trying to kill or injure those I loved—and I vowed he would suffer for it. Placing it on my forehead, I changed into a version of a snaky dragon that was like my Benefactor's true form. <<Find them!>> I commanded my Crystal Helper. <<And you will taste more blood than mine.>>

Moving swiftly through the blackness and the swirling clouds of colored mists we heard several beasts snarling and the yowl of an enraged cougar answered their challenge. When we drew near I saw the cougar that was Nachoga, up against a rock wall, being surrounded by three creatures unlike any I had ever seen before. With lethal yellow teeth and long claws they appeared to be a cross between a badger and a bear.

All were bloody, but they hadn't managed to kill the Cougar yet. He fought back with a fierce intensity that bloodied his adversaries with every swipe of his mighty claws.

I had seen enough; it was time to even the odds a bit. Drawing on Crystal's power, I allowed it to mingle with my own Qwakaiva and then as we charged the nearest beast, fire streamed out of my mouth in a mighty flood. The creature burst into flames, disappearing in a scream of agony.

Forgetting about Cougar the largest of the beasts whirled round snarling to face me. <<Yes, Azogi, the meddling pup is back!>>

My own blood lust roused, and encouraged by Crystal I spat another gout of fire, this time in his direction and had the satisfaction of seeing it burn a streak of glowing flame down his hairy face and onto his chest.

The creature roared in outrage and charged me. I would be no match for Azogi's strength if he managed to catch and sink his claws into me, so I dodged the charge, slapping a hard blow with my tail across his smoking chest as I passed. He roared again and clawed at the bleeding flesh. Following up my advantage I vomited up another gout of flame, once more hitting him in the face. When my Puwa struck, his whole beastly head burst into flame.

While I had the attention of the malicer I saw out of the corner of my eye, Nachoga leap upon the back of the other apprentice and sink his own fangs into the hairy fiend's neck.

The air around us stank of burning hair and charring meat. My nostrils flared as I backed off to gather more Qwakaiva for another strike at Azogi. I could feel my power weakening, but I didn't care. This foul malicer had tried to kill my baby sister, and hurt my father. I would die to save them if necessary.

Fortunately it never came to that. Azogi had had enough. With one apprentice dead and himself and his other helper badly wounded, he chose to vanish in a cloud of foul-smelling smoke and blood, pulling his remaining wounded apprentice after him out of the Dream.

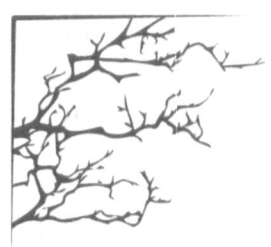

Chapter Four

In the next moment I sat up with a gasp, back in the Physical World. Mother was still sitting by the fire cradling the baby, singing to her softly and looking frightened. Nachoga too was awake now, taking deep breaths to try and ground himself, back in our place and time. As soon as he was able he went over and threw an arm around wife and daughter.

"Are you all right, My Heart? How is the little one?"

Relieved she laid her head on his shoulder. "We are fine—now." She traced a bloody claw mark on his shoulder, running down his arm. "But how are you—and Tas?"

He snorted a laugh and hugged them. "We'll be all right. I think your son and I have put an end to that old malicer this time."

I wasn't so sure; Nachoga must not have seen Azogi escape into his own body before I could gather enough power to totally destroy him. I had managed to wound him severely, both within the Dream and in his physical body. Though the burns would be visible for all to see in future, I wasn't sure he would die of them. And what did Azogi mean when he said "they" had promised him?

I resolved to tell him what I suspected, but right then... hastily getting to my feet I managed to stagger outside, before the vomiting and shaking began. I was still choking up a bitter gray liquid when Nachoga followed me out and held me up as I emptied the last of it from my body.

When I at last finished I slumped backwards into him and shamelessly rested my head on his chest like a much younger child. It felt good to have a father's strong arms enveloping me—even for only a little while. Still holding me he asked, when I'd caught my breath, "Are you all right? Did he hurt you?"

"I'll be all right. Remember, this is what may happen when I draw on my Benefactor's Gifts."

"Mm, I think I will have to offer your Spirit Guides many gifts this year. Without your help I'm not sure I would have been able to kill them all."

Looking up into his face I shook my head a troubled expression, I was sure he could see in my eyes. "Father, Azogi may not be dead. He escaped into his body before I could raise enough power for another attack that would have killed him. I'm sorry.

"He is gravely wounded—and may still die of his injuries, but he may also recover and try again to harm us. He said—"

"Don't be sorry; you did your best. He underestimated you, and paid a high price for that mistake. With one apprentice dead and he and the other badly wounded, it will take time for him to gather enough Puwa to come at us again. We will just have to be more vigilant until I can find and kill that enemy in the flesh."

"I sensed that Azogi and two other human spirits were there, but what were those creatures that attacked us?"

"The Kukiya call them, Ho'kawazi, they are unnatural beings that some Malicers create and become. They use that form to do their bidding, both in this world and in the Dream, because of the extra power they gain in the transformation."

I shivered, wishing I had killed him. In my heart I made a solemn vow to the Unseen Ones that if that malicer ever tried to hurt any of the people I cared about I would indeed kill him. I had marked him; I could find him wherever he tried to hide—in my world or the Dream.

Spring came at last with warm sunny days and cool frosty nights. Grasses and early flowers sprang up on hillsides and along the creek banks as green bud sprouted on the trees. Not wanting to be caught in the mountain hollows where we had sheltered throughout the Cold Moons when the snows melted on the peaks flooding the canyon bottoms, we packed our ponies and left those hidden places, heading for the plateau where the horses could graze and get fat again, and the People could feast on antelope and deer, and eat wild greens and salati shoots poking their russet heads through last autumn's leaves.

Of course, coming out into the open again meant we had to be more careful to avoid the soldiers who might already be hunting fresh meat themselves, or anyone who left the Preserve. As we traveled from place to place harvesting whatever local foods were available I spent a good portion of most days finding a hawk or eagle to help me scout the land through which we traveled.

The day Grandfather came to visit us Nachoga and most of the men were spread out upon the flats hunting. Samiqwas and I had been posted to watch for soldiers in their absence by Uncle Tli who'd been left in charge of camp defenses. When I saw them coming, I left the hawk to her own devices and I floated back into my body and sat up. "Grandfather is coming," I shouted to Samiqwas, who had climbed a nearby Pine to have a better view.

"I'm going back to camp to tell Uncle. I saw no one else coming, so maybe he will let you come down to visit."

"You'd better tell him to let me come down," he threatened.

I laughed and raced off to find Uncle and then to saddle my mare to guide them in.

Everyone was overjoyed to see Grandfather and welcomed him and his three traveling companions with broad smiles, when they rode into our busy camp that afternoon behind me.

Sitting beside our fire Mother placed his latest grandchild on his lap while she made tea and began preparations for our evening meal. Holding the hand of his own young son, Binahgwinn, who was just learning to walk, Uncle Tli came over to join Grandfather and the other men relaxing by our fire.

Grandfather glanced up from the baby and smiled when he saw his son, his eyes going wide when he noticed the toddling boy at Tli's side. "Greetings, my Son, I am glad to see you well." Then he turned to Binahgwinn, Grandfather held out a hand, coaxing him to come to him. "And who is this handsome young hunter, eh?"

Always eager to hold my sister, I took the baby in her cradleboard and laid her across my lap, so Grandfather could greet his new grandson and visit with Uncle.

I had let my father know that we had company and he promised to return to camp when he finished butchering the black-eared deer he had just shot. Nachoga greeted his father-in-law warmly when he returned that evening, with a pack horse weighed down with fresh quarters of meat.

For the next few days everyone traveled together. The days were long and sunny and the berries we picked were sweet upon our tongues. It was a lazy relaxed time when we enjoyed each other's company while still getting lots of work done, as we hunted, dried berries and collected other good food the Earth Mother offered us.

But it was the Berry Moon and my thoughts as well as my father's and Golannah's thoughts turned to the trader Tobek and the promised weapons. It was time to go find Tobek—more than time....

That night by the evening fire the men smoked and discussed the matter. They had to decide who would go with Golannah to get the weapons and who would stay with our women and children and protect them while they continued their slow progress south towards Saluuli Lake, the cattail harvest and the end of summer ceremonial gatherings.

The next afternoon when I came back to camp with my pack full of rabbit and grouse, Grandfather was waiting for me. After I had handed over my catch to Mother, he asked me to take a walk with him down by the creek. Most of the women and children were still out of camp gathering more berries and quail eggs while the men hunted in the nearby hills to make sure their families had plenty to eat while they were gone. I shrugged and fell into step beside him as he headed down the game trail that led along the creek.

I knew he had been watching me with a speculative eye since the first afternoon he had arrived, but I wasn't sure what was on his mind. Since he had forced me to give up my studies with Kunai's chosen mentor for me, Chumco, our relationship had been—strained.

I went with him, because I was curious, but an uneasy feeling still twisted a knot in my gut, wondering what was on his mind. When we had gone a fair distance from the cook fires and the voices of women and children were far away, he paused and invited me to sit beside him in the shade of a tall cottonwood. "My companions and I will be leaving soon. The Prophet has spoken to Sheikai in his dreams and wants us to hurry on to Saluuli Lake. Sheikai says people have already started to gather, many needing healing and our prayers. I would like you, your mother, your uncle and the rest of the boys from back home to go with us."

My mouth dropping open I stared at him as if moose horns had just sprouted on his forehead. "Why? Why would you want us to do that?"

"Because staying with these Kukiya outlaws isn't safe."

"Isn't safe?" I angrily blurted. "And how will me and Amima going with you keep us any safer, eh? You are a hunted outlaw, too, or have you forgotten that Father, Uncle and I risked our lives to keep you from being hanged?"

Grandfather sighed. ""No Grandson I haven't forgotten, but always fighting and raiding the Chamuqwani, will get some or all of you killed—maybe before you even have a chance to truly live.

"As the Prophet teaches war will not save us. We must put all our combined energies to praying and singing the sacred songs the Thunder Beings have given us. That is the only way, if we want to survive."

"Survive? People can't survive alone on prayer and song—if they want to continue to live in this Physical world. I respect Iyantsha and his teachings—and I will come if, and when, he needs my help for a difficult healing, but we claim our Qwakaiva from different sources. You know this as well as I, Grandfather, why do you pretend it is not so? I have pledged my life to Kunai, and to serve and protect my People In whatever way is needed. There are starving people to feed, and ghosts to avenge."

And to do all that we needed those Chamuqwani weapons promised us. I needed to go with my Kukiya father and the war chief, not laze about at Iyantsha's camp by the lake.

"I'm not going with you; I choose to stay with my Kukiya family, as I'm sure will Amima." Too angry to sit still any longer I stood and turned my back on him. "I love you, Grandfather, and always will, but my answer is no," I said as I stomped back down the creek.

I hadn't paid much attention to the talk around the fire the night before, because I was sure that I would be included in the war party going to meet the traders. They would need me, I reasoned, to scout for them and use my Puwa to confuse the enemy if the traders planned treachery.

Treachery... What I hadn't counted on was Grandfather having a persuasive, and treacherous tongue. And once again—as Chumco had warned—he betrayed me. Later that same evening he sought out Nachoga for another of his "talks." To my disgust, he convinced him to let him take me, Amima, Uncle Tli and his family and anyone else who wished to go with us on to Saluuli Lake.

The warband was leaving day after next I knew, and though my name hadn't been mentioned I was so sure I would be going that I'd been secretly gathering my things for the trip.

Nachoga must have told Amima his plans during the night when I was gone on night guard with the horses. Everyone was asleep, even the little one, but I could almost taste the sadness in our lodge when I returned late that night. I tossed and turned trying to fall asleep, but finally gave up. Walking outside in the gray light just before dawn I built up the cook fire and put on water for tea.

Staring glumly into the flames I waited for the water to boil and then placed a handful of leaves into the can and set it on the rocks to steep. I was going with the warband, wasn't I? damn it, I had to go. I heard the rustling of the reed mat that was our lodge door open behind me, but didn't look around as Nachoga came out and stretched. Returning from the privy he reached for the can and poured himself some tea. Looking over the rim of the cup he watched me for a long moment without speaking.

Finally I couldn't stand the waiting and said, "What did you and Grandfather talk about? I saw you go down the creek with him and Uncle Tli. I'm not going with him," I said, before he could answer, my voice low, but defiant.

Nachoga chuckled and took another sip of his hot tea. "I know you don't want to; I know you would rather go with me and the war chief—and maybe I would prefer that, too. You are a fine young warrior with many gifts—and I love you. But because you are a fine young warrior with many gifts I need you to stay and see to the safety of those others we both love while I am away."

"Nothing will happen to Amima and Kitahtla if I go with you, please let me come," I blurted.

"Son."

Refusing to answer or look at him I bowed my head staring at the fire, trying not to cry. He waited me out, and finally I looked up. Unshed tears blurring my vision I tried to explain, both to myself and him. "You are the father I always wanted—wished I had. I love you so much, and I'm afraid I may lose you if you go without me. You and the war chief are walking into danger. I feel it. I want to protect you with all the Puwa I have at my command."

"Protect me, eh?" he chuckled. "I think it's supposed to be me protecting you, isn't it?"

I'm sure he could see the rebellion plain on my face, but he answered me with gentle patience. "Tasimu, I have already lost one family; I don't want to lose another. Knowing that you, with your great Puwa, will be with my precious daughter and the woman I truly love will ease my mind and help me to focus on the traders and their hunger for our gold. Try to understand and do what I am asking of you. I'm trusting you to keep our loved ones safe. Sometimes a warrior's duty isn't to his liking, but may be for the good of all."

In a voice barely above a whisper, I choked out, "If you go—without me—I fear I will never see you again."

Nachoga acknowledged my fear, thought about it for a long moment, then shook his head. "You will see me again. This I swear. Cougar has promised. Go with your mother and the little one. Keep them safe for me."

He was right; he kept his promise and I did see him once more. Just not in the way either of us hoped. But by then it didn't matter because I had failed the trust he had placed in me.

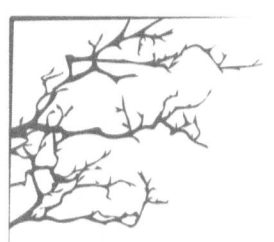

Chapter Five

Nachoga and the warband left in the gray dawn the following day. It was hard, seeing them leave, not only for me, but Samiqwas, Matoqwa and Xyilaha as well. We all had been hoping to go, but we were promised that when the warriors returned with the new weapons we would definitely be going when they next went raiding into the Chamuqwani settlements.

Grandfather's Qwakaiva was so different than mine, and I didn't know all the Otter's tricks, but I suspected that he had somehow influenced Golannah and Nachoga in their choices for who would accompany them. always before the warbands going raiding were fairly evenly split between Qwani'Ya men and Kukiya. And except for Talulsit and a few younger Kukiya warriors, this time, however, there were far more Qwani'Ya warriors coming with us to the lake than when we had left our winter home in the mountain canyons.

When I figured out what he must have done, I was furious with him. Though he never voiced his opinion about Mother marrying outside our Qwani'Ya clans, I suspected he wasn't happy about it. With invaders on all sides of their land the Kukiya were a far more war-like people than we were in the north, and with the Prophet's teachings to encourage his feelings...

Oh, I knew in my heart that he only wanted to protect his own people, but to my way of thinking he had no right to make that decision for me and the rest of us. I both resented and feared the consequences of his meddling.

In spite of his pretty words to Nachoga, Grandfather and his companions didn't seem in much of a hurry after the war chief and our men left. As we continued to make our way slowly towards Saluuli Lake, we were joined by other families, going in the same direction with injured or ailing relatives. And because of this our progress slowed even more. Now close to two hundred in number, the women had plenty of time each day to gather berries and other foods as we traveled towards the prophet's encampment.

I had barely spoken to Grandfather since we left. I played with the baby, hunted, took care of the horses and scouted the country from the sky above, whenever Uncle asked me, and tried to ignore Grandfather.

In the Seer's Pool I also kept my eye on the warband as they journeyed to Red Rock Mesa. All seemed well with them, but I still felt uneasy. Nachoga, too, came in my dreams to check on us and assure himself that we were safe.

He admitted to me that he, too, was worried. The traders and their promised wagons weren't waiting for them as expected. Golannah wasn't sure if they were late, but still coming, or they had been discovered by the soldiers and were in jail, or decided the trade was too risky and went on to the Bahasa River, expecting Golannah and the warriors to follow.

<<The war chief will wait for them a few more days, and if they don't come by then, we will rejoin the People heading for Saluuli Lake, so don't worry I will see you and the rest of my family soon,>> Nachoga told me.

And so, reassured I fell back into a deep dreamless sleep. I awoke next morning refreshed, told Amima my dream that Father and the warriors were all right. I didn't check on the warband for several days, because by next day we had troubles enough of our own to occupy my mind.

We camped that evening on a grassy slope overlooking a noisy creek swollen high with snow-melt, when Rattlesnake's warning sounded in my mind. Calling to Matoqwa that I needed to check on something I left him and Xyilaha and the others to finish caring for our horses and sat down by a large rock and searched for a winged friend to help me scout.

I found a hungry young owl who allowed me to tag along as he searched for his next meal. The noisy creek had concealed their approach, but behind a nearby ridge and around the bend of the swollen stream was a large band of soldiers settling in for the night. Fortunately for us they were on the opposite side of the flooded stream. I wasn't sure if they were aware of our camp yet, but they soon would be, though crossing the creek would prove difficult even if they spotted us.

Allowing the owl to continue his hunt I opened my eyes and sat up, taking several deep breaths to center myself. When I felt able to stand I walked over to my companions, laughing and joking with one another as they brushed and hobbled the last of our ponies. Coming over to Matoqwa, who was in charge, I said quietly, "There's trouble coming. Don't let the horses stray too far. We may want to leave soon."

"What did you see?"

I pointed with my lips across the creek. "There is a large band of soldiers just on the other side of that ridge across the creek."

Matoqwa grunted and stared in that direction, thinking. "Have they seen us?"

"Not sure—maybe not, I'm going to tell Uncle Tli." He nodded and turned to explain to the other horse guards who had seen us talking and wandered over to find out what was going on.

Heading back to camp I found Uncle Tli, Talulsit and Grandfather sitting around a fire with some of the other men, smoking and talking while the women prepared our evening meal.

Catching his eye, he broke off what he'd been saying, and motioned me to approach the fire. "What is it, nephew?"

"There are soldiers camping downstream on the other side of the creek over the next ridge."

By the time I'd finished everyone nearby had fallen silent. They may not have noticed us yet," I continued, "and the creek won't be easy to cross, but—"

"But they will find us soon enough if we stay here," he finished for me.

As Uncle started to rise, Grandfather said, "Son, it has been a long day and the children and the sick and injured are tired. The soldiers may not see us, or may be hunting other prey. We are only women and children old and sick people food gathering and wanting to pray. We are harmless and not worth their interest."

Tli snorted and gave his father an incredulous stare. Before he could say something he might regret, Talulsit said, "Yes, we are traveling with our women and children, Elder, but we are off the Preserve. However peaceful we may wish to be, I doubt if the soldiers will see it that way. We have broken one of their rules."

"And some of us are wanted outlaws, don't forget," I warned, staring right at Grandfather. "Collecting the bounty money for bringing us back to the fort will make them eager to catch us and worth the effort of chasing us all the way to the lake if necessary."

"Then we should definitely not go to the Saluuli Lake where many more of our people will be gathering for the summer harvest and ceremonies," Chittola, one of the new men who had recently joined us with his family said.

"I agree," Talulsit said. "We don't want them falling upon our sick and injured relatives like hungry wolves."

"Maybe we should head to our hideout in the deep desert," Uncle suggested.

"That would be a hard journey for the sick and old people among us," the Prophet's initiate Sheikai mused as he offered his pipe to the four directions.

The men smoked and thought about it for a while, pondering what would be the best course for us to choose. "We wouldn't have to go that far, just a few days away from here. I could mask our trail and watch them to see they don't follow."

Another of the new men who didn't know me snorted and gave me a withering look. "You? A youth can do all that?" He might have said more insulting things but he was quickly silenced by Talulsit who had seen what I could do with my Puwa.

After more discussion over the evening meal it was decided that we would all get some rest and then everyone would break camp while it was still dark and fade back into the barren hills to the north for a few days.

Uncle Tli, Qwati, several of the young men, and I lagged behind the main group as Talulsit and Sheikai led the rest of those depending on us away from the creek and back into the rabbit brush and scrub pines.

When they were safely gone I called upon Wind to help me and the warriors erase all traces of our camp. Unfortunately for us it was full day by the time we had finished and were ready to catch up with the women and children. A small party of soldiers with a Kukiya guide spotted us when we crossed the ridge top and sounded the alarm. The soldiers were unable to cross the creek, but they shot at us and Uncle and Qwati returned their fire with their own weapons killing one man and wounding another.

Over the next several days we tried our best to elude the soldiers but like a pack of hungry wolves chasing a wounded deer, they trailed us mercilessly. The sick and the old people and small children were slowing us down. There was no way they could travel as fast as trail-hardened mounted soldiers.

Drawing on the power of Uncle's Fox Spirit and Talulsit's Wolf they created many tricks to outwit them, but their deceptions and my illusions only lasted for a while, before the Chamuqwani and their own Kukiya scouts were back on our trail again.

Abandoning much of the food that we had managed to dry and preserve Tli and the other warriors urged the tired women and children up steep hillsides and over rock-strewn ledges in an effort to keep ahead of them. Others with very ill relatives chose to hide in shallow caves and thorny thickets in the hope that they would be overlooked as the Chamuqwani pursued our larger party. Wishing them well we left them with some of our extra food and hurried on.

At last when the Chamuqwani came too close, Talulsit led several young men and women, back down our trail to ambush the first group of soldiers who followed. Samiqwas, Matoqwa and his brothers were among those brave warriors who covered our retreat.

I would have gone with them, too, but I had been ordered to go with the women and use my Puwa in whatever way I could to keep them safe—especially Amima, Aunty Sagila and the babies.

Uncle had ordered Xyilaha and her thunder weapon to stay with her mother Ashiqwa and the women and the old people in case the soldiers got past their ambush. Both she and Betsiya had thunder weapons and knew how to use them as well as the bows they also carried.

Setting the horses free to run up a side canyon in the hope that we could retrieve them later, Xyilaha and I urged the women and old people up a steep gravel-strewn hillside and over the top of the ridge where we couldn't be seen from the fight below. Helping Amima climb a slippery passage I could hear the boom of the men's weapons further down the canyon behind us. When she slipped and almost fell Kitahtla started to cry. Making soothing noises Mother slid the cradleboard around to her front, fumbling to put her to the breast while still trying to climb.

"Give her to me, Amima," I urged. "You will be able to climb better without her."

At first she resisted, saying the baby would cry even more, but I insisted and at last she let me take her. This blessed little bundle was so precious to me. At that moment I was gravely aware of the trust Nachoga had placed in me to keep his beloved daughter safe. I looked down into her soft golden eyes and said a silent prayer to the Unseen Ones to protect her—always.

Smoothing back her thick brown hair I allowed some of my Puwa to flow into her little body, just as I often did to quiet our horses when they were too frightened. In another moment she was back asleep and I slung the cradleboard onto my back and urged Amima to climb.

Hurrying over the next ridge we made an exhausted camp in a tiny hollow among a cluster of water starved aspens. As soon as we were safe among the trees Xyilaha and Sheikai hurried off to find our horses.

Seeing that Mother and Aunty Sagila were resting among the trees nursing the little ones, I headed back up the hillside we had just come down. Flattening myself before reaching the crest I crawled to the top and looked down. Our trail was plain for anyone with skill to see. Crawling back a ways, so I couldn't be seen, I sat up and took my special string from around my neck and formed the pattern of the Aseutl's Gift.

Plucking the pattern I created a tiny avalanche that blotted out all traces of our passing, making the slope far more difficult to climb if anyone tried to follow us.

After I had rested for a while I summoned Rattlesnake to guard my body while I took flight to check on our warriors. Not finding a hawk or an eagle to share its sight with me I had to make do with a grumpy old crow. Through her eyes I saw that our warriors had managed to beat back the soldiers and now with some wounded were heading my way.

We had planned to meet up at Juniper Creek canyon, but without our horses we weren't going to make it that far today. I couldn't speak mind-to-mind with Uncle or anyone of the warriors covering our flight, so the only chance I had to show them the way was to have crow land on Uncle's shoulder. Unfortunately, to get his attention she cawed right next to his ear

Uncle swore in Chamuqwani and slapped at her knocking her back into the air. Crow called him a few bad names of her own while she hovered just out of reach. At last she took off down the valley where we'd sent the horses. When the warriors didn't understand and remained where they were, I had her return and try to perch on Samiqwas's shoulder this time.

He reached up and I hopped onto his hand. Cocking my head I looked him in the eye. I cawed again and took off in the direction I wanted them to follow. It took another try, but he finally understood.

"Uncle, I think the crow is Tas—and he wants us to follow him."

The warriors followed down the gulley and eventually picked up the trail of our abandoned horses and then found Sheikai and Xyilaha, who could guide them the rest of the way into our hidden camp, so I left them.

When I returned to my body Grandfather was waiting for me. He was sitting far enough away that Rattlesnake hadn't bothered him, but it was still a shock to see him. Assuring Rattlesnake that I would be all right, I urged her to go and slowly sat up.

"Are the warriors coming; are they all right?" he asked.

"I showed them the way to come and they have found Xyilaha and Sheikai. They will be with us before dark. They have wounded, one man riding double with Cohasi. We should get back." Getting to my feet I turned and started down the hill.

"Wait a moment, Grandson. I want to talk to you."

With my back still to him I said, "Talk to me? What's there to talk about? You used your Qwakaiva, got your way and I am here."

Grandfather sighed and caught up to me. "I did what I thought was right—for you and all the other Qwani'Ya people. I am sorry you don't agree with me, but it doesn't matter now, because you and your gifts are needed here. There is more to this pursuit than we can see. We are being pursued by a malicer's intent as surely as by the soldiers and their weapons."

His word stopped me cold, just as the foretelling hit me with the force of a lightning-struck tree. And like a tree, I would have fallen to the ground if Grandfather hadn't rushed forward to catch me. Behind my closed eye lids I heard women and children screaming, thunder weapons booming and men shouting. The stench of hot iron, blood and waskyja clogging my nostrils, I shuddered, my body trembling uncontrollably.

"Grandson, come back; speak to me!"

When I didn't answer he slapped me hard, shattering the sending. When my eyes flew open I saw Grandfather's face and chest covered in blood. I gasped closing my eyes again, not wanting to see the awful truth revealed by my Gift.

Death was near, coming for him and maybe more of the people I so desperately loved. <<Oh, Kunai, protect us—save us!>> I pleaded, but there was no answer, not then, nor for a long time to come.

Blinking back tears I got shakily to my feet. "We need to get back to the others," I mumbled and started down the hill.

"What did you see? Tell me—please tell me."

"Trouble and death..." I shook my head and kept on walking. I wanted to run, run away and keep on running until I could escape the Evil that was catching up to us. The Evil that Azogi had conjured with his spite and malice and now had a will of its own in our world.

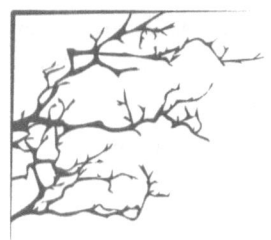

Chapter Six

Though I refused to speak of my sending when I returned to my family Grandfather must have told Uncle and Talulsit that some evil was stalking us, because as soon as we were mounted again they guided us into a maze of canyons that would confuse the most experienced of the soldiers' trackers.

When we stopped that first night I tried to contact Nachoga in the Dream, but to my dismay his mind was closed to me. I knew he wasn't dead, but I sensed only great pain, regret and despair when I reached out to him. When I wove the pattern of the Seer's Pool all I saw was darkness.

Over the next few days I kept my fears tucked away inside, my guts twisted into a tight knot of worry and despair. I barely spoke unless answering a direct question. I saw no more images of blood-covered people, which in its way was even harder, because I had no idea who to warn, or how to prevent what might happen to us—or was happening to our warriors sent for the weapons.

Our food and water was running low and those among us with thunder weapons, like Uncle, were almost out of the iron missiles they needed, but still the enemy followed.

"I don't have the Puwa that someone like the Prophet or even Utsiyonti has over the Water Spirits, but I believe I can call them to mask our passing," Sheikai said when we stopped for the children to rest in the shade of several large boulders on a high ridge top overlooking the canyons below. Far in the distance we could see the dust cloud of the Chamuqwani still following us.

Talulsit studied the wisp of white clouds hovering on the western horizon and shook his head. "Too far, maybe Iyantsha could call them, but I doubt they will listen to you or even Utsiyonti if he were here with us.

Next he turned to me his question clear. I shook my head. "I can use my Puwa to move water that is already in or upon the earth, but I have no affinity with the beings of the sky. My power comes from a different source."

"What about the men who went to collect the weapons promised us, Tas?" Chugai asked. "Have you told your new father what has happened here? Are they near; can they help us?"

I didn't want to tell them ; I had kept my fears, as terrible as they were, to myself. But they were all staring at me and I had no choice but to explain. they had to know we couldn't expect rescue from them. "I have been trying to contact my father within the Dream each night since we were spotted by the soldiers." I shook my head, my eyes suddenly moist with unshed tears. "When I look—try to find them—I see only darkness." Dropping my eyes I fell silent, letting the realization of my words sink in..

"Are they dead, Grandson?" Grandfather finally said into the silence.

Dead? Was my beloved father truly dead? My head shot up. "No, I don't believe so. But I do know he is in pain—they were betrayed, and, and he won't let me come to him."

"If they were indeed betrayed by a malicer as your grandfather and I suspect. Then he won't let you speak to him, young Puhani, because he is trying to protect you and the rest of his family—his People," Sheikai said, his voice gentle and calming. "I will pray for them."

Uncle Tli said a bad Chamuqwani word and got to his feet. "Pray if you want, but do it on your horse. We need to get to Antelope Wash before we run totally out of water, so no more time for resting."

Water, I have to laugh when I recall that. When, tired and thirsty we reached the wash that the Kukiya expected to be no more than a dry ravine with a few shallow ponds we found instead a muddy, impassible flood, raging down to connect with the Bahasa River more than two days ride away.

Behind me Chugai looked up at the clear blue sky and let out a mirthless laugh. "Well someone among our enemies certainly has Puwa to compel the Akiyazi to trap us."

And trapped we were, with soldiers close behind and no way to cross the angry water—at least for the moment. Talulsit led us back to a side canyon where we made camp in a grassy hollow at the bottom of a slope dotted with scrub pine and juniper.

I stayed close to Amima and little Kitahtla that evening while Mother cooked a meager meal of dried berries and the last of our coussa root. I held my sister close and looked into her golden eyes. She watched me with a studied intensity far beyond her young age.

Taking out Kunai's crystal I squeezed it in my fist until one of its sharp points dug into my flesh to taste my blood. When I thought it had had enough to do what I needed, I opened my palm and traced a symbol of protection onto her tiny chest with my empowered blood.

<<I promised our father that I would keep you and Amima safe, and with all the Puwa I have at my command I will do just that.>>

When I finished and looked up Mother was watching me. She said nothing, but I saw her lip quiver and the fear in her eyes. "You placed a protection charm upon her just now, I could feel it. Are we going to die?"

"I promised him to keep you and everyone safe. I won't let that happen," I assured her, fiercely hoping it was so. She nodded, maybe only to please me, because a trace of fear remained in her eyes. I opened my mouth to assure her further, but she surprised me by changing the subject.

"What has happened to my husband?" she asked next.

I hesitated not able to meet her gaze, finally I admitted, "I don't know. There is only darkness when I reach out to him."

She was quiet for a long moment, stirring the bubbling porridge. At last she took the can off the fire to cool. Turning back to me there was a note of resignation coloring her voice when she next spoke. "I have loved only two men in my life, Tasimu. If Nachoga, too, is gone, I don't want to stay in this world without him. Take care of your sister if you can, I love you, my little Rock Squirrel.'"

Her words sent a chill down my spine, but before I could reassure her once more, Uncle Tli came over needing my help. Motioning me away from the women by our family cooking fire, he drew me into the shadows and murmured, "It would be bad for us if we got trapped here, between the enemy and the flood. We need to know where the soldiers are.

"Now that our water skins are filled Talulsit says if we follow this gulley it will lead us away from the soldiers coming up the wash behind us. Can you look in the Pool and find them with your special string to make sure they don't block our escape?"

"Not with the string, but I will try the search with an owl or another winged one." I told him.

He patted me on the shoulder and I walked to a quiet place among the trees and lay down and began the search.

When I returned to the fire I was surprised to see Grandfather, the older warriors and many of the women waiting for me. Uncle motioned for me to take a seat beside him. Mother handed me a cup of tea, before retreating to sit beside Sagila and the children near our lean-to shelter.

"There are soldiers travelling up the wash as we suspected," I told them, "but that is only a part of our trouble. There are also several big tents and wagons of what look to be Chamuqwani settlers already camping near the mouth of the stream flowing into the upper branch of Bahasa River."

"If that commander of the soldiers is as smart as I think he is," Talulsit said, "he will be taking no chances and will be sending some of his soldiers across the ridges to cut us off, even if he doesn't already know about the miners."

"That may be true," I said. "Before I flew down to where the Chamuqwani miners were, I saw men on horseback climbing a hillside away from the main column of soldiers."

"If they get behind us we will be trapped here by morning," Uncle predicted, and cursed.

"Then we should rouse everyone and move away from this place before that happens," one of the new men said.

"And go where—in the dark?" Ashiqwa said.

"The children and the sick ones among us are exhausted," Betsiya said and stared at each of the men in turn. "And me, I would rather take my chances with the soldiers rather than run down the canyon into the path of a bunch of crazy miners."

"I think you both are right in a way," Grandfather said. "The women and children should stay right here and let the soldiers find us." Then turning to stare at Tli directly, he added, "But you, My Son, and the wanted outlaws among us should leave—tonight before you are trapped, or killed."

With an angry curse on his lips, Uncle sprang to his feet. "No! Who do you think I am, Old Man? I am no coward to run away and leave women and children unprotected while I save myself—no!"

"I can understand your anger, Brother," Sheikai said in a soothing voice. "Your father isn't questioning your bravery, or your willingness to give your life in the defense of the People, but think, Brother, think it through, please listen—all of you."

"When the soldiers come," Grandfather continued, "and if they find only women, children and the sick and old, what will they do to us, eh? They will take us back to the Preserve, that's what. We will go back with them and give them no trouble. Later when things are quiet and they are gone back to their fort, then you men can come help us escape again."

"That is an interesting idea," Talulsit agreed, "but I doubt if the soldiers will believe you, because there is no way that helpless women and children would be out in this desert alone without warriors to protect them."

"That may be, but it would be better if most of you go," Grandfather said. "Sheikai and I will stay with the women and maybe some of the younger warriors. We will tell them we were berry picking and got frightened when we knew they were chasing us." He hesitated, then said, "If we have to, Sheikai and I will use our Gifts to persuade them that we are alone out here."

Everyone talked about it till quite late, but finally it was decided that most of the warriors, like Tli, Chugai Talulsit, Qwati and Elder Chittola's oldest son with the rest of the new Kukiya men would leave as soon as they could pack and gather their horses. They had already been branded as outlaws and were known by the soldiers. The younger warriors like Samiqwas, Matoqwa, Cohasi and Tuumaz would stay. In spite of being a known outlaw himself Grandfather refused to go with them.

"I will disguise my face, my son, don't worry about me," Grandfather told Uncle when he insisted that if he was leaving Grandfather should, too. "I would only slow the warband down if I come. I will stay with the People where I will be of more use." Tli wasn't convinced, but let himself be persuaded by their arguments—or so I thought.

I think he had his own misgivings about leaving his young family, because later that evening I was coming back from the privy hole when I heard him and Sagila arguing. It was the first time I'd ever heard the always-smiling woman get angry and I froze where I was in the shadows, my mouth dropping open.

"You will go. If you stay the soldiers will want kill you and I no want to find another husband for my baby when they do. You will go—and keep safe. Now go!"

And to my astonishment she pushed him—hard. Tli staggered with the force of her push, stared open mouthed for a long moment, then picked up his weapons, got on his horse and left. I doubted if he saw the tears running down her cheeks as she watched him ride away.

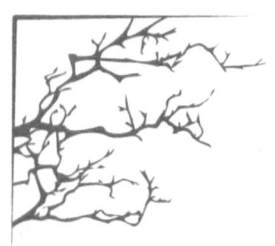

Chapter Seven

Hoping to take us by surprise the soldiers rode into the little hollow where we were camped just after Sun lightened the sky in the east. Everyone still left in camp was awake and waiting for them, though we had made no effort to pack up or take down the mats covering the lean-tos.

Holding up cut juniper branches that were the Kukiya sign of a peaceful intent, Grandfather, Sheikai and the Elder named Chittola who had joined us with a sick wife and two sons who had left with Uncle, stepped out to meet them.

Three soldiers with a lightning bolt and star badges on their chests, and the Kukiya scout Ahaz came forward to meet them while the rest of the soldiers fanned out with thunder weapons drawn to surround us.

Recognizing Ahaz from my time at the fort I stepped behind Matoqwa and Xyilaha, suddenly glad for my short stature and the ash I had smeared over the dragon tattoo on my face.

Glancing over her shoulder Xyilaha hissed, "What are you doing, stupid boy?"

"Hiding, stupid girl, the Kukiya with them may recognize me from my visit to Black Rock Fort with the war leader."

"Quiet, both of you," Matoqwa growled. "I want to hear what the dog turds have to say."

Overhearing what I said to Xyilaha Ashiqwa stepped close and murmured, "Quickly now Tasimu, come with me."

Moving slowly so as not to attract anyone's attention I followed her into her shelter, hidden among the trees. "What is it, Aunty?"

For answer she tossed me Xyilaha's old tunic dress, the one Mother had given her when she ran away with me. "Put that on and unbraid your hair." When I just stared at her, she growled, "Hurry, Nephew. Ahaz won't be looking for a young girl. You will be safer this way."

Well, she had a point, and something I hadn't thought of. I hastily pulled Xyilaha's tunic over my head and smoothed it down over the rest of my clothes. Then I sat to unravel the long braid hanging down my back. As soon as my hair was loose Ashiqwa gave it a quick comb, then began braiding it back into the two braids that a woman or girl usually wore. When she was done we crawled out of the shelter and walked over to join the rest of our family again.

Matoqwa saw me as I resumed my place behind him and Samiqwas. His eyes widened then he smirked. "Don't look at me, dog fart," I hissed. "That Kukiya scout knows me. He probably suspects that I was the one who set the Earth monsters on the soldiers when they tried to trap us at the fort. And if he recognizes me now it could mean bad trouble for me and everybody."

"Be quiet both of you," Betsiya whispered and nodded her approval at the change in my appearance. I was small for my fourteen years; no one who didn't know me would suspect I wasn't the girl I was pretending to be.

Returning my attention to our leaders and the soldiers, I heard a tall Chamuqwani with a big nose and patchy hair on his upper lip, who seemed to be their leader, say in a youthful, but gruff voice, "I am, Sub-Commander Hillberk. You zaunks are in violation of the law. You have left the Tribal Preserve and you have killed one of my soldiers and wounded two others."

Sheikai nodded to the Chamuqwani and then said. "Sub-Commander it is true we left the Preserve, but only to pick berries and pray. We are peaceful people; no one among us has killed any soldiers."

Sub-Commander Hillberk made a show of looking around at the dry pine and brush hillsides then he turned back to Sheikai and said, "Peaceful berry pickers, eh. I see no berry bushes out here. Don't play games with me. I want the murderers of my men."

"Yes, there are no berries here, but we only came this far into the desert away from Swampy Lake, because we were frightened when we saw that you were trailing us.'

The soldiers' leader looked around our night camp with its hastily built lean-tos covered with last year's cattail mats, our few belongings and snorted his disbelief. "You look like runaways and outlaws, and I find your presence off the Preserve most suspicious.

"Tell your people to come out of the shelters, put any weapons in a pile there," he pointed to a place of cleared ground in front of him," and then sit by the fire while my men go through the shelters. I don't believe your story, and I want to know what you are hiding."

"Sub-Commander, we don't want any trouble," Grandfather said and Ahaz translated. "We will go with you back to the Preserve, if that's what you want. We aren't hiding thunder weapons or anyone."

The commander ignored Grandfather and barked an order for his men to begin examining our belongings.

The soldiers searched, and they were rough about it, violently shoving women, sick old people and little ones out of the way when someone was too slow about obeying their commands. Tossing our blankets into the dirt, tearing clothing, and deliberately flattening with their hard boots, the big cans we used to make tea or cook stews and mush.

The destruction was malicious, unnecessary, and thorough. They even went so far as to rip open the rawhide bags and cloth sacks containing the last of our food, spilling the contents onto the dusty ground. While they hunted for hidden weapons they also pocketed anything they found that suited them.

Sobbing children crawled into the laps of women huddled in their blankets with only their frightened eyes peeking out. Beside me I could feel the anger radiating off Matoqwa and the other young men near me. When a soldier with orange hair on his face pushed a sick woman to the ground, I felt Matoqwa's muscles tense and I gripped his arm. "Don't be stupid. You will only get yourself and some of us killed if you try to fight them now. Wait!" I murmured next to his ear.

He cursed and angrily jerked away, but he stayed where he was, and sat beside Samiqwas and Cohasi when a brown haired soldier motioned with his thunder weapon in his direction.

Everyone muttered as they watched the soldiers turn up a few thunder weapons that were old and had no missiles to shoot from them. They also collected all our bows, war spears and Xyilaha's thunder weapon that she had tried to hide under the dirt and dried leaves in the lean-to she shared with Ashiqwa.

I saw the beautiful bow and quiver of arrows Nachoga made for me added to the pile and my heart cried out with the pain of it. Not knowing his fate it had been a comfort to at least have that little part of him to hold onto and give me strength. Now it, too, was gone as I helplessly watched the soldiers set fire to the pile.

When Grandfather protested that our young men needed those weapons to hunt for us, the commander answered, "You can eat oat-mush and hard cake like the rest of the zaunks on the Preserve."

After completing their search our camp was in shambles. Except for Xyilaha's little weapon the soldiers hadn't found any usable thunder weapons or known outlaws among us. Angry and frustrated that the men they were sent to hunt weren't here their youthful leader threatened to start killing children if someone didn't tell him where we had hidden all our good weapons, and where he could find the outlaws who killed Agent Daglish, and the man who had murdered his soldier.

His words made us afraid, but no one spoke up. None of us knew where the warriors had gone, though I suspected Uncle and a few of the others from back home were near.

After the commander screamed more threats, he noticed Tuumaz giving him a rebellious glare. Enraged by his act of defiance he ordered one of his men to take Tuumaz and Matoqwa, the tallest and strongest of the young men left behind, tie them to a sturdy pine and whip them.

"Commander Hillberk, please, Sheikai cried after only a few strokes. "The boys don't know any more where these outlaws are than the rest of us. We are peaceful zaunks we don't know anything about men getting killed."

Grandfather protested their treatment as well and I felt the change when he quietly used his Qwakaiva to make the soldiers stop. Released from the tree at last, they staggered back to the fire where Grandfather hurried over to see to their wounds.

It was after that that I overheard Ahaz trying to appease his angry young commander. "Sir, most of these people are northerners. They can barely understand me, because I only know a little of their language. They may be telling you the truth—or at least partly the truth. None of them were at the fort when Commander Rossman called the peace council. I doubt if they had anything to do with the killing of Agent Daglish."

"Maybe not, but they are lying about being alone out here. There were warriors with them, and those men killed one of my soldiers. I want the murderer."

"I understand, and I agree with you, but I doubt if the women know where their men are now any more than we do."

Sun-Commander Hillberk swore, then snarled, "Then what do you suggest we do, Lead Scout, just let them go back to 'berry picking' hmm?"

Ahaz shrugged. "There isn't much we can do, but take these people back to the fort, resupply and keep looking, Sir."

When they completed their search to no one's satisfaction the Chamuqwani allowed the women to collect the food and belongings that weren't destroyed during the weapons search. And then they herded us down a trail towards the river.

Afraid we might escape the Chamuqwani took all our horses and made everyone walk except for the weakest of the sick ones who were allowed to ride, but their horses were roped together and lead by a soldier on horseback.

Instead of retracing our path back to Summer Swampy Lake and from there to the Preserve, the sub-commander after checking his map decided to take a shorter route down to the Bahasa River and onto Black Rock Fort, where agency soldiers could be summoned to take us the rest of the way, while he continued to hunt for outlaws.

Unfortunately for us this route would take us past the new Chamuqwani settlement. I never knew if the commander knew about the miners before making that fatal decision, but he did little to protect us from the Evil lying in wait for us once we arrived at the camp up from the river.

The young warriors like Samiqwas, Tuumaz, Matoqwa and Cohasi walked roped together under the vigilant eye of two veteran soldiers with hard expressions and cruel eyes. Much to her grim satisfaction, Xyilaha, in her boy's clothing was taken for another of the young warriors and roped in the line along with all the others.

Still in my girl's disguise I spent the day walking beside Amima and my Aunties. For much of the day I carried little Kitahtla on my back tucked safely into her cradleboard, while Mother put an arm around Chitola's sick wife to help her walk. Being near the rear of the column the dust was bad, so like many of the people I covered my lower face to keep out the dust as well as hide my tattoo. Unfortunately for the sick woman, a cloth on the face wasn't enough. She had to stop often, doubling over with fits of coughing throughout the day.

When we at last made camp just before dark in a sandy spot among the rabbit brush, the babies and young children were fretful and everyone was exhausted. But we weren't allowed to rest. Pointing their weapons in a threatening way the soldiers commanded Ashiqwa and a few of the older women to cook for them as well as for our own people.

To my amusement Betsiya folded her arms across her chest and demanded, "Soldiers throw me food in dirt. Now no good. You give soldier food to hungry children and old people. Then me cook for you."

The sub-commander didn't like it, but she had a point. If they were going to take us alive back to the Preserve then they had to feed us.

I was ordered, along with other girls to take the soldiers' pails and water bottles and fill them at the nearby muddy stream. Grandfather and Elder Chittola promised that no one would run away if he released the young men. The sub-commander finally agreed on the condition that they do camp chores like digging privy holes and gathering dung and sticks for the night's fires.

Just before I was going to curl up beside Amima and the baby and try to sleep, Grandfather called me over to him and asked me to do some scouting of my own, with an owl or bat. "I'm afraid for your uncle and Elder Chittola wants to know about his sons who left with the outlaws. Can you try and check on them?"

Worried about the new settlement we would reach by tomorrow afternoon, I wanted to do a bit of scouting of my own, so I willingly agreed. Mother was lying on her side at the back of the tiny shelter nursing the baby when I crawled in and spread my blanket in front of them, offering what little protection I could, should any of the Chamuqwani try to bother her. All day I'd been hearing the soldiers joking when their officers weren't near, that they planned sleeping with a cloocha whore that night—and it wasn't going to be my mother.

A young owl answered my call and we flew off searching for our warriors. I found them making a fireless camp over the next ridge. I spotted Chugai on sentry watch and their horses munching on bunch grass in a sheltered hollow a little further down the slope.

Assuring myself that they were well and undiscovered the owl and I flew on down the creek past our camp to where the stream connected with the Bahas River. The Chamuqwani settlement had grown since my last look if the many cook fires were any indication. Urging my companion closer I soon saw why, and that knowing tore my heart wide open.

Tobek and his partner were there with their wagons. They were doing a brisk trade, trading waskyja for gold.

Next day Sub-Commander Hillberk seemed surprised when his scouts reported the new settlement at the mouth of the creek where it flowed into the muddy river. "What are those people doing out here?" I heard him grumble to his gray-haired sergeant as they rode up the column past me.

The man wiped the sweat off his forehead and shrugged. "According to the new treaty the country around here is open for settlement now." The sergeant glanced at the dry hills covered with rocks, scrub pine and rabbit brush, and laughed. "Or at least for mining claims, I doubt if anybody but these stupid savages could ever call this accursed land home."

Hillberk grunted his agreement. 'Treaty opening be damned. With the hatred for the savages and their raids growing among the settlers these people's presence here is going to complicate our situation. We will have to keep a close eye on the..." I heard no more as they rode further up the column of exhausted people.

Sun was shining with a warm golden light when the soldiers ordered us to make camp by a rocky bottomed creek up from the new settlement. In the distance we could hear shouting male voices and the pounding of hammers on wood, and other mechanical noises. Leaving us with a strong guard of his men to make sure we didn't run away, the sub-commander and a few of his men rode down the creek, heading for the settlement.

Taking the baby from me when she began to fuss, Mother asked, "Tasimu what's happening; do you know?"

"There's a new settlement of miners just ahead. I saw them through bird's eyes when I scouted for Grandfather last night." I told her. "I don't think the soldiers' leader knew about it, before his own scouts told him earlier. And, he didn't seem happy about the news if what I overheard is true. I suspect he has probably gone to see for himself.'

I wasn't happy either; rattlesnake was whirring her warnings in my mind and the foretelling was making my whole body tremble.

Next day we remained in our camp while the soldiers discussed what to do with us. We were nearly out of food, so the sub-commander sent some of his men to buy supplies from the traders in the new settlement for his men and us, while he figured out what to do next.

We were all restless and unsettled, wanting to go—anywhere—even back to the Preserve, rather than remain here so close to the Chamuqwani. The water in the creek had a bitter metallic taste that the little ones didn't want to drink, which some of the old people blamed on the miners.

When I asked next day why we were still camped here rather than going on the Preserve, Grandfather told me, "This soldier leader is young with little experience. He doesn't know this land or the people. I think he wants to do right, but is also afraid of making mistakes that will anger his superiors.

"So he is cautious he waits, and sends word to the fort, asking Commander Rossman for more soldiers and boats to float us down river to Black Rock Fort. And after that agency guards will come and return us to the Preserve, while he and his men continue to patrol for outlaws, and anyone else who might be heading to see the Prophet—and join in the Spirit-Calling Dances."

"But the longer we stay here the more danger we are in. Grandfather we need to go away from those miners down there," I protested.

He must have read the urgency of my warning in my Spirit Fire, because he patted my shoulder, and said, "I will speak to the others. We will try and convince him to continue on down river as soon as possible.

It hadn't taken long for the news of soldiers guarding a bunch of what the miners referred to as, "cloochas or whores" to reach the new settlement. Half drunk and leering men kept showing up in small groups to call us names and make rude gestures of invitation to the women and girls.

And much to Cohasi and Matoqwa's amusement that included me. Though I have to admit they defended me with threats and rocks until a soldier came to investigate, when I was approached by a couple of dirty mean-eyed Chamuqwani while hauling water. The soldiers had orders to chase them away, but their hearts weren't in it, so the men always came back.

I could tell from the soldiers' talk that some had lost companions to my creatures the night of our escape. The light in their Spirit Fires' said they would welcome an excuse to take their revenge, and it didn't matter if that reckoning was carried out on innocent people.

After hesitating to add to my Elders' worries I told them more of my observations and fears. Some Grandfather had observed for himself and he had already spoken to the sergeant in charge, but the man hadn't seemed to take him seriously enough to do anything about the situation.

As the day wore on, and no orders came to move, hoping to ease everyone's fears, Sheikai, Grandfather and a few of the others who knew the Prophet's sacred songs sat down by our cook fire, and began to sing. Having no drums or rattles—they'd been burned along with our weapons, Elder Chittola, and a few others, picked up a rock in each hand and clicked them together to accompany the singing.

In an act of defiance, Tuumaz and Samiqwas and the rest of our young men formed a circle and started dancing and singing, too. After a slight hesitation women and children joined in. as the power grew people relaxed and Betsiya brought a few of the very ill into the center of the circle, laid them down and laid her hands on them for a healing. Grandfather left his place among the singers and joined her.

When I asked him if he would like my help, he politely, but firmly refused. <<We can't do much for the very sick ones. They will have to wait till they can find their way to the Prophet. Save your strength; your kind of Qwakaiva might be needed later.>>

At the time I was hurt by his rejection. Once more the old hatred Otter's Qwakaihi had for my Seal father and his lineage had surfaced—or so I thought. Looking back, in a way it was better I didn't drain my strength in a futile attempt to save lives. My Gift was needed later, and the price I personally paid by summoning my power nearly destroyed me.

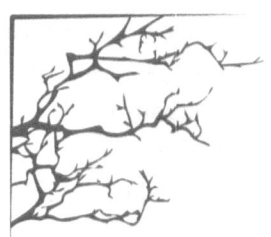

Chapter Eight

As the singing and praying continued that day I could tell the soldiers guarding us were growing nervous and didn't like it, but they didn't stop the dancing, either. The sound seemed to attract more Chamuqwani from the miners' settlement. They stood around talking and joking with our guards until the sub-commander came back and put an end to the dancing and made the gawkers go away.

Next day when the sub-commander was busy elsewhere the singing and dancing began again, the pattern continuing as the days went by and we remained, waiting, for the boats—or something, while the Evil stalking us came ever closer.

Restless, bored and frustrated by being confined and guarded by soldiers my friends came to me with a plan to test their prowess as hunters and warriors when I was at the creek collecting water for the soldiers' use. "Tas, can you help us? We want to have a look at the Chamuqwani settlement tonight—maybe steel some food, weapons," Samiqwas said, as the one, of the five suddenly stepping out of the brush, appointed to convince me. "Can you use your Gift, so we will get past the soldiers without being discovered?"

I set down the bucket and kept them waiting while I thought about it. I did want to see the settlement, or more specifically Tobek or his partner. I was still trying to contact Nachoga, whenever I had a quiet moment. He was alive, but his whereabouts was still unknown to me. I was determined to find out from one of those traders what had happened. "Maybe, but I will have to come with you—and don't tell Grandfather."

"If you are coming, then leave your dress in your mother's shelter," Cohasi smirked and then Matoqwa snickered. But he yelped in the next moment as Xyilaha punched his arm and called him a dog fart.

I gave him a disgusted look, picked up my water bucket and headed back to the soldiers' camp to give the sergeant the water he wanted.

I had no intention on wearing Xyilaha's dress, but before we met later to sneak past our guards, I wanted some quiet time to speak to my crystal and maybe Rattlesnake. If the warband's disappearance was indeed caused by the traders betraying the warriors for the imperial man's bounty , then it was left up to me to make them pay. I promised myself that they weren't going to live long enough to enjoy their bloody reward. Tobek had been warned; there were consequences for a betrayal of my People and I planned to see that the traders were punished if they were responsible.

I got my chance after our meal when Mother went back to our shelter to nurse a fretful Kitahtla and then fell asleep. Grandfather and the other older men and women among us were by the central fire talking to the sub-commander, the sergeant and a couple of his senior aides.

In the darkness among the trees I removed the dress, but kept my hair braided in a girl's fashion, and then tied the braids together, so they hung out of the way down my back. Still holding the dress under my arm I tossed my blanket over my shoulders and returned to lie in front of Mother and the baby by the shelter's entrance. Under the blanket I took Crystal Being out of the bag around my neck and held it in my hand, summoning its power.

My emotions churning I conveyed to the being my fears, my anger, my desperation, and my need for vengeance if my father had indeed been betrayed. I held the crystal so tight that blood from my palm coated its points adding intensity to my communication. Then I waited for its answer.

I was about to break the contact and go to meet the others when it finally spoke, <<What you suspect is true. They were betrayed for the reward. If you wish my help with your personal vengeance there will be a debt owing for my assistance that is more than the taste of your blood, young Siyatli. Are you sure you have the courage to pay it?>>

Its words were sobering, but what choice did I have? <<I feel like my whole world is disintegrating around me, Shining One. I have to punish the ones who betrayed my father and the warband. It's up to me now to do whatever I can to protect those I love and stop the Evil.>>

<<Stop the Evil, are you sure you can do that by taking your vengeance now? To act at this time will make a change in the Pattern true, but it may not have the result you intend, young one, are you sure?>>

<<Yes, I will have to take that chance. The men who betrayed us must be punished. I see no other way; I promised him. I have no choice.>>

<<Kunai may not be happy with you, if you change the Pattern at this time,>> the crystal being warned. <<And if you evoke the Great One's ire you may forfeit the aid of one of your spirit allies if you proceed. Do you still want my help for your dangerous plan.>>

Looking back I wonder if I could have prevented disaster if I hadn't been so impatient, but back then I allowed my feelings of anger and fear to rule me in spite of the Shining One's warning. <<Yes, I am sure.>>

<<So be it then.>>

Later that night when all was quiet and most everyone asleep in our combined encampment, five young warriors crept through the shadows past the guards dozing at their posts to meet in a pine thicket overlooking the creek. As I waited for the others Rattlesnake found me and curled herself around my chest under my shirt. She licked my cheek with her forked tongue. <<This is the last time you will be able to call on me, young Siyatli, but I will do your bidding before I leave you forever.>>

Forever? I had been a lonely and frightened boy with hostile enemies all about me when I had arrived in this desert land so different from my northern home. Rattlesnake had been the first to offer me her assistance and the thought of her leaving me twisted a knot of fear and despair in my gut. Was my revenge so important to me? Should I wait and hope the pattern would favor my intent later? <<Leave me—forever?>>

<<It is a portion of the sacrifice owing for my aid, young one. Are you sure you want to take your vengeance now?>>

Part of the sacrifice owing? My heart sank at her words and a chill ran down my spine. What else would the Unseen Ones ask of me? I trembled fearing what else they might want in payment. Then Nachoga's and my sister's faces appeared before my inner eye. I had to protect my family from the Evil stalking us—no matter the cost to me personally.

<<Thank you for your guidance,>> I took a deep breath to strengthen my resolve. <<You and the other Spirits of this land have honored me with your kindness, but I feel I have no choice—Nachoga—I will miss you, Honored One.>>

She touched my face again with her forked tongue and tightened her coils around my chest for a brief moment. <<So be it then, young Siyatli. I think maybe I will miss you, too.>>

As they arrived, I heard Cohasi murmur to his brother, "This reminds me of our raids to steal the stupid chicken birds from the Chamuqwani when we were traveling to the Preserve."

"Yeah, well don't trip over your own feet like the time we almost got caught," Samiqwas grumbled. "I don't want to get shot."

"Be quiet, both of you," Xyilaha hissed. We are still near enough for the soldiers to hear us if one of them goes to pee."

Using my Gift I was able to guide us through the darkness to the edge of the new settlement without being detected. From what we could see as we approached this place wasn't much more than a cluster of large white tents like the soldiers used, and smaller huts thrown up by lashing saplings together and then covering them with pieces of hide, cloth or whatever else the miners could find.

But much to our disappointment, unlike our own camp where women, children and off-duty soldiers were sound asleep, here many people were still awake and walking around, talking and shouting at one another.

This was due mostly to the traders' wagons that were clustered together near a large fire. Tobek and his partner Lennard were there, but there were three other traders as well.

Each wagon had a long table placed next to the side facing the fire on which the trader had placed items he had available for trade. All had bottles and jugs of waskyja to sell but the items on display also included knives, axes, thunder weapons, blankets and sacks of flour and oat-mush. Most of the men still awake and standing around the fire talking were drinking or already drunk, or nearly so.

"We should split up and search the camp in groups of two," Tuumaz said. As the oldest and most experienced raider among us he was in charge. He took Xyilaha with him and headed off to circle around the tents and come into the settlement from the north. Matoqwa and his brother headed in the opposite direction.

"I want to get near the traders' wagons," I murmured to Samiqwas as we headed for the first row of tents. "The fat one with the black hair and big laugh is Tobek. He is the one that promised the war chief new thunder weapons. I want to know why he is here and not at Red Mesa."

"With all those Chamuqwani around it's going to be hard to get close to him," Samiqwas said.

"I will use my Qwakaiva to mask our coming. When we get close we can go around the back and hide in the shadows. Then I will climb into his wagon and wait for him to come get more waskyja."

"Tas, that's too dangerous," he protested. "We only have our belt knives for weapons. What if he sees you?"

"Then I will kill him—he betrayed my father, and the war leader."

"You don't know that for certain."

"Then I need to find out." Making a cutting motion with my hand I faded into the night. He could follow or not as he chose. He sighed and trailed along after me.

As I promised, I used my Puwa and we made it to the shadows behind the wagons without being noticed. There was a crowd of men gathered around the more sociable Tobek's wagon, so I chose to climb into his partner Lennard's wagon instead. Samiqwas faded back into the shadows to wait for me.

As I waited inside I glanced through the trade goods arranged there. Opening a box that contained a few small thunder weapons and their missiles I stuck my head out the back of the wagon and motioned Samiqwas over. I handed him a loaded weapon, a pouch of missiles and a couple knives I'd pulled out of another box.

"Be careful," he murmured before returning to the shadows.

It was in the next box I opened that I found it and knew for sure I'd been right. Under a scratchy blanket was the smoking mixture pouch that Golannah's first wife Shinuuta made for him and painted with sacred designs. When he left to meet the traders I knew it contained yellow rocks, not its usual smoking mixture. The war chief would have never willingly taken it off, or traded it.

My vision turned red as a fire ignited in my gut, and my hands shook as I tied the pouch onto my own belt. This was all the proof I needed. Fearful of what I might find next I flung open other boxes, and I wasn't quiet as I looked. I was searching for something belonging to my father, while heart-sick and afraid I would also find it.

It wasn't long before my presence was discovered, by the trader out front. With a curse he clambered into the wagon and peered into its dark interior. "Hey! Who's that? What'cha doin' in here?"

When I didn't answer and remained only a dark silhouette against the lighter cloth of the wagon cover, he climbed in and lit a lamp I hadn't noticed hanging on a wooden rib that was holding up the cloth top.

Staring open mouthed at the destruction I had made of his goods, it took him a moment to focus his attention on me. What he must have seen on a first glance was just another zaunk brat, hoping to steal a few trinkets before running away. But the Tasimu that was just another dirty zaunk boy was no longer in the control of the body he saw standing in the wreckage of his things.

No that Tasimu had stepped aside to allow the power I had summoned with my blood and my intent to take control of the person he now saw. "Hello, Betrayer," the voice, that was not my voice said in his language. I smiled, showing lots of teeth.

"Did you have to share the reward with Tobek? Too bad neither of you will live long enough to enjoy it." I came a little closer to let him have a good look at my face in the lantern light. I pointed to the tattoo on my jaw, and his eyes grew wide when he recognized it.

"My father warned you what would happen if you broke your promise and betrayed us."

As I'd been speaking Rattlesnake had crawled out from inside my shirt and wound herself around an upraised arm pointed straight at his face. Becoming aware of her for the first time, Lennard stared, shaking his head in denial. "And for your greed and betrayal I've come to give you the painful death you deserve."

I came closer, still smiling. Whatever he saw in my eyes made him shake uncontrollably. "W-witch! Leave me alone. I didn't d-do nothing to the war chief—or your father."

"Who did, then, Tobek?"

"N-no. The soldiers were just there. They must have followed us—but we didn't know—I swear!"

I laughed, and there was no mirth in the sound. I stepped even closer. "Too bad, I don't believe you."

As he would have turned to clamber out of the wagon Rattlesnake flung herself at his face and sank her fangs into the flesh of his cheek just below his left eye. Wrapping herself around his neck she continued to pour her poison into him as he tumbled out of the wagon. The men still around the fire fell silent as Lennard toppled to the ground screaming and writhing, Rattlesnake still wrapped around his neck.

<<Good bye, Honored One, thank you for your Life-Gift,>> I said as I watched her disappear, accepting her death. Then taking advantage of the distraction out front I quietly jumped down from the back of the wagon.

I was about to look for Samiqwas when I felt the muzzle of a thunder weapon press against my side, and a voice said, "When my partner didn't come back right away, I knew there was something wrong. So I let the boy take over. I come; I listen."

The Crystal Being still directing me I heard myself laugh, as I ignored his weapon and turned to face him. "And what did you hear, Chamuqwani, hmm? Did you hear that I have come for you, too?"

Tobek chuckled and pushed the muzzle of his weapon into my chest to make his point. "Ah, but it is me holding the rifle—Mathrom's rifle actually—and now that your snake is gone you have nothing with which to defend yourself, Witch."

Yes he spoke true; I could feel the essence of my father still clinging to the weapon I had so proudly gifted him moons ago. "When last I saw you, you didn't believe in the power you call witchcraft. Should have believed before you betrayed them. Didn't you want the gold they offered?"

"I got the gold and the miners and soldiers will pay well—with more gold—for the weapons I have."

I laughed again and the sound seemed to unnerve him. "You are a brave little zaunk, I will grant you that. Maybe I won't kill you. Maybe I give you to the soldiers and collect another reward for you. They would like me to give them the one who killed so many at Black Rock, and then you could join the others waiting for the hangman."

"Not going to happen, Chamuqwani. This is a hard and ancient land. The Unseen Ones who guard it rarely forgive. You are a dead man."

This time I felt his mood shift and saw the spikes of rage in his Spirit Fire. He was going to kill me. <<Oh, Father, Amima, I'm sorry I didn't recognize the great evil arrayed against us. I should have guessed, done better at protecting you and the People,>> I told them, and the spirits I could sense hovering around me in the darkness.

Resigning myself to accept my fate, I snarled, "Do it, Chamuqwani, if you dare."

"Hey stupid dog turd," someone shouted from the darkness. And then a large rock hit the back of Tobek's wagon. When he turned I thrust the muzzle of the weapon into the air and then rammed my head into his fat gut. The weapon fired as he wheezed and doubled over and I took off running. Catching his breath the trader fired the weapon again, trying to see me in the gloom. I kept running and behind me I heard another smaller weapon fire twice, but the big thunder weapon was silent after that.

The sound of the weapons caused an uproar behind me, confused and drunken men stumbled about, firing their own weapons and shouting they were being attacked by the savages.

Samiqwas caught up to me as I was heading for the creek. "Did you kill him?" I asked as I knelt in the shallow water and splashed water onto my hot face and chest. I was feeling weak and a little dizzy, but I couldn't give into my sickness yet.

"I think so. I hit him once in the chest and once in his fat gut, but I didn't stay around to make sure," Samiqwas said. When I stood and started past him he grabbed me and spun me around to face him. "Tas, what were you thinking? You could have gotten yourself, and me killed back there. If you hadn't found that weapon and given it to me...."

He left the rest of his thought unvoiced, but I knew he was angry with me, and maybe afraid, too. I took Golannah's pouch off my belt and showed it to him. "I found this in amongst the trader's things. They betrayed our people and collected a reward from the soldiers for their capture.

"My father warned them what would happen—and now..." Swallowing hard I continued, unable to totally mask the tremble in my voice. "And since, since he-they are gone, it was left up to me, to carry out the punishment."

"Oh, Tas, I'm sorry."

I knew he meant it, but right then I didn't want sympathy from him, or anyone. I was trying too hard to keep from breaking down and bawling like a baby to accept any kind words—even from him. "We need to find the others and get back," I repeated and headed up the bank.

In the distance I could still hear the boom of thunder weapons and now there was a red glow rising from several fires. All this commotion would soon attract the interest of the soldiers, and we needed to be back in camp before that happened.

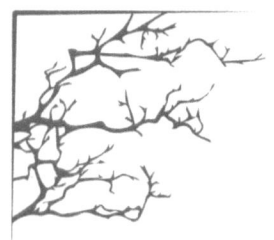

Chapter Nine

The rest of our little warband were waiting for us by the scrub pine thicket where we had planned to meet. As we crept in among the trees I heard Xyilaha breathe a sigh of relief. "Stupid boy, I thought I was going to have to come rescue you."

Cohasi snickered. "What happened? One of you dog turds trip over your own feet this time?"

Ignoring the jibe Samiqwas growled over his shoulder, "Shut up, ptarmigan-brain, and get moving." Then he headed out of the thicket and I followed, ending their chance to ask more questions.

As we crept through the darkness with only star light as a guide I noticed that both Tuumaz and Xyilaha had managed to find weapons of their own. Cohasi and Matoqwa had no thunder weapons, but they had knives and Cohasi an axe on his belt and Matoqwa carried a heavy sack of oat-mush or flour on one shoulder.

When we were nearing the top of the ridge that overlooked our camp in the creek bottom below, two shadowy figures rose from the rabbit brush and confronted us. Startled, Tuumaz raised the thunder weapon he carried, but in the next moment it was snatched out of his hand by a third man who smashed a fist against his jaw, dropping him to his knees.

Xyilaha was fumbling her weapon out of its holster when I closed my own hand over hers. "Don't! That's Uncle Tli," I hissed next to her ear. She relaxed her grip and I breathed a sigh of relief.

"Alright, dog humpers," Tli growled, "what are you doing out here?"

No one answered at first, but finally Tuumaz, still rubbing his jaw, rose to his feet and answered, "We wanted to look around the new Chamuqwani settlement—that's all."

Chugai snorted. "That's hardly all, the Chamuqwani over there are acting crazy, like somebody kicked a wasp nest."

"They are just drunk, mostly," I said. "There several traders down there selling waskyja and a lot of men are trading gold for the drink."

Tli grunted and returned his attention to me. "And you know this, how?"

"Because when Samiqwas and I were exploring I recognized two of the traders, selling waskyja. They were the two that promised the war chief and Father they would come with new weapons to Red Mesa."

I let that information sink in for a moment then continued, "The traders betrayed the warband for the reward money offered by the imperial man at Black Rock Fort. He claims they are the ones killed the fat agent."

Xyilaha gasped. "But they didn't do it. Why your father was with us recovering from his wounded shoulder—and the rest of the warband was with you and Golannah in the desert."

"Yes, I know that—we all know that, but who among the Chamuqwani would believe that a bunch of dirty zaunks didn't kill the greedy pig who starved and cheated us out of our treaty goods, eh?"

She thought about it, then sighed and nodded her agreement.

Well, there might be one or two Chamuqwani who possibly would believe us, I thought. I would try to contact Collin within the Dream when next I slept.

At the sound of my name I returned my attention to Uncle and the matter under discussion. Tli was saying, "Nephew, are you sure?"

"Yes, I was with Nachoga when I heard the war chief show the traders a sack of yellow rocks he took from the miners' pit house at Sandy Bottom creek, when we traveled to the fort. Golannah and Father warned Trader Tobek and his partner to bring the weapons and not to betray them."

Reaching to my belt I untied Golannah's pouch from my waist and showed it to them. "I found this in one of the trader's wagons when I was searching, and then he later admitted the betrayal—before I killed him."

Everyone recognized the pouch. I let the significance of my words sink in, then added. "The other trader had Nachoga's thunder weapon—the one I gave him. He, too admitted to collecting the reward money, before Samiqwas shot him."

Turning attention to Samiqwas, Chugai asked, "Did you kill him?"

Samiqwas shrugged. "I don't know for sure; we didn't stay around to check. But I hit him two times, once in the chest and once in his fat belly." Chugai smiled his approval.

Uncle swore and held out his hand for the weapon, which Samiqwas reluctantly gave him. Then he held out his hand for Xyilaha's. When she resisted he cuffed her and took it anyway. Then he pointed to Cohasi and Matoqwa and told them to put down any plunder they had collected while exploring the miners' camp.

"You are all brave young warriors and we are proud of you, but you can't return to the women with weapons or other plunder, because the soldiers will search again, after the trouble tonight," the Kukiya man with them explained, trying to smooth over our angry feelings at being treated so roughly.

I wasn't so sure I was proud of me, I thought, as I followed the others back to our camp. As I'd promised I had carried out my revenge for the betrayal of the father I had grown to love beyond reason, but I hadn't considered the consequences of my act on the other vulnerable people left in my care. And, to complicate the matter further, I still didn't know where Nachoga and the warriors were being held—if they weren't already dead.

No, Nachoga and Golannah at least were alive—somewhere. Tobek had said as much, before Samiqwas killed him. Maybe when we returned to Black Rock Fort I could learn more and find a way to rescue them.

Sad and fearful, I crept back into the shelter I shared with Mother and the baby when the stars faded in the grayness just before dawn. I put on Xyilaha's dress and covered myself with my blanket, hoping for some sleep before the soldiers would have us up to begin the day.

Her voice soft in the darkness, Mother said, "Where have you been all night, My Son?"

I thought about pretending to be asleep and not answering, but I couldn't lie to her, even though I knew what I had to tell her would cut her to the bone. My voice choking on the words, I said, "I went with Samiqwas and a few of the warriors to explore the new Chamuqwani camp."

She gasped. "Oh Tasimu that was so dangerous—if they had caught you... Why?"

Ignoring her question for the moment, I swallowed hard, trying to control the silent tears running down my cheeks. Finally I took several deep breaths and answered, "He isn't coming back to us, Amima. The soldiers captured him; the Chamuqwani traders betrayed him and the war chief for the imperial man's reward and the yellow rocks the miners found at Sandy Bottom Creek."

She fell silent after that, maybe not wanting to believe me, and then I heard her quiet sobbing from her bed in the shadows. All thoughts of sleep abandoned I scooted over and reached out to hug her, unable to hold back the flood of my own tears any longer. We clung together sharing our grief, each trying to console the other for another terrible loss of someone we loved. When I could speak I choked out, "Amima, I'm so sorry. I should have been there—gone with them—but Grandfather, damn him—"

She put a finger over my mouth to stop me. "Hush now, my Dear One, my Little Rock Squirrel, if you had gone I might have lost you, too. Stubborn man, I had a bad feeling from the beginning about that trip—and I told him so. He said he didn't want to leave me and the baby, but sometimes loyalty to a kinsman means a person has obligations that bind more tightly than love. I wish..." she started crying and never finished her thought.

Wanting to cheer her and give her hope, I said, "Amima, he may not be dead. If the soldiers take us to Black Rock Fort I'll use my Puwa to make someone tell me where he is, and then I'll rescue him for us."

She kissed my forehead and patted my shoulder. "He may not be dead, but he will be in prison far away—too far away to come back to us. I think you had the right of it when you said that he was lost to us—and it's forever this time."

Mother and I clung together grieving until sensing our distress, the baby woke and demanded our attention. Cradling the little one, Mother put her to the breast, tears still flowing down her cheeks.

It was light by then, I could hear doves cooing their greetings to the new day in the trees by the creek, and someone over by the main cook fire laughed and poured water into a battered can for tea. Mother looked over the baby's head and met my eye. "What are you going to do now, My Son? Are you going to tell your grandfather and the Elders what you discovered about the warband?"

I sighed, crawled outside our shelter and got to my feet. "I suppose I should warn them, because the soldiers will be coming to search for outlaws or stolen weapons after what happened last night."

Suddenly afraid her eyes grew wide as she realized the danger. "What happened last night that you haven't told me about? You boys didn't bring weapons or anything else back with you, did you?"

"We did, but fortunately Uncle Tli and some of the warriors met us and made us give them the weapons and other plunder we collected. But the real problem is that me and Samiqwas killed the ones who betrayed the warband. And the miners were so drunk they started shooting at anyone, so there may be more dead than the ones who deserved our vengeance."

Mother took in a deep breath and let it out slowly. "Tli and the outlaws are still nearby? Oh, Tas, do you realize what this means? Now the soldiers will be looking for our men even harder. They probably think it was them attacking the Chamuqwani last night—not a bunch of foolish boys."

Well, that was another thing I hadn't considered when I conjured my vengeance. My gut twisting in a knot of fear and remorse , I said, "I'd better go find Grandfather and the others." And then before she could say anything else I turned and went to look for the Elders.

By the time I washed by the creek and hauled a couple buckets of water back to our camp Sheikai, Grandfather and the rest of the Elders were awake and sitting around the main fire drinking tea and talking, waiting for Betsiya to finish with the pot of mush she was cooking.

When I walked up Grandfather smiled at me and patted the ground beside him, inviting me to sit with them. "You look worried, my dear one, what's troubling you this morning?"

Ignoring the cup of tea Betsiya offered me I swallowed hard, took a deep breath and began, "There's trouble coming and I need to warn you. Sometime soon the soldiers will be here to search for our warriors and any plunder taken from the Chamuqwani settlement last night.

Betsiya looked up from her cooking and studied me carefully with her Spirit Gift. Finally Grandfather put down his tea and asked, "Did our warriors attack the miners—was anyone killed?"

"Uncle and the others are near. They've been following sense the soldiers took us, but they didn't attack the miners—though I'm sure they will be blamed for the deaths last night."

"And you know this how, young one," Elder Chittola asked.

Taking another deep breath I looked down at the fire and admitted, "Because I was there in the settlement last night and am responsible for at least one of the deaths."

They all fell silent, staring. "Tell us what happened." Grandfather said in a gentle voice that added another stone of guilt to my growing pile.

To answer him I removed Golannah's pouch from under my dress and showed it to them. When Betsiya held out a hand for it, I gave it to her to examine. "Some of the young men came to me yesterday and asked if I would use my Puwa to help them get past the sentries so we could explore the new settlement last night," I began. "I found Golannah's pouch while searching through one of the trader's wagons. He and his partner were the ones supposed to be meeting the warband at Red Mesa with the new thunder weapons. Instead they were selling waskyja to the Chamuqwani miners.

"When I recognized them I wanted to know what had happened to my father and the others. What I found out was that those two betrayed them to the soldiers, kept the weapons and took Golannah's gold. The one called Lennard admitted that to me before I killed him."

"Oh, Grandson, you shouldn't have done that." There was such a note of disappointment in his voice that it snapped something inside me, and I forgot all my teachings of respect for Elders.

"Maybe you should have never meddled and let me go with them. I could have prevented this evil, and then there would have been no need for me to take my revenge on the greedy Chamuqwani responsible for our warriors' deaths and capture," I snapped.

Hearing my words Betsiya gasped, dropping her spoon into the dirt. Though her face remained unreadable I could see the sudden fear and grief swirling in murky clouds within her Spirit Fire. Knowing that had been no way to tell her about her husband made me ashamed once more. Mother and I weren't the only ones who would be mourning the loss of beloved relatives.

"I'm sorry," I mumbled to no one in particular and dropped my eyes to the fire once again.

Retrieving her spoon and wiping it off on her tunic before placing it back into the can of bubbling mush she focused her gaze on me, demanding I raise my eyes and look at her. "Is he dead then, young Puhani?"

I shook my head. My voice trembling with the power of my emotions I told her the truth as I knew it. "When I search for the warband within the Dream or by using my special string, there is only a gray mist of Evil, covering my sight. Because of my closeness to my father I sense he is alive but in great pain. I don't know where he is, and I didn't find out from the traders, before we killed them.

"The war chief, your husband, honored woman, and the others I can't be sure of their fate. They may be captured, dead, or escaped back into the desert and will return to us later. I keep trying—have been ever since the soldiers found us, but always it is the same. I'm sorry."

Betsiya lifted the mush off the flames and set it on the ground to cool. She picked up Golannah's pouch and stood. Unwilling to meet anyone's eye she said, "I will take this to Shinuuta and Second Wife. They will want to know what has happened to the war chief."

Sheikai rose as well. "I will go with you, Sister. I will sit with them and the other families. We will sing and pray."

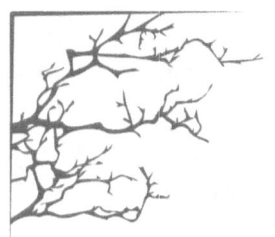

Chapter Ten

The sub-commander and some of his soldiers stormed into our encampment when Sun was past the midpoint in the azure sky and heading for his night-time sleep. All day we had been expecting them. We had heard a distant commotion coming from the Chamuqwani settlement, but until then we had seen only the soldiers ordered to guard us.

People were nervous, keeping a close eye on the guards while going about daily chores and caring for small children. No one talked much. They had been warned about the trouble in the miners' settlement and the expected visit from the soldiers.

We were sitting around our cook fires preparing or eating a late morning meal, and merely looked up with resigned expressions at their arrival. Grandfather, Elder Chittola and Sheikai rose and stepped forward to meet them.

Sub-Commander Hillberk, the interpreter Ahaz, two of his senior men and the sergeant in charge of our guards marched in and stopped in front of our Elders. The rest of the men they brought with them into our camp were already fanning out to search our shelters for men, weapons, or other plunder, tossing our meager possessions and the food we had left into the dirt like last time. Little ones cried and mothers enveloped them in their blankets to hold them close and try to sooth them.

His face nearly as red as a salati berry the sub-commander shouted at the Elders in front of him, "Where are they—I want them—NOW!"

Ahaz didn't need to translate, we all knew what he was shouting about, before he finished, but no one knew where the outlaws were at the moment. And I prayed that Tli and the others had had the good sense to disappear into the desert's badlands—at least for a little while.

"Sub-Commander," Chittola began, "as we've told you before we don't know where the outlaws you are searching for are hiding."

Without warning the angry sub-commander stepped forward and smashed his fist into the Elder's face. "Don't lie to me, you zaunk Bastard. There are eight men dead in the settlement down there," he gestured with his other hand down the creek towards the new miners' encampment. I want those who are responsible, and I want them NOW!"

I remained sitting by the main fire with my bowl in my lap and my head down. I tried to finish my meal, but my hands were shaking so bad I couldn't lift my spoon to my lips. I felt eyes upon me and I dared not look up. I knew it was Ahaz and he was searching for, me—the witch.

I guessed he knew I wasn't with Golannah and the warriors sent to retrieve the promised weapons, and after Lennard's unnatural death last night I was sure he knew I was somewhere near. I doubted the Chamuqwani commander would believe him if he accused me of being a malicer, though if there were any soldiers here that had been at Black Rock, they might. Whatever his personal reason was, I was sure he wanted me found—and killed, maybe.

Returning my attention to the soldiers, I felt Grandfather exert his Qwakaiva to try and calm down the angry men, and as he did so I heard him saying, "Sub-Commander, please no hurt we are only women, old people, and children. We no kill Chamuqwani miners."

Sheikai pointed with his chin to the sergeant stepping over the wreckage his men had created to come and report. "Sergeant say same. No outlaws, no weapons, like we tell."

The sergeant saluted and told his commander in more detail what Sheikai had just told him. The Sub-Commander's face became even redder, barely able to control his mounting frustration. He said through gritted teeth, "If they aren't here, then mount up a patrol and search the surrounding hills until you find them, damn it, find them! That settlement down there is about to explode."

The sergeant saluted, and hurried off with most of the soldiers to carry out his commander's orders. He had barely left, and the sub-commander and his aides were leaving when another soldier raced up the creek trail towards us. Halting in a cloud of dust he flung himself off his horse and hurried over to the sub-commander and saluted. "What is it, Soldier?" Hillberk snapped.

"There's a mob of settlers comin' this way. They are liquored up pretty good. Been drinkin' since before the funeral you ordered me and Patrolman Jonus to attend. They say they're gonna find and kill those outlaw bastards. And, if you can't do your job, then they'll do it for ya.

"They say they'll do what's necessary—even killin' some of the cloochas and brats if that's what it takes to get the truth out of the rest of the damn zaunks."

Sub-Commander Hillberk swore, using a lot of Chamuqwani bad words I'd never heard before. "I'll be damned if I'm gonna let a bunch of drunken filthy miners tell me what to do. I'll find the men responsible for the murdered men—all the murdered men—and punish them as the law says. I don't need any help from a bunch of drunken, ignorant assholes."

He was trying to act hard to convince his men he knew what he was doing, but I doubted they believed him. He didn't fool me or the others with a Gift among my people. We could see the fear and indecision twisting in his Spirit Flame, in spite of his harsh words.

The young sub-commander was still issuing orders to his aides when the first of the shouting miners came staggering into view on the creek trail. Someone must have seen the soldiers still lingering by our fires and told the others. A shout rang out and they surged forward, brandishing thunder weapons and clubs and shovels. The sub-commander's face paled, but he stood his ground the other senior men coming up to flank him. "Halt!" he shouted. "Go back to your camp. You men have no business here. We have the situation under control. I have my orders to find the murderers."

"Your orders? That's a joke. If it's your 'orders', Rich Lord's Pampered Son, then you're doin' a piss-poor job of it," a dirty miner with a floppy hat and a tangled mass of brown hair on his face roared. We want the filthy zaunk bastards that killed the traders and the other men in our settlement. "

"Well they're not here" the sub-commander yelled right back, and placed a hand on the butt of his weapon. "My men have already checked. There are no outlaws here.

"Then make one of the cloochas tell you where to find them," someone shouted from the back of the mob. "Slap'em around a bit and they'll talk!"

"Yeah, especially one of the pretty young ones." There was a chorus of agreement with that suggestion and the crowd surged forward.

The sub-commander and his aides drew their weapons and stood their ground. "HALT!" he roared. "Get out of here and sober up. I've already sent out a patrol to find the murdering outlaw scum that attacked the settlement. Now go.

"Find the murdering outlaw scum?" someone yelled. "You lot couldn't find your way out of a privy shack at noon."

"I said, we will take care of this."

"Take care, my ass," a miner shouted. "Like you soldiers did at Black Rock when you let that Golannah outlaw and his warriors escape?"

"I know nothing about that incident; I wasn't there at the time."

The gray bearded leader snorted. "Don't know, or don't want to know, 'cause like the trader killed last night those deaths at the Bahas River Ford were unnatural—I don't care what the priests and Commander Rossman are saying—even your own zaunk scout says so."

"Why one of them could be usin' some devilish heathen witchery and the outlaws could be right here under your nose and you'd never know."

Sub-Commander Hillberk whirled and glared at Ahaz. The scout dropped his eyes and cringed. "You, Scout Ahaz are on report," I will deal with you later," Hillberk snarled under his breath. Returning his attention to the angry men in front of him he repeated, "Go back to your settlement and let us handle this. Don't be more stupid than you already are."

"Stupid are we?" a miner yelled and drew his thunder weapon and pointed it at Grandfather's chest. "I say it's you, ya high-born, ignorant whelp that is the one who is stupid. I was tradin' at the Willow Creek Agency when that zaunk right there was supposed to hang, until more of his outlaw kin broke him out o' the agency jail. So don't talk to me about handling this. You can't even find an outlaw when he's right there under your nose."

"Why he's probably the one who witched and killed those traders," another man cried.

"Please," Sheikai said in his best Chamuqwani, "We good zaunks. No hurt, no kill. We only want dance and pray."

"Pray, ya heathen bastard, and what'cha prayin' bout, uh? You singin' to make us all disappear?"

"Ain't gonna' happen, zaunk," another miner shouted.

"Yeah, the ones gonna disappear is you," someone else growled.

By that time my whole body was trembling like an aspen leaf in the wind. The visions of my foretelling hovered at the edge of my awareness, demanding my attention.

The mood of the crowd had worsened the longer the sub-commander showed his weakness by arguing with them. They wanted violence—blood, and I feared they weren't going to be satisfied with just talk.

The hatred and anger swirling about us at that moment clogged my nose and thrust its dirty, icy fingers down my throat, leaving a foul metallic taste in my mouth. I could hardly breathe I was so frightened, for Grandfather, for Amima and the baby, for all of us.

"You give us that one," their leader shouted and pointed his weapon at Grandfather again. "We'll make him tell where the rest of the outlaw scum went, before we hang him for the filthy heathen malicer he surely is."

"Me no bad malicer, no kill anybody," Grandfather said, standing tall and speaking out for himself. "Warriors no here, don't know where go."

"I told you men to leave, before I have to shoot some of you myself," the sub-commander roared, but by then nobody was listening to him.

The potential for violence sparked in the air like lightning before a rain storm. Where was Amima? There huddled with Sagila, Ashiqwa, Xyilaha and some of the children near the edge of camp by the junipers. Conjuring a simple charm not to be noticed, I put down my bowl and slid slowly backward away from the fire toward them. I was nearly to them when my world disintegrated into chaos.

"Lying zaunk Bastard," someone shouted and then a thunder weapon boomed. I turned just in time to see Death's Raven land on Grandfather's shoulder and his chest explode in a red flower—like in my vision. There was another boom and Sheikai, too fell to the ground covered in blood. I heard the sub-commander yell an order, but his words were drowned out by another volley of weapon fire.

Someone screamed, maybe me—maybe Amima—maybe someone else, I didn't know. But what I did know was that I had to try and get my mother, the babies, family and friends away from there!

From what I pieced together later when I lay grieving in the dark of a jail cell, the soldiers that Sub-Commander Hillberk had sent to search up the slopes heard the shots and must have thought that the outlaws had crept around to attack them from below. From their position they heard the weapons' fire and answered with their own thunder weapons, firing down into our camp killing the innocent, as well as their own friends and drunken miners.

Meanwhile the miners assumed that the shots coming from up the slope were fired by outlaws and began returning fire. And, since they could barely see who was up there or where the shots were coming from they fired their weapons at anything that moved. Women, children, soldiers, the sick and old, it didn't matter. This was their chance to take revenge on an enemy beyond their understanding.

Caught in the middle between two groups of angry men we had no place safe to hide. Everyone panicked, running and screaming, children blown apart by powerful weapons. Miners coated in blood dragging struggling women into the brush to fuck and kill.

Pulling off Xyilaha's dress I mumbled a protection prayer and raced to the women in my family, urging them up the slope and into the cover of the trees, while I lagged behind to hastily conjure what protection I could offer with my illusions. As we reached the cover of the junipers Matoqwa, Cohasi, and Samiqwas appeared, carrying thunder weapons. They fell in behind us to cover our passing in case we were followed.

Already hiding within the trees Betsiya and a few of the younger girls and boys found us. Bloody and disheveled the younger ones hovered close to Betsiya their eyes wide with fear. She spoke to them gently, urging them to be strong, and that she was proud of them as the group of us made our way further into the brush.

Tuumaz found us, too; he had managed to take a weapon from an enemy. And as we approached a barren rocky place where the junipers couldn't grow he and Matoqwa crawled forward on their bellies to peer through the sagebrush at the open ground ahead.

Behind us, down the slope we could still hear more weapons firing, women screaming and men cursing and yelling. I wasn't sure, but it sounded like some of the weapons being fired were coming nearer.

After what seemed like a very long time our scouts crept back to where the rest of us lay flat under the sheltering junipers. Samiqwas and Cohasi moved away to watch our back trail while Ashiqwa and I crawled closer to speak to Tuumaz and Matoqwa.

"We can't stay here," Ashiqwa said. "I think the Chamuqwani are coming up behind us. What did you see? Can we make it safely across that barren rocky ground, before the enemy catches up to us?"

"Maybe. I saw no soldiers on the ridge above," Matoqwa said. "But they could be hiding up there, waiting... Tas, can you find a bird to help you check on where they are?"

Before I could answer, Tuumaz said, "What we need are horses."

Yes, I thought, trust a Kukiya to think of horses first. But he was right with horses we could escape into the desert and hopefully find the warriors, before we could be captured again.

Then I remembered, "When I flew with Owl I saw a deep run-off gulley near the edge of the junipers a little further to the south. It flows down to meet Creek on the other side of the soldiers' camp. In the spring it would be full of snow melt, but if there is water there at all this time of year it will be easily crossed. The gulley is away from the fighting—and close to where the soldiers were keeping the horses last time I looked."

"If we could reach it we could hide in the brush and cacti and no one climbing the ridge would be able to see us. Then after dark we could make a try for horses," Matoqwa suggested.

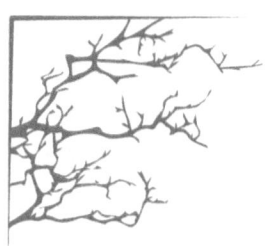

Chapter Eleven

It took us a while with the little ones, but we finally crept into the brush along the creek bank and headed into the steep-sided wash to wait for darkness. Both Kitahtla and Uncle's boy Binahgwinn, the youngest among us, were terrified, wanting to cry and fuss, sensing, no doubt, their elders' fear and upset. To keep them quiet, so they wouldn't give us away I used my Gift and put them to sleep. The older children stayed close to Betsiya, and she managed to keep them from giving in to their fear.

"You must be like Rabbit and Little Mouse, hiding in the brush and being very, very quiet, so that hawk and Eagle can't find and eat you," she whispered to them as they huddled next to her.

For the rest of that terrible afternoon thunder weapons boomed sporadically up on the ridge behind us, but not like when we first ran. Men shouted and swore, women cried and pleaded, and the soldiers barked orders from the direction of our shelters. With only our ears to guide us it was difficult to know exactly what was going on and if it was safe to either go back to the soldiers' camp and hope they would protect us from the crazy miners, or if we should stick to our original plan, steel back our horses and run for the desert.

Still undecided, as the evening shadows lengthened in the wash Tuumaz, Xyilaha, Matoqwa and Samiqwas left our hiding place, heading for the grassy spot down from the soldiers' camp where our horses were being kept. I had found a friendly owl to search the land around us for soldiers or other enemies. I discovered another small group of people hiding like us, but no soldiers or miners seemed to be near. I told the warriors that when I returned to my body, before they crept back into the brush.

It took our warriors most of the night, but in the grayness before dawn we heard the clop, clop of several horses hooves coming up the wash towards us. Someone barked like a fox and I answered with the cry of a hunting owl.

Soon after that Tuumaz and Xyilaha appeared on the trail below us leading four horses and Samiqwas and Matoqwa followed with a few more.

When they came near Cohasi and I stepped out of the brush to meet them. "There aren't enough for everyone to ride, even doubling up," Samiqwas said, echoing what I could see with my own eyes.

"There weren't many horses left in the clearing, and those were guarded. We had to wait till the stupid guards fell asleep, before we could even get these few. Most of the soldiers are out hunting outlaws, and the women and children who survived the fight earlier today."

"And what do they plan to do with us if they find us?" Ashiqwa asked as she came over to us.

Tuumaz shrugged. "Take back to Preserve I guess."

Samiqwas snorted. "I'd rather take my chances in the desert." There was a chorus of agreement to that idea.

Now that the children were asleep, Betsiya, Sagila and Mother came over to join us as we talked by the grazing horses.

"I will stay here with the little ones, maybe find the others you told us about, Tas, and go back to the soldiers' camp when I think it will be safe for us," Betsiya said after surveying the few horses the young warriors had managed to find.

"Sister, is that wise?" Ashiqwa asked. "What if they kill you, or—"

"I will have to take that chance," Betsiya said interrupting. "Without food blankets and shelter the children won't survive at all out in the desert. And besides we would only slow you down. You will have a better chance without us."

"Maybe I should stay, too; I'm not a very good rider," Mother said into the silence that followed her pronouncement.

"Amima, no!" I gasped. "You can't do that."

"Your son is right, Sister, "Ashiqwa said. "You're too young, too pretty. You, and Sagila need to go with the young warriors."

"You need to go as well, Ashiqwa, back on the Preserve that convert bastard who beat you might try to claim that you are still his woman. And, besides Talulsit is out there somewhere," Betsiya argued.

Looking around at the lightening sky Tuumaz urged, "We have to go. Be day soon and soldiers will find us here."

When the young warriors took the horses from the soldiers they hadn't been able to bring saddles or bridles. Riding bareback with only a piece of rope around the pony's nose would do for the warriors, and I could manage if I used my Gift, but Amima was going to have a difficult time of it. She glanced at the horses and frowned with dismay. Ashiqwa came over atop one pony and leading another. If you will feel better I can lead your pony."

Mother considered, then nodded. "That would be good, at least until I get used to riding like that."

Sagila had already chosen a fine brown mare and mounted with ease, taking the rope Xyilaha handed her, and then reaching for Binahgwinn placing him to sit by the pony's neck in front of her.

Then with Kitahtla's cradleboard in her arms Amima approached and held the baby up to her. "Sister, will you take her, as well? You are the better rider; I think she will be safer with you if we have to run."

Sagila studied Mother for a long moment as if she knew the deeper meaning of what Mother was asking. At last she reached down for the cradle board and put it on her back. "I will keep her safe for you until you come for her, My Husband's Sister. She be like my own daughter."

"Thank you. That does ease my mind."

"Amima, I can lead your pony," I offered.

Mother smiled, but shook her head. "You will be needed to help defend us should the soldiers discover us. Ashiqwa and I will be fine. And with that last soon to be broken promise, she mounted her pony with my help and we followed Tuumaz up the wash.

We urged our horses up the gulley until it became too clogged with fallen rocks and debris for the horses to manage, then we found an animal trail and climbed up the rest of the slope. All was quiet around us. We had reached the next ridge top, and had traveled most of the way down, thinking ourselves safe, when the soldiers found us.

Led by the experienced gray-haired sergeant whose scouts must have seen us coming down the trail, they charged out of a side ravine as we reached the flat ground. They drew their weapons and demanded that we stop. Someone, I never knew who, fired their thunder weapon. Xyilaha's horse reared, she gripped his belly tighter, snapped the end of the rope against its flank, and the pony then took off running with her bent low over its neck.

I saw Tuumaz raise and fire his own weapon in the soldier's direction, then took off after Xyilaha, with the rest of us following close behind. I could hear the babies crying somewhere ahead of me in the growing dust cloud, but there was no time to stop and sooth them.

I was near the rear of our little band; I'd planned to use my Puwa and call Wind to wipe out our back trail once we were down the ridge, but the soldiers found us before I had the chance. The Chamuqwani chasing us were firing their weapons, so to encourage them to keep back, those of us who were the best riders, shot their weapons in return.

Then suddenly Uncle Tli and the outlaws appeared out of nowhere, returning the soldiers' fire and urging us to hurry. As best I could tell in the haze, Samiqwas and Xyilaha were keeping pace with Tuumaz, trying to shield and protect Sagila and the babies. Matoqwa and Cohasi flanked me, firing their weapons behind us until they ran out of iron missiles. Just ahead of me, Ashiqwa and Amima were struggling to keep up, but their horses weren't up to the race and were falling behind.

"Give me Amima's lead rope," I shouted to Ashiqwa as I urged my stubborn pony closer to hers. She reached out to me, but at the last moment, her pony shied. I saw blood trickling down its flank as the wounded beast leapt away from me. Saying several bad Chamuqwani words under my breath I urged my horse closer to Mother's.

I could see her frightened eyes grow wide as she clung to her mount, her hands clutching its main, the lead rope far out of reach dragging in the dirt between the pony's front hooves. My plan was to call upon my Qwakaiva to help me abandon my own pony and safely climb onto hers, a feat well beyond my skill without spirit help. Then we would escape with us both atop her pony.

Sadly the Evil conjured against us had other plans. I had dropped back to come alongside her, when she gave a startled cry, threw up her hands and fell backwards off the horse, a crimson stain suddenly covering her back.

Feeling my world torn apart once again, I yelled and leapt for her, but it was too late. And then my own horse shrieked and fell. I managed to roll off it just before my leg would have been broken and trapped under its dying weight. I must have hit my head a stunning blow as I landed. When I woke sometime later I felt dizzy and my body ached all over. It took me another moment to remember, and then I frantically looked around searching for her.

She was lying in a crumpled heap not far from me. Unable to stand I crawled over to her and pulled her into my arms as best I could. Forgetting my own physical pain I pushed her hair out of her eyes and pressed my forehead against hers, the tears flowing uncontrollably down my cheeks. My sweet, beautiful mother, so brave, so kind, was gone to the Beyond.

At that moment I cursed my service to Kunai, and my pledge to work for the protection of my own and other worlds. I wished the soldiers would find and kill me, too. I didn't care what happened to me. Amima was dead, Grandfather and probably Nachoga, too. I didn't want to live in a world without them.

Seeing her ghost hovering, I cried even harder. <<Oh, Amima, I'm so sorry. I didn't protect you like I promised him.>>

She came closer and I felt her cool lips kiss my forehead. <<I love you, my little Rock Squirrel. Don't blame yourself; you did your best. I go to wait for him with my sister-wife. Take care of Kitahtla as best you can, my dear one.>>

I might have stayed there with her cooling corpse in my arms until Death's Raven found me too, but that was not to be. While I lay there grieving the soldiers had ridden up and surrounded me. Jerking me roughly to my feet. Still covered in my mother's blood, they grabbed my hands and tied them together and tossed me onto a horse.

"This little bucki don't have no weapons," one of his men told the sergeant.

He grunted and pointed to Mother's corpse. "What 'bout that one?"

"Just a cloocha and she's dead—no weapons either," the man answered. He motioned with his chin. "Not like those two."

Through my haze of grief I noticed for the first time the two other bound riders among the soldiers. Cohasi and Matoqwa beaten and bloody were also tied atop horses being led by other soldiers.

As we were about to leave more soldiers rode up and I learned that the rest of my relatives had escaped. I wished them well, but my heart also felt like it was going to fall out of my chest onto the ground. I knew with the certainty of another foretelling that I would never see my beautiful baby sister again in her lifetime. I wished her well and prayed that Cougar would keep her safe for many, many years to come.

I don't remember much about our ride back to Black Rock Fort and then eastward to a Chamuqwani settlement where Train visited. Broken inside and selfishly lost in my own grief, I did what I was ordered to do by my guards. I refused to speak and only ate the little Matoqwa made me swallow with his threats.

"I'm not going to let you kill yourself, you stubborn Siyatli boy," he growled one evening, his battered face twisted into a fearsome mask when I just stared at the bowl of slops thrust into my hand by an indifferent guard.

"Us Big Ice Lake boys gotta stick together, remember? You gotta eat, Tas," Cohasi coaxed, and I'd never heard him speak to me with such gentleness in his voice before.

I raised my head and glared. I wasn't ready to give in yet. "Why should I eat? They're only taking us to a bigger Chamuqwani settlement so more people can watch us hang."

"Shut up, dog turd, you don't know that for sure—do you?" he said.

Well, no, I didn't know that. I just felt like dying and wanted the Chamuqwani to save me the trouble of doing it myself.

Matoqwa growled a curse and punched me. "Stop feeling sorry for yourself, and think about the rest of us for a moment, Siyatli dog turd. We need you if we are ever gonna escape out of here."

Escape? Suddenly more aware of my surroundings I looked around. In his gruff way Matoqwa was right. I was being a selfish dog turd. In the dim and stinking jail where we'd been locked up after several dusty days of travel, there were more Kukiya and Qwani'Ya warriors and boys here besides me and my two friends.

Picking up my spoon I took a bite of the burnt mush and forced myself to swallow.

After Matoqwa's gruff chastisement I started paying more attention to my surroundings. I learned that we had been brought to one of the Chamuqwani bigger settlements east of the Tribal Preserve. Some of the warriors imprisoned with me had been captured by soldiers when they went raiding the ranchas to take back some of our stolen treaty beasts so they could feed their families.

Many of the warriors in the barred cells in the row had already had a "trial," and knew their fate, they were just waiting to be hanged. Others were being sent to a Chamuqwani prison even further away from our people, and they'd been told by the taunting guards that they would have to stay there for the rest of their lives.

One night after we had been confined in this jail for several days I asked an older warrior in the cell across from me that I knew by sight, but not by name, about Golannah and my father.

"Your uncle, Golannah, is dead," he told me.

My heart was saddened by the news. I knew tears were pooling in my eyes and was glad the dim light hid them. Golannah had always been kind to me and my family. With his death the Kukiya People had lost a great man. He had been the hope for a free and better future for all of us. "What happened; do you know, Uncle?"

The man shook his head and sighed. "Not sure, Nephew. Some say the Chamuqwani beat and tortured him, trying to make him tell where he got the yellow rocks he wanted to trade for thunder weapons."

"But he never told them," another warrior sitting nearby said. "His Puwa was strong. He died like a true leader of the People."

"And what about his brother, Nachoga, do you know what happened to him?" I asked the second man, who seemed to have heard more of the gossip than the first warrior.

The second man shrugged. "The Chamuqwani? Who knows; who cares. Probably betrayed the warband for a share of the gold."

Unable to control the rage bubbling up like a dragon's molten fire inside me, I rose, stepped to the bars of my cell, gripping them tight enough to turn my knuckles pale. Peering into the dimness of the other cell I glared murderously at the man. "Have a care what lies you spread about my father or you will regret it," I snarled.

Whatever the warrior saw when he looked at my face made him shrink back. Someone murmured to him who I was and that I was a powerful Puhani. He swallowed hard and stammered an apology.

Matoqwa grabbed me or I might have done the man some harm in spite of his apology. "Settled down, Siyatli dog fart, or you will have the soldiers coming in here to investigate," he growled.

He was right, and what had happened to my boasts that I would never use my gift for personal vengeance? I sat back down and covered my head with the raggedy blanket I'd been given, feeling both angry and ashamed. What was happening to me? I was out of harmony with the world; my grieving had unbalanced the Qwakaiva of my Spirit. I needed to remember my Elders' teachings and get myself under control.

Sometime after the evening meal when all was quiet and dark I heard some of the men who had been here the longest talking when they thought me and most of the new arrivals were asleep.

"Is that young northerner truly the Puhani that Ahaz was looking for? He doesn't look like much—too young."

"The Unseen Ones give power to whoever they wish—no matter their age. Surely you know this." Another voice in the darkness said.

"Yes, I know, but why was that dog turd Ahaz looking for him so hard anyway? None of the Chamuqwani would believe him if he claimed the boy was the witch that killed all those soldiers at the ford."

"I heard he was looking so hard for the malicer, because another Puhani told him that if he didn't find and kill the witch he was going to die."

"Hmm, and where is that traitor of a zaunk now?" someone asked.

"Dead. Somebody shot him when those crazy Chamuqwani miners and the stupid soldiers killed all those women and children when they were chasing outlaws."

Someone laughed. "Then what the Puhani told him was true, eh?"

"Well, watch what you say around the one in here with us, or you might not wake up some morning."

"I will be careful, but he will die with the rest of us, no doubt. The Chamuqwani's Puwa is stronger than any Puwa he might have."

That warrior might be right, but if I could, I would save as many of the others as possible before I let Death claim me, I thought and closed my ears to the rest of their talk.

Later that night I tried once more to contact Nachoga. I sensed that he was somewhere to the east of me, but I learned little else. When I tried an enraged Cougar chased even me away. As I drifted sad and alone at the border of the Dream I felt the crystal being I wore around my neck awaken and speak to me.

<<Have no fear, Siyatli Boy the Cougar will keep his promise to you. You will see him again.>>

Hope flared like a bright light in my soul.<<When, Honored Spirit? Will I be able to save him—will we be able to escape?>>

<<You will see him as he promised; when it is time. Now pay attention,>> It admonished. <<Tomorrow they will come for you and the others. There is help being sent to you, but you must not let the Evil Ones who threaten your world find and take me when they search you. If they find me, not only you, and your people, but because I am also linked to his power even the Great Kunai himself may be in danger.

Its words sent an icy spear of fear into my heart. <<Honored Spirit, I am confined by the Chamuqwani in their jail. What can I do to prevent this? Should I dig a hole by the brick wall and hide you there?>>

<<No! The Evil One's agents will sense my Qwakaiva and come for me after the soldiers take you away. You must not leave me here, or anywhere else.>>

<<Then what do you want me to do?>>

<<You must swallow me and the shell your Seal father gave you; keep us safe inside your body, Siyatli boy. That is the only way,>> the crystal being said.

Swallow the crystal? It was nearly as large as a hawk's egg and the points on both ends were sharp enough to draw blood when I needed a blood gift. <<Spirit, my human body isn't designed to carry such a being as you inside my flesh,>> I protested. <<Surely there is another way.>>

The Crystal Being's radiance flared with its impatience. <<Take me out of the pouch around your neck and you will see. You must learn to curb your rebellious nature and trust in the Qwakaiva gifted you by your great Benefactor, young one. Do as I instruct you.>>

So I did. To my surprise when I emptied the contents of the pouch onto my hand the crystal and shell that fell out onto my palm were the size of juniper berries. Before anyone around me could take an interest in what I was doing I brought my hand to my mouth and swallowed them.

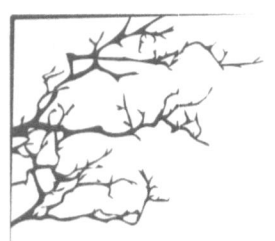

Chapter Twelve

At dawn the crystal being inside me warned me of their coming. Sitting up I spoke to the others in my cell in a low urgent murmur, "Get up and get ready. The soldiers will come for us soon."

I heard several groans, but no one questioned my prediction. We had all used the bucket in the corner and were sitting with our blankets folded over our shoulders when several burley men came in and opened our cell door. "Get up you dirty zaunks, today's the day you're gonna get what's comin' ta' ya." A man with a patch over one eye growled, and motioned us out the open door.

As we emerged another of the soldiers did search us as Crystal predicted, and took away my pouch, then like the rest he bound my wrists with iron bands, and connected us together with a long chain. Outside we were escorted to a large wagon through a crowd of curious Chamuqwani who shouted bad words at us and through garbage, in spite of our guards' half-hearted attempts to keep them away.

Matoqwa and another Kukiya youth named, Chatoka, as the tallest among us were the ones the onlookers picked on the most. Ignoring the jeers and thrown awful as best we could, we made our slow way across the open space. Then the chain linking us together was removed and soldiers with weapons drawn ordered us into the wagon. The ride was a short one, only through the dusty streets of the settlement to the place Train visited.

Train was already there waiting, puffing dirty black smoke, impatient to be on its way. There, too, a crowd was waiting to yell abuse at us. On the platform we were hustled into a closed cart on Train and locked in to find our own places on dirty straw that stank of animal dung. No one came to offer us even water or check on us for the rest of the trip.

Hungry and thirsty I tried to sleep as best I could, but it was hard. Fear and worry stalked me like hunting wolves. Did they really plan to hang us like the warriors in the next cell had claimed? I feared it might be true and in spite of Crystal nesting inside me, I found myself helpless to prevent it, if that was to be my fate.

And to be honest, I didn't care. I had been through so much, my homeland, my family, all that I valued seemed lost to me right then, and my sleep was tormented with images of bloody women's bodies and dead children missing limbs and faces. I craved the oblivion I hoped Death would grant me when it came at last.

Train climbed through hills and twisted and turned on its iron road and the stench of its smoke choked my nostrils when Wind blew it back on us. It also stopped and started up again several times during that trip. I could hear people talking and laughing as they entered and left other carts Train pulled when we stopped. The good smells of fried food being sold to the Chamuqwani riding Train was an added torment at such times.

As we traveled ever eastward the scent of the land outside my dark, rumbling prison changed. I could smell water as we crossed a big river and the green smells of unfamiliar plants and trees assaulted my nose as we left the dry land behind.

It was dark when we reached our final stop, and were herded, stumbling out of the stinking cart with thunder weapons pointed at us and new Chamuqwani soldiers shouting at us to form a line. The chains were return to fasten us together, and then we were ordered to march to a large stone house with no windows on its sides.

The roads in this place were all illuminated with bright lanterns on poles here and there. We could see what was around us almost as well as if it were day. Though Sun had gone to his bed some time before many women and men of different skin colors, but wearing similar clothing, were still awake and walking around.

When these Chamuqwani saw soldiers marching a line of dirty zaunks down their clean road many stopped to stare, but only a few of the onlookers shouted abuse and no one threw things. Mostly they were just curious when they noticed us, but otherwise seemed happy and relaxed, going in and out of stores and places that we could tell by the good smells served food. My stomach rumbled with its emptiness. I tried to ignore it. These people were indifferent to our suffering. I wouldn't give them the satisfaction of showing any weakness.

Chained between the two brothers, when we were nearly to the big jail I heard Cohasi ask his brother, "Is this place the same big town we came through when the soldiers took us to the Preserve? I think I remember that big temple over there." He pointed with his lips to a massive building with the fearsome stone monsters still perched on its roof.

Matoqwa looked and grunted. "Maybe. But back then I was more interested in the sweet dried fruit the priests were giving us to pay much attention to carved stone."

Cohasi snorted. "I wish we had some of that sweet fruit right now," he said wistfully, "and some tea to wash it down." Matoqwa grunted his agreement.

Tea, how I wished for tea, or even the dirty water of the big river we had just crossed before stopping here. I agreed with them, and would have said so, but my throat was too dry to talk.

Then I made the mistake of glancing in the temple's direction and nearly stumbled to my knees. A knot of fear twisted in my gut, taking my breath away. Yes... it was the same temple where on our journey to the Preserve, those monsters had studied me with fierce cold eyes and warned me that I one day was going to pay for the evil I had done to one of their holy men.

<<Soon,>> they promised when I stared too long at their grotesque faces. <<This time you will not escape our vengeance, Heathen Witch.>>

I gasped, suddenly dizzy and would have truly fallen if a sharp tug on the chain hadn't saved me. Jerking me upright, Matoqwa muttered, what's a matter with you, dog turd, watch where you put your feet."

"Hey, no talking, you stupid zaunks!" a red-faced soldier shouted and back-handed Matoqwa to make his point. "Keep moving."

Matoqwa spat out a mouthful of blood and did what the soldier commanded, but he cursed him and his whole family under his breath when the guard's back was turned.

When the man was called to speak to another soldier with a lightning bolt and stars on his badge I murmured my apology to Matoqwa.

"Oh shut up, stupid Siyatli," he replied.

In the morning we were given tea and fed then more buckets of water were handed in and we were told to wash and make ourselves look presentable for the Chamuqwani chiefs that were coming to watch our trial and the hangings. Trial, no one had bothered to explain to us what that Chamuqwani word meant. But, whatever "trial" was, it was happening today.

At that point I was indifferent to what the Chamuqwani had planned for us. I just wished it would be over. Now that Rattlesnake had abandoned me I was feeling guilty that my power hadn't been capable of freeing us, and I was terrified of the punishment Djoven's creatures had been taunting me with all night. I was also still grieving the loss of my home, my way of life and nearly everyone I loved.

Still in our bloody and stained clothing we were chained and marched out of the big jail and into the sunlight. Like before there was a crowd waiting to see us. Men in dark clothing with pale faces and light eyes, a few of them also had the little black boxes like Willum carried at Black Rock Fort. I wondered if these men would also put me in a book, like Willum wanted to do.

We were marched slowly down a wide street with the crowd following, shouting questions at our guards all the way. At another big house with wide stone steps leading up to massive wooden doors flung wide to swallow us up like the gaping jaws of a giant creature born in the darkness, we were told to climb the stairs and enter.

<<We are coming for you, Evil, Heathen Witch,>> Djoven's creatures had spotted me as we passed their temple and now their voices were once more yammering inside my head.

<<Your power and your life belong to us, we will feast on your flesh and drink up all your power for our master, soon, soon,>> they taunted.

<<You can have this body, if you want, foul monsters, but I will never give you, or your god my Qwakaiva, never!>> They only laughed and continued to taunt me with their threats. I tried not to listen to them, but their insistent clamor was distracting in spite of my efforts to ignore them.

I was only half aware of being led down a long smooth-floored hallway that echoed with the clink of our chains and the soldiers' heavy boots. We entered a long room with wooden benches placed in rows and a high platform at its front. Our guards ordered us to sit on a long wooden bench by the wall then the guards left us, still chained and wandered off to talk and joke with other soldiers wearing similar uniforms in the room.

A while later a commotion started by the door by which we had entered, but I paid the shouting men over there little attention, still engrossed with my inner battle with Djoven's demons.

Then I heard someone call my name. "Tas? Is that really you?"

At first I didn't look up, thinking what I'd heard was only another demon sent to annoy me. "Tas, I did what you asked; I found the intercessor for you, remember, you wanted me to do that for you. Tas?"

When I still didn't raise my head, he pleaded in the coaxing voice someone might use when speaking to a hurt child, "Please look at me, Tas. You know, I still have my string and have been practicing my figures. Want to see?"

"Leave 'lone Chamuqwani dog turd!" Matoqwa snarled. "Him no want talk you!"

At Matoqwa's gruff words I suddenly realized the voice I heard wasn't in my mind. I jerked my head up and stared into Collin's concerned face. Yes, he was really there crouched before me, his brown hair tied back from his beardless face with the cord he'd used to make the string figures I'd taught him back at the fort.

I laid a hand on Matoqwa's leg and said in our language, "It's alright; I know this Chamuqwani." Then in the Chamuqwani language I hesitantly said, "Hello, Friend Collin."

What he saw on my face must have shocked him, because I saw unshed tears spring into his expressive eyes. "Oh, Tas, what have they done to you?"

His kindness made my own tears well up to clog my throat, making it hard to speak. "Soldiers kill mama, grandfather, father gone, baby sister—all gone now. When we run so no kill, soldiers chase." As best I could I waved my bound hands to include all the boys and young warriors sitting next to me. "Rattlesnake, she die, too. Me no can help People. Bad malicer cursed me."

"Sorry to hear about your helper, Rattlesnake." Then the importance of my words must have sunk in, because Collin gasped and his eyes grew wide. "Wait a moment, are you telling me that you and these other boys were there at the Gold Creek Massacre?"

I wasn't sure where gold creek was or what a massacre was, so I just repeated what I said before. "Soldiers and miners kill everybody."

"But the settlers and Sub-Commander Hillberk are saying they were attacked by outlaws and they had to defend themselves. They swore to the Court representatives and the press that you and these others had weapons and killed the women and children as well as the soldiers and settlers who died that day."

The others who had been listening and trying to follow our conversation as best they could, growled in protest. "Not true, Chamuqwani," Matoqwa spat. "Outlaws no kill. Soldiers and miners kill. Outlaws far away in desert when bad mans come and kill womans, babies and old sick people."

"But the soldiers claim they took weapons away from some of you when they captured you," Collin insisted.

"Soldiers lie. We no have weapons till take from dead mans. We only want protect womans and little ones from crazy mans," Cohasi angrily blurted, before his brother told him to shut up.

"Is this true?" Collin asked me.

"Yes. Is true, People berry picking then want go see Prophet with sick Elders. Then soldier come. They chase—kill."

Collin thought for a moment, glanced around then hesitantly asked, "Tas if I take your hand could we speak—mind-to-mind like we did in the Dream? I know Yon Bronworthy and the others who are here in protest of your treatment will want to hear about this in more detail than your knowledge of my language will allow."

His was an interesting idea, and one I'd never tried before, but maybe. With my crystal urging me to agree I had just said I would try, when the guards arguing with the other men by the door noticed Collin talking to us and shouted for him to get away from us. When he didn't move away fast enough the soldier headed in his direction a hand on his weapon.

"I said move away from the prisoners, before I arrest you and then you can join them in a cell, you stinking troublemaker."

Collin stood up and began walking towards the door. "Don't worry, Tas, it's going to be all right; don't give up hope."

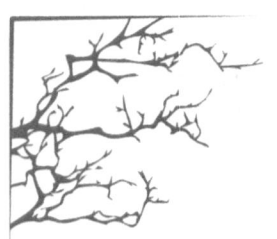

Chapter Thirteen

Not long after Collin left us to take a seat on a bench near the front of the room next to his friends, a fat Chamuqwani in a black robe with long curled white hair came in to the room from a door behind the tall platform and a soldier shouted for everyone to stand up.

We were ordered to rise with the rest of the people who had come in while Collin and I were talking. After the fat man took his seat on the platform the rest of us were told to sit down again.

Everyone was speaking in the Chamuqwani language, and no one was there to translate for us, so I paid little attention to what was happening after that. Other men in black robes rose and shouted at one another and occasionally the fat man on the platform pounded his table with a little hammer and told everybody to be quiet. Not understanding them I sank back into my own personal misery as the Thunderer's monsters continued to torment me with visions of the horrors they had planned for me.

At last it was over. Everyone rose and the fat man in the black robe left through his little door. People were talking to one another, and some, including Yon Bronworthy were trying to push their way through the people so they could talk to us. But our guards were having none of that. Ordering everyone to, "keep back" we were hustled out of the room through another door I hadn't noticed before.

The hallway we entered this time stank of stale vomit and unwashed bodies. A soldier guard opened a door into more cells. We were released from the chain and shoved into a dirty cell, and the door closed behind us. From the cells further down the row imprisoned Chamuqwani jeered and shouted at us.

Where was Collin? Could he really help us? Feeling discouraged I sat next to the brothers on a bench against the far wall. As soon as we were left alone, tall and thin as a pine sapling Chakota began to pace, like a caged animal, shouting curses right back at our tormenters. I could see his Spirit Wolf howling and snarling at another confinement.

Disheartened most of the rest just sank to the floor and stared at nothing. Some sang softly their Puwa songs, preparing themselves for the death that was surely to come.

"Tas, do you know what these Chamuqwani plan to do with us?" Cohasi finally gathered the courage to ask me.

I shook my head. "I've had no foretelling if that's what you are asking. I don't know any more than you do."

"Those men go to decide whether to hang us or just put us in a prison somewhere," a Kukiya youth named Inishkim said overhearing.

He had studied with a priest on the Preserve, before he had run away to join the outlaws, I remember him telling me. He spoke their language better than I did, so maybe he was right.

"And what do you think they will decide," Cohasi asked.

Inishkim shrugged. "Who can say, those crazy, unnatural people are capable of anything."

While waiting to hear our fate we were given dry bread and chunks of some kind of hard yellow stuff that smelled of sour milk. Most of the warriors didn't want to eat theirs and just soaked the hard bread in the water we were also given. I ate my share of the yellow stuff and a couple more pieces given to me by those who didn't want theirs. It tasted good, though later I got sick with cramps from eating such an unfamiliar food.

That afternoon after our meal the soldier guards came to bring us back to the big room to hear what the Chamuqwani had decided to do with us. On the way they taunted us with predictions of hanging , being burned alive and other terrible tortures, until a man in a black robe, who said he was our friend made them stop.

As we took our places again on the hard bench, this same man, and another wearing clothes like the settlers near the Preserve wore stood in front of us. To our surprise the settler spoke to us in a halting version of the Kukiya language. He said he had learned our language because he was married to a Kukiya woman. He would translate for the other man in the black robe standing beside him.

The black robed one was a short square man with a trimmed gray beard and the same long white hair as the other men. He had kind green eyes and told us, "My name is Attorney Ricosen. Your friend Lord Bronworthy has asked me to plead for you. I have one last time to speak and hopefully I can convince the court to take into consideration your youth and not to hang you.

When the fat black robed man came in and took his seat on the platform the talking began again. The man who was our translator stayed near us and Collin joined him when our guards were distracted. while Ricosen returned to his table near the platform.

<<If you call Collin closer we can link with him,>> my crystal said.

When I caught his eye, I motioned for Collin to come to me. He did, and crouched in front of me. "What is it, Tas?"

I reached to take his hand between my bound hands, but he pressed mine between his own instead. I felt a current of Puwa flow down my arm and into his covering hands. His eyes widened as he felt my power.

<<Give me the cord from your hair and then go back to your place next to Bronworthy, before they get angry and make you leave this room,>> I instructed. <<I will maintain our contact through the cord, so I can better understand what the black robes are saying about us.>>

He nodded, quickly untied his hair, pressed the cord into my hands and stepped away.

"What were you doing just now with that Chamuqwani," Matoqwa muttered in a voice no more than a whisper.

"He is translating mind-to-mind with me in case our translator doesn't speak true I will know now."

Matoqwa snorted. "What does that matter. You'll just know we're going to hang that much earlier."

I called him a dog fart then returned my attention to Collin.

Just before it was Ricosen's turn to speak a young man wearing the white shirt and black coat that seemed to be normal Chamuqwani clothing here entered the room. The young man walked to the table where he sat and whispered something to him. Ricosen looked surprised, then glanced back to the closing door and saw two priests enter and take seats in the backrow of benches. I didn't know the older of the two, but the other I knew all too well. It was Intercessor Raymonel.

When the black robed fat man called his name, Ricosen rose and walked to the open space in front of the platform. He cleared his throat and said, "Your Honor before I conclude my remarks in the defense of these young men I would like to call a member of the distinguished clergy forward to present to you his observations on the savages. He also may have a possible solution to our dilemma."

A black robe at another table near the front jumped up and objected. After some arguing back and forth, the fat man they called Judge banged his hammer and they fell silent.

Glaring at both men with his cold blue eyes, Judge said, "I understand your objections, Distinguished Prosecutor, but I don't like condemning men to death unnecessarily, especially as young as these defendants are. So, I will hear what the priest has to say in this matter."

Ricosen bowed then turned to face the room. "Intercessor Raymonel, would you please come forward to address the Court?" The Intercessor rose and slowly walked up the row of benches to stand beside Ricosen.

The Intercessor had changed since last I'd seen him. there was gray in his pale hair now at the temples. He was thinner than before with deep lines of pain and suffering carved into his face. But his blue eyes still burned with an inner fire that told me he was willing to fight for justice for any cause he believed was right.

Standing beside Ricosen he bowed to Judge, then began, "Your Honor, for many years my mission was among the northern tribes. I learned their language and lived among them, making many converts to our blessed faith. When their leaders signed the emperor's treaty and agreed to give up their northern lands, and move to the Tribal Preserve that our glorious monarch, in his wisdom set aside for them, I travelled with them, sharing the hardship of that terrible journey until sickness and injury forced me to remain in this fair city while my charges went on to their new homes."

Turning to face us he smiled then returned his attention to the man on the platform. "I recognize many of these boys from that trip. They were good boys, working hard to help their families with the difficult conditions through which we were forced to travel.

"Ah but once on the Preserve conditions for them were no better. They were cruelly treated by the agent this government appointed to care for them. And we wonder why they were led astray by evil men who want only to continue their futile war with the Empire?

"These boys and their families have been starved and cheated out of the goods they were promised to make a new and civilized life in their new home. And that is our sin!" he thundered.

"How can these young people and others like them learn to be peaceful and productive citizens of the Empire when those who were trusted to show them the error of their heathen ways have failed so miserably at the task entrusted to them?

"I have spoken to his Divine Holiness Prelate Minduel and he in turn has contacted the director of Saint Yon's Live-Away School at Barner's Crossing. The Divine tells me that Director Harriscot will gladly take these boys if the Court will have mercy and assign them into his care. He promises to keep them for six years, and instruct them in the skills they will need to live prosperous lives within the Empire, if the court is willing to indenture them to him."

What an irony, I thought as the men talked on. Intercessor Raymonel, the priest that Chumco had wanted killed when he directed me to place his malicer's bundle in the priest's bedding was now here to save me from hanging. In my mind the tormenting monsters called the intercessor a traitor and jabbered and wailed. But their cries were suddenly drowned out by Kunai's rumbling laughter.

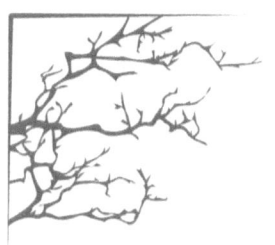

Chapter Fourteen

It took more time for the black robed men to argue with each other, but it was finally decided that the majority of us would be sent to the live-away school Intercessor Raymonel mentioned to Judge. So, I was being sent to the prison the Chamuqwani made for children after all. Chumco was right; six long, torturous years as my punishment, and Kunai wasn't going to save me. What a laugh, I thought, but there was no mirth in the knowing.

The interpreter told us that priests from the school would come to fetch us in a few days. Until then we would remain inside the jail, though our new friend Ricosen did get Judge to let us have visitors.

For Chakota and another Kukiya warrior named Wachata, who was small for his age, like me, but older than the rest of us, Judge's decision was different. They would hang along with several older warriors that were also being held somewhere in the big jail waiting their turn to be hanged.

Prosecutor had argued that those two Kukiya were known outlaws that had been seen by many soldiers after murdering two innocent women and a child living on a rancha near the Preserve.

Though Ricosen argued hard for them to go with the rest of us to the school Judge finally gave in to the Prosecutor's wishes and condemned the pair to hang.

When his fate was translated for him Chakota jumped to his feet and cursed Judge and all Chamuqwani with every bad word he knew. Several soldier guards rushed to him and he fought them like the wolf of his Spirit Fire, as they dragged him away. Wachata, the other one of my group going to die remained stony faced, showing no display of weakness.

I had listened to him singing his power songs back in the jail cell and I guessed he knew what was coming and had made peace with his death. He gave the guards no trouble as they escorted him from the room.

Ricosen had seen to it that the rest of us were put into a clean cell that had a small high window that offered us some light and fresh air. He also arranged for us to get better food than just water and dry bread, for which we were grateful.

That evening after our meal of fresh white bread and a stew with lots of meat floating in a rich brown liquid, Yon Bronworthy, Collin and the cloocha-man translator appeared outside our cell door.

With a bit of coaxing and an exchange of script-money our guard unlocked our cell and allowed the visitors to come in and sit with us for a while. Knowing that these were the men who had saved us from hanging everyone was polite, even dragging over a wooden bench for them to sit upon.

Bronworthy asked about the new food and other arrangements he'd made for our comfort, then he got down to the true reason for their visit. "The people whom I represent at the Emperor's Court would like to hear more about conditions on the Preserve and what happened at the Gold Creek Massacre. Would you be willing to talk to us about that if we come back tomorrow?"

There were nine of us left in this cell, five Kukiya youths, me, Matoqwa, his brother and a Qwani'Ya boy from down the Socanna River. The others all looked at me, as if I was suddenly their leader. I blinked, startled. Matoqwa and Cohasi never had allowed me to speak for them, or let me tell them to do anything. They often punched me if I tried.

When the silence dragged on uncomfortably long Inishkim murmured, "What should we do, Puhani?"

"Yeah, Siyatli dog fart, should we talk to these Chamuqwani?" Matoqwa growled.

I sighed and nodded. "You come back tomorrow, Friend Bronworthy, we tell," I said in my halting Chamuqwani.

Bronworthy had caught the Kukiya calling me, "Puhani." And he knew the meaning of that word. His eyes sparked with renewed interest as he focused on me as the group's appointed leader.

"I remember you from the treaty negotiations," he said to me. "How is my friend Golannah doing?"

Well that seemed to be another thing the soldiers were keeping a secret. "Golannah, him dead. Chamuqwani soldiers and miners catch..." I didn't know the Chamuqwani words for what I'd been told happened, so instead I sent pictures of the war chief being tortured into Collin's mine.

Collin gasped and Bronworthy whirled to stare at him. "Collin, what's wrong?"

Taking a shaky breath he said, "Tas tells me that our friend was tortured and murdered for the secret of a gold deposit he knew about."

Turning back to me, he frowned as he studied me more carefully. "Do you know who did that?"

I shrugged and shook my head. "Long time want war chief dead. Traders tell soldiers where to find. Catch—kill, but him no tell where gold."

Later when the guard returned and it was time to go, I called Collin over to me one last time. Handing him back his cord, I said into his mind, <<Collin, be careful who you and Bronworthy tell about me—especially any of Djoven's priests. Even Intercessor Raymonel might want to burn me for a witch if he knew what I can do.

<<Your friend lacks the Puwa to speak with me as we do, but you have told him about me. Though he finds it hard to accept who, and what I am, he is curious. I sense that he can also be too trusting of people who secretly do much evil. Please warn him not to talk about me—to anyone—or the Evil Ones will hear and come for me at the live-away school.>>

Collin nodded and patted my arm. "Don't worry, Tas, I'll warn him. Everything is going to be alright. You're going to learn so many new things while at the school. And when you're older you can come live with me, if you want.' He smiled at me hopefully. "Then you can teach me more string figures, eh?"

I smiled and nodded, just to please him, but he could still see the dread and fear in my eyes.

"Don't worry I also went to a live-away school myself when I was young. That's where Yon and I met and became friends. You will be fine once you get used to it, truly it will be good for you and your friends there."

He was being kind and trying to reassure me, but he was also lying. I could see it in his Spirit Fire. It had not been good for him at the live-away school he and Bronworthy attended—not good at all.

Next morning Collin and Bronworthy arrived with several important-looking Chamuqwani. There were too many to meet in our cell so the guards chained us and marched us to a big room with planks of wood on its walls and long pieces of dark cloth hanging from atop its glass windows.

Bronworthy and Intercessor Raymonel argued with the guards to remove our chains, but they refused, claiming they had orders. The Intercessor did at least convince them to remain outside the closed door while they talked to us.

Eight Chamuqwani of different skin tones sat in comfortable chairs facing the long bench on which the guards had ordered us to sit. Collin, Bronworthy, his cloocha-man interpreter, the Intercessor and the older priest I'd seen in the room where Judge visited, as well as two others: a dark-haired older man and a woman with yellow braids wrapped around her head, wearing a long blue dress were with him. Bronworthy introduced the newcomers, telling us they were "reporters" who were going to help him tell our story to the rest of the people in the Empire.

We stayed in that room, answering questions until just before Sun went to sleep. Twice during the day Chamuqwani servants with dark skins brought everyone kafa and small round cakes Collin called cookies. They were very sweet and good. At midday we were marched back to our cell to eat and pee, then we were returned for more questioning throughout the long afternoon.

In the morning the people wanted to know about the conditions on the Preserve after our arrival. We all told them about the lack of food, and missing treaty goods. We spoke about the sickness that killed so many and how warriors had been forced to raid the settlers' ranchas because their families were starving.

As we spoke I was able to send Collin images of the sick and starving people through our mind link. He began the day by writing what we said in his book, but as we told our stories in more detail and I fed him mind images to enhance our words, he put down his writing stick and just stared at the floor.

I knew I was being cruel to him, a man who had always been kind to me, but the crystal being inside me commanded that I keep going. <<If he truly wishes to join us, then he must accept all that the power demands. This is his time of testing. Continue.>>

In the afternoon when we returned to the room Bronworthy and the two reporters were more interested in what they called, the gold creek massacre. I suspected that might be coming, so I warned Cohasi and Matoqwa to be careful how they answered any questions about that night.

"If they know we were in the settlement they might change their minds about hanging us," I warned.

Matoqwa snorted a laugh. "You mean change their minds about hanging 'you,' Siyatli Boy. We didn't do anything but steal knives and mush." When he saw the expression on my face he laughed again.

"Don't worry, Tas. I'm not going to tell them about you, because you were right to kill those traders. I would have done the same thing if I'd had the chance.

"Yeah, like I told you before, dog turd," Cohasi said, "us Big Ice Lake boys gotta stick together."

I gave them a relieved smile, but the knot of worry in my gut still hadn't uncoiled completely. "Good. Then I won't have to make your ears grow as long as a snowshoe rabbit's, before they burn me." Matoqwa growled a curse and punched my arm.

The afternoon session was a difficult one for all of us because our emotional wounds after the massacre were still so raw and unhealed. Like the Chamuqwani this was the first time I had heard the Kukiya boys' story. It was similar to the others I already knew. It turned out that most of them had been hiding with some of the people Owl and I saw, just before Tuumaz led the raid for horses. They were captured when they stayed behind while the women and old people ran away from angry miners.

When it was my turn to tell of that time I nearly disgraced myself by breaking down like a baby. However, I did mind-share with the unfortunate Collin all the vivid details of Grandfather's, and Amima's deaths and later my capture. The reliving was as hard on me as it was for poor Collin linked with me. As crystal commanded I didn't spare him.

When I finished my throat was raw and I could barely speak. Collin experiencing the full-force of my visions and feelings was openly sobbing, and others in the room were wiping at their eyes, having unwillingly absorbed some of the Puwa of my sendings as well.

Feeling drained and empty I was glad when Intercessor Raymonel and Bronworthy rose, finally calling an end to the day's session. As someone went to tell the guards to come and get us, Collin came over to say good bye to me.

"Yon and I will be leaving in the morning on an early train. We have to get back and report our findings to our representative in parliament, but Attorney Ricosen will be around to make sure you boys are treated fairly till you leave for the school."

Still holding my hand he studied me carefully, his eyes moist with unshed tears. He swallowed several times before he could get the words he wanted to say to come out. "Oh, Tas, I'm so, so sorry for all those terrible things that some of my people did to you—and your family. I think you are the bravest and most honorable person I have ever met.

"I hope we meet again, and I will check on you from time to time at the school, if that's alright with you." Then he surprised me by bending over to hug me.

The guards had entered and were shouting for us to stand up. I took his hand one last time and said, <<I'm sorry, too, for what I did to you today, Collin. I know it wasn't easy for you experiencing our struggles like that, but Kunai demanded that I share with you those things.>>

"Kunai? That's your dragon friend, isn't it?"

<<Kunai isn't my friend; he is my Benefactor, and one source of my Power. Years ago I pledged my life and my Puwa to work with him for the good of all beings.

<<Since you told me you wanted to see a real dragon—>> I gave him a lopsided smile, <<maybe someday that might happen. Right now he is testing you to see if you are worthy of his regard, and your Puwa is strong enough to become a warrior against Evil like me and my Seal father.>>

He chuckled and dropped his eyes suddenly shy. "A Chamuqwani Puhani, eh? I feel honored that you think so well of me, I'm not sure I deserve it, but I will try to be worthy of your, uh, Benefactor's regard, and yours too."

<<You have already proven yourself by completing your first task when you found the priest for us.>>

Then as the premonition took hold of me I slipped off my special string, the one woven from my mother and Seal father's hair, crumpled it small and hastily placed it in Collin's hand, before the guard could see.

At his startled look, I explained, <<Priest's take away at school. I don't want them to have it. Keep this safe for me. It's made from my parents' hair. It has Puwa, great Puwa. I come back for it—someday.>> I gave him a mischievous smile. <<Maybe Kunai come and teach you magic with string, eh?>> His eyes grew wide at my mention of magic, but I didn't explain, only continued to smile.

At last he closed his hand around the precious item then put it in his pocket. "Yes, I will keep it safe for you, always," he promised.

Would I find my string again sometime in the future? Maybe—I wasn't sure—I just knew that if the enemy took it from me bad things would surely happen to all of us.

Still, giving him my precious string was one of the hardest things I had to do. By doing so I knew I was severing all the physical links I had to my old life and the people I had loved, and loved me. Tears filling my eyes, I said, "Safe journey, Friend Collin."

Letting go of my hand as a red-faced soldier approached us, Collin said over his shoulder, "Good bye, My Friend."

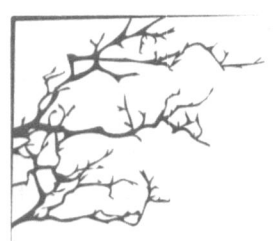

Chapter Fifteen

After our protectors left Town the Evil demons had one more torment waiting for me. The hanging of the outlaws was to take place the day before we were to go to the live-away school. Over our friend, Attorney Ricosen's protests prosecutor talked Judge into making a part of our punishment that we witness the event. He claimed that it would make us always be "good zaunks" if we knew what happened to bad ones.

Judge agreed, and so as dawn colored the sky a deep crimson we were ushered out of our cell and marched in chains to stand in front of a high platform where seven looped ropes dangled down from a crossbar overhead. Behind us I could hear a crowd of Chamuqwani gathering, talking and laughing among themselves.

My back as rigid and straight as a mountain pine I refused to show them any weakness, or let them see my grief and fear. Out of the corner of my eye, I saw Cohasi turn to watch the assembling people, but I chose to stare at the platform and ignore them and their hurtful comments. They could call us filthy heathen savages and dirty zaunks all they wanted. I didn't care. They all were rotting fish guts, and stinky dog turds anyway.

My sleep had been troubled with terrible nightmares, ever since Collin had left with his friends. Within the Dream I sang my Puwa songs and fought off the fearsome monsters sent to taunt me. I knew Nachoga was here, somewhere deep underground in this big jail, because our guards had been joking about the pale-skinned renegade they'd caught with the savages and what was being done to him, and teased us that we would be next, if we weren't good little zaunks.

Knowing all that, I searched for him within the Dream until I found him. Prowling the Unseen World his Spirit, like the mighty Cougar he truly was, snarled and raged at the frail human body still confining him. He knew I was near, but was unable to speak with me in a human language. The cougar part of him, in which he had found refuge from the pain and torment, could only yowl at his helplessness and pace with tail slashing, impatient to be free.

<<Soon,>> I promised him as I swam in my seal form beside him. <<It will be over soon.>>

As Sun's golden light shone into the jail's courtyard a soldier blew his horn and everyone fell silent, turning to face the plat form where several large muscular soldiers were bringing seven chained men out of a black doorway and across a cleared space behind the platform.

A hooded man was already atop the structure to place the loop around each man's neck as two soldiers unchained them and escorted them with hands still bound behind their backs up the wooden stairs.

Until that moment I hadn't known for sure who had been captured when the traders betrayed the warband. Now I knew. A stone-faced Eqwohi and his nephew Shliwa were the first to mount the platform and have the ropes pulled over their heads to fall around their necks.

Feeling sad for Betsiya, I was also glad she wasn't here to see her husband hang. I prayed she and the children were safe back on the Preserve or running free in the desert. I would try later to tell her in the Dream that he was gone.

Wachata, and two other scarred warriors, kin to Golannah, that I knew by sight but not by name came next. And then the defiant and still cursing Chakota was dragged onto the platform.

Eqwohi looked over at the boy and his eyes flashed with his contempt. In a stern voice he told him in his language, "Stop, behaving like a spoiled child. Be a brave Kukiya warrior and make me and your ancestors proud." After that Chakota stopped fighting the soldiers and took his place alongside the others.

Nachoga was the last. Unable to walk without help, because of the continuous beatings and tortures he'd had to endure since his capture, he could barely stand and was unable to mount the platform without the guards' help. Once atop the platform and the rope in place he used his last bit of strength and straightened. Standing defiantly his bruised and bloody face calm, he looked out at the shouting crowd as if searching for something, or someone.

<<I am here, my father,>> I told him. Then he looked down and saw me also chained and bound below him.

His face twisted into a painful grimace that I think he meant to be a smile. <<As you can see, my son, I have kept my promise when I left you and your mother. You are seeing me again... Just not in the way either of us hoped, eh? Are you here to hang as well?>>

Grief suddenly welling up to nearly overwhelm me, I cried, <<Oh, Father I wish you would have let me come with you, instead of being swayed by Grandfather's meddling. Maybe none of this would have happened if...>>

<<Perhaps, but we can't change what the Unseen Ones have chosen for us, my son. Be at peace.>>

As we communicated with one another using our Puwa a Chamuqwani in a black robe came forward to address the assembled crowd, telling them about the warriors' terrible crimes against the people of the Empire. I paid him little attention, continuing my talk with the man I'd grown to love above all.

<<No, the Chamuqwani friends your brother and I told you about came and got Judge to only send us away to a live-away school instead of hanging us.>>

<<That's good. And what of your mother, and my daughter?>>

After he asked that question I nearly broke down and cried. I'm sure with his Spirit Sight he could see my grief. <<Father, I've failed the trust you put in me. I couldn't keep them safe after all. Amima, Grandfather, so many dead at what the Chamuqwani are calling a massacre. I'm sorry.>>

I saw his body shudder as he took in my news. Then he straightened once more and asked, <<And what of my sweet baby Kitahtla, is she waiting for me in the Beyond, too?>>

<<Being the better rider, Amima gave her to Sagila to carry when we stole back our horses and tried to escape. Kitahtla was with her aunty just before we were spotted and I was taken. Last I saw Uncle Tli and some of our warband had Sagila and the babies and were racing off into the desert with Xyilaha, Samiqwas and more of our people.>>

He gave me a mental chuckle. <<Your mother was always a terrible rider, in spite of my many lessons. Ah well, I will see her again soon enough. I will have to continue trying to teach her, eh?

<<That's good that the little one is still in this world. Tli will keep them as safe as anyone can. And you must use your power to keep her safe, too,

where ever they take you. Kill that evil malicer Azogi who has cursed us, for me, my Son. Promise to do that one last thing for me.>>

Before I could answer him, in the world around us the door was opened under Eqwohi and then Shliwa's feet. Choking for air they swung and kicked as the rope tightened. At last they hung still, their faces turned purple and dark stains forming on their crotches and legs.

Watching their bodies dangle lifeless and the crowd jeering around me, my grief turned to rage and I agreed. <<I will kill that evil man. He will not find and hurt my baby sister,>> I promised him. <<I have already dealt with those lying dog turds that betrayed the warband. They aren't alive to spend the reward or the gold they stole from Golannah.>>

He tried to smile. <<Good. That eases my mind. I can face my death easier now, knowing you will be here to watch over her and the rest of our People in the years to come.>>

By charging me with the protection of Kitahtla he was placing a great burden on my shoulders. Hadn't I learned the consequences of personal vengeance already? I had failed him once by not protecting Amima, I prayed I was strong enough not to fail again.

When it was his turn, he kept his eyes on me as the hooded man tightened the rope around his neck. We didn't say good bye; we would see each other again one day.

But as his body swung lifeless from the rope at last, I couldn't help the tears that blurred my eyes. I trembled like a leaf in the wind. My heart felt like it would burst out of my chest and fall upon the dusty ground. I was going to miss him and Amima so much. How could I go on living without my family, my people, my home?

I wanted so badly to jump up on that platform, tell all those ignorant, hateful Chamuqwani that they should kill me, too. I was the one, the malicer that had killed the soldiers at the ford, and I was the one who took my selfish vengeance on the traders and set into motion the massacre that followed. I was the one that needed to die...

Knowing a little of what I was feeling my two friends, that were bound on either side of me, stepped as close to me as our chains would allow in an attempt to comfort me. I was grateful, but it still hurt so much I could barely breathe.

I could also hear the echoes of Djoven's creatures' laughter in my mind, enjoying my pain. They taunted me by saying how they would soon be welcoming the warriors' souls into Djoven's fiery place of eternal punishments.

<<No, Evil Ones—never, these souls belong to the ancestors and the desert land that gave them birth. With the Qwakaiva gifted me by my Qwa'Nayhi Seal father and the Great Kunai, you will not have them.>>

As Crystal Being awoke within me I raised my bound hands to catch Sun's light within the circle my fingers made, and then I began to sing the sacred songs that would open a portal for my dead to pass through.

In an act of defiance Matoqwa, Cohasi and the others chained with us joined in my song.

The End

Tasimu's story is continued in Book Four: *Bitter Echoes of Memory*

ADDITIONAL INFORMATION for the books telling Tasimu's Story
Words in the Qwani'Ya Language:

Qwani'Ya Tsa'adi, or Fish People, what the Indigenous people living by Big Ice Lake call themselves

Qwa'osi the Otter Warrior, a guardian spirit protector of the Qwani'Ya

Co'yeh the Lake Seal, the Otter's rival, a spirit with both light and dark aspects

Siyatli, a child born to a human woman whose father is a lake Seal

Qwakaiva, a difficult word to translate in its full meaning, similar to what we might refer to as magic, chi, life force or shamanic medicine

Qwakaihi, someone gifted with great power whouses their gift for the good of others

Aseutl, a snake-like dragon figure some say lives at the bottom of Big Ice Lake

Kunai, a shape-shifting magical being of great power, and benefactor of Tasimu

Qwa'Nayhi a shape-shifting being able to travel between many realms of existence, like the Qwa'Nayhi Seal man who is Tasimu's father

Amima, mother in the Qwani'ya language

Appi, father

Ami grandmother

Ati, grandfather

Coshelah cousin, a person's patrilineal cousin. The Qwani'Ya claim their descent from their mothers, so the father's kin aren't as close and referred to differently

Chamuqwani, a term the Indigenous people use to refer to the Imperial invaders of their land

Asiya, a greeting like hello

Unfamiliar Terms in the Chamuqwani Language

Zacatik, what the imperial conquerors have named all the Indigenous peoples they have encountered as they have expanded the Empire's borders.

Zaunk, a degrading term used by soldiers and settlers from the empire to express their contempt for all Indigenous peoples they discovered during their conquest

Bucki, a derogatory term for an Indigenous man or boy

Cloocha or Cloocha-whore a demeaning term for an Indigenous woman or girl

Words in the Kukiya Language

Kukiya, what the Indigenous people living in the desert and mountain country out of which the Empire created their Tribal Preserve call themselves

Puhani, a person with magical powers, the same as a Qwakaihi in Tas's people's language

Puwa, the magical power, like Qwakaiva, that a Puhani can use

Akiyazi, the magical beings that have power over the rain and the water in lakes and creeks

Don't miss out!

Visit the website below and you can sign up to receive emails whenever Celu Amberstone publishes a new book. There's no charge and no obligation.

https://books2read.com/r/B-A-YGQM-EOLUC

BOOKS 2 READ

Connecting independent readers to independent writers.

Also by Celu Amberstone

Rituals
Blessings of the Blood: A Book of Menstrual Lore and Rituals for Women
Deepening the Power: Community Ritual and Sacred Theatre

Tales of Tasimu
Taste of Memory
When Memory Dies
Abandoning Memory

Tales of the Kashallans
The Dream-Chosen
The Hunted Kashallan
The Outlawed Bond
Uncertain Refuge
Prey of the Umwira
Blood Magic's Snare
Kashallan Alliance
Treacherous Campaign

Standalone
Refugees and Other Stories

About the Author

Celu is of mixed Cherokee and Scots-Irish ancestry. Celu Amberstone was one of the few young people in her family to take an interest in learning Traditional Native crafts and medicine ways. This interest made several of the older members of her family very happy while annoying others.

Legally blind since birth, she has defied her limitations and spent much of her life avoiding cities. Moving to Canada after falling in love with a Métis-Cree man from Manitoba, she has lived in the rain forests of the west coast, a tepee in the desert and a small village in Canada's arctic. Along the way she also managed to acquire a BA in cultural anthropology and an MA in health education. Celu loves telling stories and reading. She lives in Victoria British Columbia near her grown children and grandchildren.

About the Publisher

Kashallan Press is an independent publisher releasing books by author Celu Amberstone. Among her books are critically-acclaimed works now re-released by Kashallan Press, and new works showcasing her talents in writing both fiction and non-fiction.